ROBERT M. PHILMUS is Assistant Professor of
English at Loyola College, Montreal.

INTO THE
UNKNOWN

INTO THE UNKNOWN

The Evolution of Science Fiction
from Francis Godwin to H.G. Wells

ROBERT M. PHILMUS

University of California Press
Berkeley and Los Angeles 1970

University of California Press

Berkeley and Los Angeles, California

University of California Press, Ltd.

London, England

Copyright © 1970 by The Regents of the University of California

SBN 520–01394–8

Library of Congress Catalog Card Number: 70-84790

Designed by Steve Reoutt

Printed in the United States of America

To my Amanuensis and Wife

Preface

Any approach to the study of a genre as heterogeneous as science fiction will necessarily be polemical. The most neutral access would seem to be by way of literary history, but one can not even write a history of science fiction without making assumptions about the nature of this type of fiction. Sooner or later the critic must establish criteria of selection to differentiate science fiction from other categories of narrative; the use of "science fiction" as a catchall term comprehending all utopian romances, celestial voyages, futuristic predictions, accounts of technological marvels yet to come, and so forth, allows no standard for excluding (to take a few instances at random) *News from Nowhere,* the *Paradiso* from the *Divina Commedia,* the Book of Revelation, or the records of the U.S. Patent Office.

The starting point of this essay, therefore, is to define how science fiction essentially differs from other kinds of fantasy. My conclusion, based on examination of works generally regarded as examples of the genre, is that the distinguishing feature of science fantasy involves the rhetorical strategy of employing a more or less scientific rationale to get the reader to suspend disbelief in a fantastic state of affairs. Such a strategy is, of course, only a means to an end; but it is an emphasis on this rhetorical means, it seems to me, rather than the subjects science fiction treats of or the writers' attitudes toward them, which gives a definition of the genre discrimination and latitude.

In qualifying and at the same time extending my preliminary definition, I proceed from the strategy to its purpose, and hence to the areas of coincidence of science fiction and other classes of fantasy. This transition is provided by describing the strategy as one of displacing the real world with a fantastic myth that, through the process of displacement, interprets elements of reality. That is to say, the concept of mythic displacement (somewhat analogous to Freud's *Verschiebung*) permits me to account for the convergence of science fiction and fantasy in general, and to analyze especially the relation of science fantasy to satiric and utopian fiction.

This argument outlines my opening chapter and structures the discussion in the chapters that follow. After considering how the strategy of science fantasy emerges in the early fictional voyages, and projects for voyages, to the moon, I go on to illustrate some of the continuities of theme and myth subsisting among works that belong to the history of science fiction, and then take up the myths of science fantasy as speculation in their own right, as what Hans Vaihinger calls *Philosophien des "Als Ob."* My concluding chapter deals with *The First Men in the Moon,* where H. G. Wells reviews synoptically the myths of his earlier "scientific romances" and thus confirms the tendency for science fiction to be self-regarding.

As I indicate throughout my essay, Wells's science fantasies, and *The First Men* in particular, epitomize a tradition that in English goes back to Francis Godwin. An interest in Wells, which supplied the impulse to undertake this study, has directed my attention toward satiric science fiction and has also determined in part the limits set for my essay. As a rule, I have confined my discussion to works published in England roughly up to 1900, including a number of translations. But my intention has been to determine the nature of science fiction, not to write a literary history; so that I have often dispensed with chronological precedence for the sake of logical order and have gone beyond my assigned chronological boundaries whenever it seemed consistent with my intention to do so. Specifically, I have taken into account some modern science fiction: since much of the material that appeared before the turn of the century is not science fiction in any strict sense, I have checked bearings on the direction of the genre from contemporary instances, mentioned chiefly in footnotes and in the Postscript.

Had I approached my subject from some other point of view, say that of the writer of science fiction, a few of my concerns would no doubt have been quite different. I should then have focused on twentieth-century examples and been more attentive, for instance, to the problems involved in translating scientific ideas into fiction. Similarly, if I had set out to write a history of ideas, I would have concentrated more on background material and probably should have found the evidence latent in the history of science fiction before 1900 insufficient for my purpose. As it is, I hope I have contributed something to an understanding of the genre which may be of benefit to other students of science fiction.

Acknowledgments

Among those who helped me in preparing this study, I am particularly grateful to Robert C. Elliott for patiently going over my manuscript a number of times in its various stages of incompletion and offering valuable criticism of my arguments. I would also like to thank Bruce Franklin, George P. Mayhew, Roy Harvey Pearce, and Andrew Wright for their suggestions and encouragement. In my research I have of course incurred a debt to the staffs of many libraries, especially the University of California library system, the Henry E. Huntington Library, the Library of Congress, the Folger Shakespeare Library, and the British Museum.

Extracts from the works of H. G. Wells are quoted with the kind permission of A. P. Watt and Son, literary agents for the Wells estate, and their New York affiliate, Collins-Knowlton-Wing, Incorporated, and passages from *The Time Machine* are quoted by a further arrangement with Heinemann and Company Limited. The Oxford University Press has also been cooperative in allowing me to cite several passages from Geoffrey Strachan's translation of Cyrano de Bergerac's *L'Autre Monde*.

Contents

"Nous voici en route . . . en route vers . . ."
"L'inconnu . . . l'inconnu qu'il faut fouiller
pour trouver du nouveau, a dit Baudelaire!"

JULES VERNE

Nous voulons . . .
Plonger au fond du gouffre, Enfer ou Ciel,
qu'importe
Au fond de l'Inconnu pour trouver du *nouveau!*

BAUDELAIRE

I

Science Fiction as Myth

> Long since on Mars,
> and more strongly since he came to Perelandra,
> Ransom had been perceiving that the triple distinction
> of truth from myth and both from fact
> was purely terrestrial—was part and parcel
> of that unhappy division between soul and body
> which resulted from the Fall.
>
> C. S. LEWIS

Ostensive definitions of science fiction are not hard to come by. One can always indicate what the term means by pointing to an example: H. G. Wells's "The Country of the Blind," for instance, or Isaac Asimov's *I, Robot.* In attempting to give a more precise definition, however, the boundaries of the genre, like those of Ahab's doubloon, are found to be highly ambiguous. Because one can single out some fictional utopias, say, or some tales of the future as examples of science fiction, there is a temptation to include all stories of these sorts in any stipulation of the proper limits of the genre.[1]

---

[1] Thus, for example, Mark R. Hillegas announces toward the beginning of *The Future as Nightmare: H. G. Wells and the Anti-Utopians* (New York, 1967) that "the great anti-utopias of the twentieth century constitute, with Wells's scientific romances, future histories and, to some extent, utopias, a single kind of fiction, for which there is no other name than science fiction" (p. 5). (It is not clear from the context whether Hillegas is referring to all "future histories" and "utopias" or only Wells's, especially since he afterward speaks of Wells's scientific romances and utopian fiction only.)

1

To avoid the confusion of categories, which such an un-
critical and inclusive definition leads to, I propose to call
attention to science fiction first as a strategy of narrative presentation—a rhetorical strategy in Wayne Booth's sense[2]—which
may be shared by works belonging in other respects, such as
content, to different generic classifications. From the point of
view of rhetorical strategy, science fiction differs from other
kinds of fantasy by virtue of the more or less scientific basis,
real or imaginary, theoretical or technological, on which the
writer predicates a fantastic state of affairs. The strategy, then,
involves what Wells somewhat deprecatingly calls "the ingenious use of scientific patter"[3] to justify a literally fantastic
situation; it might entail the hypothesis of a machine for
traveling through time, the evolution on other planets of beings superior to man, or sundry other "inventions" (Wells's
term again) of the author's imagination.

This definition would admit most of the stories generally
accepted as science fiction; it would leave out, along with fiction that no one would consider grouping under this generic
rubric, fantasies sometimes mistaken for science fiction either
because of accidental resemblances to representatives of the
genre or because their author has written other works that have
rightly been classed as science fiction. The definition, that is,
would subsume only those fantasies depending essentially
upon a scientific rationale to account for the imaginary situation that the writer projects into some spatial or temporal
region of the unknown; and not novels that scientific theory
informs or structures without contributing necessarily to their
plausibility (e.g., Darwinism in the novels of Thomas Hardy),
or fiction that contravenes the limits of the possible without
offering any scientific excuse for the extraordinary (e.g., *Alice
in Wonderland*). Also excluded would be tales of the future
in which speculations about advances yet to come in theoretical science or technology are incidentally put forward (as
in William Delisle Hay's *Three Hundred Years Hence*); or
tales of the unknown wherein the author makes no attempt
to depict the unusual and mysterious as anything but super-

[2] See Wayne C. Booth, *The Rhetoric of Fiction* (Chicago, 1961), pp. 105-106.
[3] H. G. Wells, Preface to *The Scientific Romances* (London, 1933), p. viii.

natural or otherwise inexplicable (as in many of the short stories of Ambrose Bierce and Ray Bradbury). Nor need any number of fantastic romances be regarded as more than peripheral which, ignoring scientific justification altogether, use "remote planets or even galaxies as the backcloth for spy-stories or love-stories which might as well or better have been located in Whitechapel or the Bronx"[4] (as in the case of Edgar Rice Burroughs' Martian saga and its subliterary descendants).

But apart from such exclusions, this preliminary definition of science fiction as a rhetorical strategy does not presume to adjudicate among the diversity of subjects and attitudes found in fantasies deploying that strategy. As I have already stated, the diverseness of the ends achieved by means of this strategy permits, in many instances, the convergence of science fiction with other types of fantasy. To determine the nature of a few of these interconnections, I intend to analyze the rhetorical techniques of science fiction, together with some of their implications, as the genre emerges historically as a strategy for satiric and utopian fiction.

Such an analysis is also meant to qualify and augment my initial formulations about science fiction through an investigation of the character of the science fictional fantasy—an investigation necessarily proceeding from the means essential to science fiction, namely the scientific rationale, toward the end common to all fantasy. My conclusions, it may be said by way of anticipation, accord with what Northrop Frye observes of science fiction, that it is "a mode of romance with a strong inherent tendency to myth."[5] In the next sections of this chapter, and in the chapters that follow, I will try to establish the sense in which science fiction mythicizes not only the science that it appropriates, but elements of historical reality generally.

Science Fiction and Satiric Fantasy

The concurrence of science fictional techniques and a satiric attitude can partly be attributed to the overall effect of rhe-

---

[4] C. S. Lewis, *An Experiment in Criticism* (Cambridge, 1961), p. 109.
[5] Northrop Frye, *Anatomy of Criticism* (Princeton, 1957), p. 49.

torical strategy. That strategy, from the writer's point of view, often requires him to dislocate the fictional participants in time or space, or to disorient them ideationally in the face of some hypothetical innovation. The disorientation within the fantasy, and in the mind of the reader to the extent that he becomes involved in the fictive situation, creates the conditions for satire; commonsensical notions of what constitutes reality do not seem to apply to the fantastic state of affairs. Thus in many satiric science fantasies, a seemingly improbable social order (or chaos), sometimes the logical result of an imagined technological discovery, displaces what is commonly thought of as social reality;[6] and the consequent deformation reveals aspects of the true nature of the existing social order.[7] The scientific rationale, in other words, does not simply mediate between fantasy and reality; it may also indicate a satiric correspondence between the two.

An interpenetration of the real world and an apparently fantastic state of affairs is an essential feature of all science fiction, but especially of satiric science fiction; and this fact should qualify any hypothesis about the purposes of establishing an illusion of plausibility. The more or less scientific explanation proffered by the writer of science fiction to account for the world of his fantasy acknowledges a reality outside the fiction; but sometimes the acknowledgment itself can serve an ironic intent. In Edmund Crispin's words, "almost the whole of [the explanatory] apparatus may constitute a horrible assault not just on probability but on possibility as well,"[8] with a view to exposing the limits of recognized reality.

The Time Machine can be taken as a paradigmatic instance. Both the theory which renders time travel a possibility and the vision of the distant future which the Time Traveller narrates

[6] I use *displacement* by analogy with the Freudian term *Verschiebung*. Compare, for example, Sigmund Freud, *The Interpretation of Dreams*, tr. James Strachey (New York, 1961), pp. 307-308.

[7] Thus Isaac Asimov observes of Fritz Leiber's *Coming Attraction* that one is "horrified at the society" depicted, "moved by its reality and profoundly disturbed at the realization that it is an extrapolation of some of the worst features of our present way of life." ("Social Science Fiction" in *Modern Science Fiction. Its Meaning and Its Future*, ed. Reginald Bretnor [New York, 1953], p. 185.)

[8] Edmund Crispin, "Science Fiction," *TLS*, Oct. 25, 1963, p. 865.

contradict the complacent assumptions of his fictive audience; so that in introducing that audience to the principle of his machine, the Time Traveller adumbrates the effect of the vision to follow. His admonition that "I shall have to controvert one or two ideas that are almost universally accepted" (I, 3),[9] while specifically meant to prepare for his argument that there exists a fourth dimension, applies equally well to his tale of the future. The fact that the Time Traveller's hypotheses proceed from their own suppositions, however, does not prevent his fictional auditors from incredulously rejecting his theories.

In this last-mentioned respect, *The Time Machine* suggests another satiric strategy: what may be called an inversion of credibility. That is, by trying "in every possible unobtrusive way to *domesticate* the impossible hypothesis" *(Scientific Romances,* p. viii), the writer of science fiction may bring about a satiric reversal of fantasy and actuality. Ray Bradbury succinctly defines that reversal as his general aim: "To make the extraordinary seem ordinary, and cause the ordinary to seem extraordinary."[10] This statement, it can be said, describes in part the achievement of almost all memorable satire; and such reversals have been employed for satiric effect at least since the time of Lucian.

Wells illustrates the ironic result of satiric inversion in dramatizing the reactions of Edward Prendick, a literary descendant of Lemuel Gulliver. Prendick treats circumstantially the fact of the existence of the Beast People on Doctor Moreau's island, whereas he first regards their origin and customs, which the reader recognizes as deformations of evolutionary theory and social convention, as strange and unheard of.

The Island of Doctor Moreau, with its unmistakable allusions to *Gulliver's Travels,* provides an instance of the historical basis for associating a science fictional strategy with satire. From the point of view of literary history, the technique of

[9] All quotations from Wells's science fiction refer parenthetically to volume and page numbers of the "Atlantic Edition" of his works (28 vols. [New York, 1924-26]) unless otherwise specified.

[10] Ray Bradbury, "A Happy Writer Sees his Novel," *San Francisco Chronicle,* Nov. 22, 1966, p. 41. Bradbury here records his reaction to the film version of *Fahrenheit 451.*

"extrapolating" from present reality develops as a satiric strategy in some of the literary antecedents of science fantasy. Among these predecessors are Lucian's *Icaromenippus* and the numerous fictional voyages to the moon in the seventeenth and eighteenth centuries. Often didactic in tone, such accounts view from a lunar perspective events on earth or discover in a lunar world societies and institutions that become the measure of their sublunary counterparts.

I will discuss a few of these fictional lunar voyages in the following chapter, where I will attempt to indicate in some detail what they contribute to the thematic preoccupations and rhetorical techniques of science fiction and the more immediate precursors of the genre. For the moment, it is sufficient to note that the idea of depicting a remote world to stand in for this one realizes a strategy akin to that of satiric science fiction. As Kepler expresses his conception of the strategy in a private letter (he was considering writing a lunar fantasy of his own): "Would it be a great crime to paint the cyclopian morals of this period in livid colors, but for the sake of caution, to depart from the earth with such writing and secede to the moon?"[11] Later fictional journeys to a world underground[12] and to other planets,[13] along with aerostatic voyages

[11] Kepler to Matthias Bernegger (a translator of Galileo), quoted in *Kepler's Dream*, ed. John Lear (Los Angeles, 1965), p. 77. The original German text can be found in *Johannes Kepler in seinen Briefen*, ed. Max Caspar and Walther von Dyck, 2 vols. (Munich, 1930), II, 199.
I deal with Kepler's *Somnium seu Opus Posthumum de astronomia lunaris* in passing, as it impinges on works more central to my concerns. The speculations about lunar astronomy that it contains have long been clear (see chap. 2, n. 2 and n. 8); as for its allusions to astrology and demonology, if they are meant to be more than a protective disguise of the true import of the *Somnium*, their intent is so obscure as to be thus far indecipherable. See Lear's Introduction, and also D. P. Walker's review of Lear's effort (*N.Y. Review of Books*, Sept. 22, 1966, pp. 10, 12).
[12] Chiefly Ludwig Holberg, *Nicolai Klimii Iter Subterraneum* (Hafniae & Lipsiae, 1741), translated anonymously as *A Journey to the World Underground. By Nicolas Klimius* (London, 1742); and its anonymous English imitation, *A Voyage to the World in the Centre of the Earth* (London, 1755).
[13] Interplanetary voyages have, of course, become commonplace in science fiction. Representative of the motif before Wells are Percy Greg, *Across the Zodiac*, 2 vols. (London, 1880), an imaginary rocket voyage to Mars, and the anonymous *Politics and Life on Mars* (London, 1883), typical of the pseudo-histories of life on "other planets."

around the known world,[14] assume Kepler's strategy, which Lucian and his successors in England had already gone far to translate into example.

Equally relevant to the development of science fiction as a satiric strategy is Thomas Shadwell's, and later Jonathan Swift's, method of selecting actual experiments from among those performed or proposed by members of the Royal Society —usually as set down in the *Philosophical Transactions*—and adapting them to the purpose of ridiculing certain contemporary conceptions of science. Particularly in synthesizing two or more such experiments, or in transforming their details so that they might appear more absurd, Swift extended Shadwell's satiric use of science and thus prefigured the technique of projecting scientific discoveries into the imagined unknown. To be sure, neither *The Virtuoso* nor *Gulliver's Travels* shares the opinion that natural philosophy can contribute lasting truths to human knowledge—and this quite apart from the views that either Shadwell or Swift might have expressed publicly or privately elsewhere. Yet although writers of science fiction, from Wells onward, cannot agree with this estimate of science, still the idea of extrapolating from scientific theory and practice for the purposes of fiction goes back to the satire of science in Shadwell and Swift especially, rather than to works more favorable to science, such as the esoteric fantasies of Cyrano de Bergerac.[15]

Concerning the projects of Shadwell's virtuoso, Sir Nicolas Gimcrack, all but one derive from the records of the Royal Society or from other accounts of then recent experiments. Claude Lloyd, who extensively documents Shadwell's sources, says that "for the details of his treatment, usually for his very vocabulary, he drew mainly upon three sources—Sprat's *History* [of the Royal Society], Hooke's *Micrographia,* and the

[14] Among the usually anonymous works to appear shortly after the first aerial ascensions are *The Modern Atalantis; or, The Devil in an Air Balloon. Containing the Characters and Secret Memoirs of the Most Conspicuous Persons of High Quality, of Both Sexes, in the Island of Libertusia . . .* (London, 1784); and *The Aerostatic Spy,* 2 vols. (London, 1785).

[15] Though a few writers borrowed details from Cyrano, there is no indication it was recognized that his *Autre Monde* disguised serious philosophical speculations. I take up Cyrano's metaphysical fantasies in chap. 6.

Philosophical Transactions."[16] The one instance of "virtuosity" that is apparently Shadwell's own invention introduces the virtuoso in his laboratory. Bruce and Longvil, the two Restoration lovers trying to arrange an assignation with Sir Nicolas's wards, pretend to be virtuosi themselves as a pretext for entering his house and discover Sir Nicolas during his swimming lesson. Sprawled upon a table and exercising his limbs spasmodically, he is all the while attached by a cord to the frog in a nearby tank, whose motions he attempts to imitate. In the conversation that ensues, Sir Nicolas discloses what makes him a virtuoso.

> *Bruce.*   We are both your admirers. But of all quaint inventions, none ever came near this of swimming.
> *Sir Formal.*   Truly I opine it to be a most compendious method that in a fortnight's prosecution has advanc'd him to be the best swimmer of Europe. Nay, it were possible to swim with any fish of his inches.
> *Longvil.*   Do you intend to practice in the water, sir?
> *Sir Nicolas.*   Never, sir. I hate the water. I never come upon the water, sir.
> *Longvil.*   Then there will be no use of swimming.
> *Sir Nicolas.*   I content myself with the speculative part of swimming. I care not for the practic. I seldom bring anything to use; 'tis not my way. Knowledge is my ultimate end.

Despite Sir Formal Trifle's florid acclamations of his friend's accomplishments, however, Shadwell does not allow that proponent of "pure" science any glory; and at last Sir Nicolas himself is forced to admit that he has never invented anything in his life. What finally prompts that confession, and generates the satire also, are what the playwright considers to be the practical—or rather, *impractical*—consequences of the "speculative part" of natural philosophy: blood transfusions, "engine looms," and the like. It is presumed that the audience will find these projects as impractical, as incapable of being

---

[16] Claude Lloyd, "Shadwell and the Virtuosi," *PMLA*, XLIV (1929), 475. See also Marjorie Hope Nicolson's introduction ("Satire on the New Science") to the edition of the text of *The Virtuoso* prepared by David Stuart Rodes (Lincoln, 1966), pp. xix ff. The quotation below follows this edition, pp. 46-47.

brought to use, as Gimrack's learning to swim upon a table, and therefore will be amused at the weavers' anxiety about a possible mechanical loom no less than at the virtuoso's abject denial (in the face of their wrath) that he ever originated such a loom, or anything else.

Like Shadwell, Swift too extracts accounts of experiments from the *Philosophical Transactions* and similar records, and these he freely adapts in the Third Book of *Gulliver's Travels*. But whereas many of the experiments Sir Nicolas describes still seem laughable only because they are primitive, Swift establishes a context in which such projects must necessarily appear deranged. The absurdity of all the projects at the Academy of Lagado has its source not merely in that the "speculative" part of learning cannot be put to practical use, but also in that the ends desired by the projectors are not consonant with the means they employ—in other words, the fault is in their theory as well.

One professor, for example, purposes "to give the World a compleat Body of all the Arts and Sciences" by working with a frame into which "the whole Vocabulary" has been emptied and deployed according to "the strictest Computation of the general Proportion there is in Books between the Number of Particles, Nouns, and Verbs, and other Parts of Speech." By manipulating this frame in a haphazard fashion and then recording any "three or four Words together that might make Part of a Sentence," the professor hopes to "write Books in Philosophy, Poetry, Politicks, Law, Mathematicks and Theology" (pp. 166-168).[17] Aside from the satiric insinuation about how books on these subjects are cranked out "without the least Assistance from Genius or Study," what makes this computer a ridiculous waste of effort is not just its primitiveness, but the supposition on which it is based: that truth in these matters can be arrived at accidentally by mechanical means.

In this and other projects at the Academy, Swift turns the idea of man and the universe as mechanisms against itself. He thereby reveals that attempts to compile "a complete *Body* of

---

[17] Jonathan Swift, *Gulliver's Travels*, ed. Herbert Davis (Oxford, 1941). Subsequent quotations from the *Travels* refer to this edition.

all the Arts and Sciences" by mechanical means, or to "improve" the language by substituting things for words, would reduce the operations of the spirit to those of the body, thus mechanizing those operations and abolishing mind from the universe. But not accomplishing this reduction, such projects merely discover an absence of mind in whoever proposes them.

The ultimate mechanical operations Swift surely means to impugn are those of the Newtonian universe and its mathematical God. To this end, he portrays the Flying Island of Laputa, whose dimensions are proportional to those of the earth as calculated by Newton.[18] They also correspond to those of the "terrella" with which William Gilbert conducted experiments in magnetism, but "concerning the actual motion of the island, there is little help from Gilbert."[19] The motion of the Flying Island, however, which its inhabitants govern by means of a "Loadstone of prodigious Size" located "at the Center of the Island" (pp. 151-152), might well be explained if Swift has associated Gilbert's attractive and repulsive magnetic forces with Newton's theory of gravitation. Because of the doubts Newton himself had about the nature of the attractive force of gravity and, more importantly, the widespread misunderstanding of the nature of that force among his contemporaries,[20] such an association on Swift's part is not unlikely.[21]

In fact, there are several details about the Flying Island which Swift might have supplied with little more than a casual perusal of Newton's *Principia*.[22] The tendency, for instance,

[18] See Marjorie Hope Nicolson, *Voyages to the Moon* (New York, 1948), p. 193.

[19] Marjorie Hope Nicolson and Nora Mohler, "Swift's 'Flying Island' in the *Voyage to Laputa*," *Annals of Science*, II (1937), 414. A discussion of Swift's use of Gilbert is to be found here (pp. 413-419) and in *Voyages*, pp. 192-194.

[20] See Alexandre Koyré, *From the Closed World to the Infinite Universe* (New York, 1957), pp. 175-198.

[21] Most histories of science at least mention that Gilbert's theory of magnetism provided an analogy in the seventeenth and early eighteenth centuries for what Newton fomulated as the law of universal gravitation. See, for example, A. C. Crombie, *Medieval and Early Modern Science*, 2 vols. (New York, 1959), II, 153-154. Also, if one accepts the conclusions of Professors Nicolson and Mohler, Swift was alluding to both Newton and Gilbert in determining the dimensions for the Flying Island and its motivating loadstone.

[22] A copy of the second edition (1713) of the *Principia Mathematica* is listed in the sale catalogue for Swift's library in 1742 (entry no. 326). How and when he might have come into possession of Newton's work is not clear (Swift himself did not record it in the sale catalogue he made up in 1715).

of the Flying Island to move "in an oblique Direction," rising and falling as it passes across the mainland of Balnibarbi below it, can be interpreted as a satiric distortion of Newton's "resolution of any one direct force . . . into two oblique forces" (I, 22),[23] a principle applied to the analysis of planetary orbits. Swift's own diagrammatic exposition of the Flying Island's movements, in the chapter headed "A Phenomenon solved by modern Philosophy and Astronomy," seems to parody the *Principia* stylistically also.

> By this oblique Motion the Island is conveyed to different Parts of the Monarch's Dominions. To explain the Manner of its Progress, let *AB* represent a Line drawn across the dominions of *Balnibarbi;* let the Line *cd* represent the Loadstone, of which let *d* be the repelling End, the Island being over *C;* let the Stone be placed in the Position *cd* with its repelling End downwards; then the Island will be driven upwards obliquely towards *D.* When it is arrived at *D,* etc. (P. 151)

For comparison, here is a portion of Newton's analysis, toward the beginning of the *Principia,* of the orbit of a body whose motions are acted upon by centripetal force:

> Let the time [i.e., the interval] . . . be divided into equal parts, and in the first part of that time, let the body by its innate force describe the right [*recta;* i.e., straight] line *AB.* In the second part of that time, the same would . . . proceed directly to *c,* along the line *Bc* equal to *AB.* . . . But when the body is arrived at *B,* suppose that a centripetal force acts at once with great impulse, and turning aside the body from the . . . line *Bc,* compels it afterwards to continue its motion along the . . . line *BC* obliquely from *AB.* . . . By the like argument, if the centripetal force acts successively in *C, D, E,* &c. and makes the body in each particle of time, to describe the . . . lines *CD, DE, EF,* &c. they will all lye in the same plane . . . the centripetal force by which the body is perpetually drawn back from the tangent of this curve, will act continually. (I, 57-58; the Latin text can be found in *ed. cit.* I, 34-35)

[23] Quotations from Isaac Newton follow *The Mathematical Principles of Natural Philosophy,* tr. Andrew Motte, 2 vols. (London, 1729). The original

Swift never pretended to understand mathematics, but his
facetiously scientific explanation of the progress of the Flying
Island does sound somewhat like Newton's demonstrations in
the *Principia*; and if it does not parody Newton's demonstrations specifically, it clearly intends to ridicule explanations of
that sort. On the assumption that this is so—and the passage
in the *Travels* would otherwise be gratuitously nonsensical—
the satire is all at the expense of Newton and his fellow philos-
opers. For his Laputian colleagues, those self-absorbed astron-
omers with their one eye turned upward and their other
inward, have not actually discovered the laws of the cosmos;
they literally give law to their precarious universe and attempt
to act as gods over its motions.

Although *Gulliver's Travels* is not science fiction, strictly
defined, in details and episodes like these a technique of presenting science as fiction can be perceived which anticipates
the science fiction of later writers. Whereas Shadwell at most
changes merely one or two details in the scientific accounts
from which he borrows, Swift imaginatively transfigures scientific theory and experiment by describing the literal state of
affairs that they suggest. This literalizing of the abstract, which
tends to enlarge metaphor into myth, does not originate with
Swift. But it is a feature in the evolution of science fiction in
the nineteenth century most prominent in writers like Samuel
Butler and H. G. Wells, whose careful reading of Swift is
apparent for other reasons.[24]

Science Fiction and Utopian Fantasy

Although the satiric attitude enters into science fiction in
the historical development of the genre, that attitude is an incidental, not an essential aspect of science fiction. Where satire
is found, though, the fantasy is likely to reflect, and critically
reflect upon some of the predominant ideological and axio-
logical dogmas of a society. The writer often dramatizes his

Latin text, supplied where necessary, follows the second edition of the *Philosophiae Naturalis Principia Mathematica*, 2 vols. (Cambridge, 1713).
   [24] Thus Wells recorded that "My early, profound and lifelong admiration
for Swift, appears again and again in this collection" (Preface to his *Scientific
Romances*, pp. viii-ix).

critical detachment in the point of view of an observer who stands outside the fictive social order, a point of view that may be achieved, following Voltaire's *Micromégas,* by introducing on earth creatures from other planets, but which is usually realized by means of voyagers to some imaginary land presumed to be cut off from the known world by seas of space or time.

These voyagers sometimes discover a utopian world: in the moon, at the center of the earth, on another planet, or in the hypothetical future. The utopias in science fiction and its antecedents, however, are as a rule part of the apparatus of criticism directed at the existing social order rather than blueprints of an ideal social structure.[25] Moral or intellectual beings whose superior virtue or power is defined in opposition to the state of affairs on earth inhabit most of the utopias in early works related to science fiction; and against these beings the iniquities or backwardness of men is explicitly measured.

This sort of utopia, with its evaluative, often satiric orientation toward the present, gives rise in the late nineteenth century to utopian science fiction that condemns existing social and moral evils by depicting the enlarged scope some imagined technological innovation might give them or by presenting those evils as consequences of some more or less scientific theory or discovery. At about the same time, writers of utopian fiction that describes an ideal society also begin to adopt a science fictional mode of presentation (though optimism about the future realization of any such positive ideal is relatively short-lived).

The first utopia encountered in the history of English science fiction is the Edenic lunar world to which Domingo Gonsales voyages in Francis Godwin's *The Man in the Moone* (1638). In Godwin's lunar utopia, the inhabitants, whose lifespan is thirty times longer than that of Tellurians ("which proportion agreeth well with the quantitie of the day in both worlds, theirs containing almost thirty of ours")[26] have ad-

---

[25] The (heuristic) distinction between the "ideal" utopia and the "critical" utopia is somewhat analogous to Friedrich Engels' analysis of socialism as "utopian' or "scientific."

[26] Francis Godwin, *The Man in the Moone* . . . (London, 1638). All quota-

vanced so far in natural philosophy as to have perfected the Philosopher's Stone (pp. 100-101). Further defining his utopia, Godwin makes it clear that conditions there are in direct contrast with those on earth. As in Eden, "There is no want of any thing necessary for the use of man" and "Food groweth everywhere without labour" (p. 102); but also these Lunarians commit no murder and "it is not found that their is either Whoremonger amongst them" (pp. 102-103). Indeed, "Through an excellent disposition of that nature of people there, all, young and old doe hate all manner of vice, and doe live in such love, peace, and amitie, as it seemeth to be another Paradise" (p. 104). This domestic tranquillity they of course insure by transporting anyone thought likely to offend it to earth.

Lunar utopias for a long time after Godwin's are more a vantage point for the satiric observation of earthly affairs than an organic part of that satire. Samuel Brunt, for example, the pseudonymous author and hero of *A Voyage to Cacklogallinia* (1727), discovers his Selenites to be the vegetarian souls of the virtuous dead, who live on the moon until the soul dies and the understanding returns to its Creator (pp. 148-149).[27] Accepting one Selenite's offer to "shew the World unmask'd" (p. 155), Brunt looks down on earth and beholds diverse forms of human wickedness, "nor was there a Vice, a Folly or a Baseness, practiced in this World below, tho' ever so secret, which I did not see there represented" (pp. 164-165). This unmasking is consistent with the satiric world of the Cacklogallinians, which imitates *Gulliver's Travels;* but it is hard to fathom what the sketchy details of Brunt's lunar utopia have to do with the terrestrial island of Cacklogallinia.

---

tions are taken from this edition; and as with other early texts that I cite, I have silently amended the more obvious printing errors and adapted printing conventions (but not orthography) to accord with modern practices.

[27] The references here are to Samuel Brunt, *pseud.*, *A Voyage to Cacklogallinia. With a Description of the Religion, Policy, Customs and Manners of that Country. By Captain Samuel Brunt.* (New York, 1940). This is a facsimile text with an introduction by Marjorie Nicolson.

Brunt's lunar utopia perhaps owes something to Cyrano's *Estats et empires du soleil*, "Englished by A. Lovell" as *The Comical History of the States and Empires of the . . . Sun* (London, 1687). The account of the dying "soul" of a philosopher can be found in the second book of Lovell's translation, pp. 92-93.

The lunar perspective on the sublunary world, as illustrated at the end of Brunt's narrative, is a motif repeated throughout the seventeenth and eighteenth centuries, most imaginatively in Swift's Lilliput. In *Gulliver's Travels* and, perhaps concurrently, in Ludwig Holberg's *Journey to the World Under-Ground*,[28] utopia reappears as integral to the satire of human life. Holberg's work, replete with echoes of Godwin, Cyrano, Kepler, and any number of other writers who had previously considered with seriousness or ridicule the feasibility of celestial human flight,[29] precipitates its hero Nils Klim through the crater of a volcano and into a subterranean solar system, where he becomes temporarily a satellite of the planet Nazar and finds first among the nations of that planet an arboreal utopia.[30]

Holberg proffers a mock explanation for the existence of this world underground—"that the Conjectures of those Men are right who hold the earth to be concave, and that within the Shell or outward crust there is another lesser Globe, and another Firmament adorn'd with lesser Sun, Stars, and Planets" (p. 7).[31] But Holberg's utopia of rational trees in fact relies no more on science, real or imagined, than Houyhnhnmland does.

Not until the second half of the nineteenth century does one come upon utopias in fiction which depend in some essential respect on scientific theory or hypothetical technology. In the first few decades following the appearance of Darwin's *Origin of Species* (1859), writers of utopian fiction gradually adopt a strategy of projecting utopia as a consequence of the theory of evolution as they understand it. On the basis of the theory that strange new species slowly but continuously evolve from older forms of life, and that some one of these new forms may be destined to surpass, if not supplant, Homo sapiens as he is at present, writers of utopian science fiction imagine an order

[28] Though Holberg's Latin text was not published until 1741, the actual date of composition is generally put a good deal earlier. William A. Eddy, *Gulliver's Travels: A Critical Study* (Princeton, 1923), pp. 67-68, argues the possible influence of Holberg's work on Swift; but this is highly doubtful. See Harold Williams, *Dean Swift's Library* (Cambridge, 1932) p. 91.

[29] See Miss Nicolson, *Voyages,* pp. 227-229.

[30] Compare Cyrano's talking trees in his *Voyage to the Sun.*

[31] See above, n. 12.

of beings in the unknown reaches of time or space whose characteristics, both individual and social, differ greatly from those of man at his present evolutionary stage.

The attitude of these writers toward the changes they envision is not one of univocal approval. "The presumption," writes H. G. Wells, "is that before [man] lies a long future of profound modification, but whether this will be, according to his present ideals, upward or downward, no one can forecast."[32]

Some authors of utopian fiction, however, do view these prospects as more or less millennial. The man of the future will have transcended his present capacities to the degree that they now exceed those of the ancestral ape. As Richard Gerber observes in his study of utopian fantasy,

> The stress on evolutionary utopian progress is to a great extent biological, for this seems to be the most proper, radical and efficient way for man to gain greater power, and more and more various life. . . . The evolutionary quest is less for an ideal man making the best of present possibilities than for a superman whose intellectual and moral superiority is founded on his superior development.[33]

Robert Cromie's Martians of *A Plunge into Space* (1890), for instance, have attained a level of civilization that is far in advance of any on earth. They have no need for government to maintain peace and order; their flying machines can take them to any location in a matter of hours, at most; and their self-control allows them to leviate their bodies at will. "One look at a Martian's face would convince the most obstinate sceptic that in them the *animal* had been suppressed and supplanted by the intellect" (p. 112).[34]

[32] H. G. Wells, "Zoological Retrogression," *The Gentleman's Magazine* (Sept. 7, 1891), p. 253.
[33] Richard Gerber, *Utopian Fantasy: A Study of English Utopian Fiction Since the End of the Nineteenth Century* (London, 1955), p. 13.
Martin Schwonke, *Vom Staatsroman zur Science Fiction* (Stuttgart, 1957), pp. 42-50, also describes the transition in utopian fiction to a science fictionalized strategy for presenting utopia, without, however, providing any theoretical basis for this shift or any close analysis of the works involved in it.
[34] Robert Cromie, *A Plunge into Space*, 2d ed. (London, 1891)—with a Preface by Jules Verne.

Cromie does not disapprove of this suppression, but he says that the "restless beings from striving Earth" who witness these developments on Mars are not yet ready to renounce the struggle for existence to realize them. Going one step further, he continues, in this chapter called "The Millennium": the voyagers from earth "were fresh from a combatant age. They were not ripe for an age of complete fruition—and dawning decay" (p. 170).

If Cromie, foreseeing the decline that he thinks must succeed the millennium, takes an ambivalent attitude toward his imaginary world on Mars, other writers of utopian science fiction perceive in the possibilities for reshaping man enlarged opportunities for totalitarian control. Immediately thought of in this regard is Aldous Huxley's *Brave New World* (1932), with its description of a society wherein human desires have been thoroughly conditioned and reduced almost wholly to biological needs, that they might at once be gratified. Less obviously, there is Doctor Moreau's island, where the god Moreau, having turned animals into men by means of surgery, dictates their thoughts and their behavior. But before Huxley and Wells, Edward Bulwer-Lytton had described in *The Coming Race* (1871) a society in which the evolving power of man over his environment and other men leads to voluntary submission to social constraint.

Lytton imagines a subterranean people who have discovered the power of "vril" and utilize their knowledge to transform themselves and their environment. "I should call [vril] electricity," explains the American who has adventitiously descended into the world of "Vril-ya," "except that it comprehends in its manifold branches other forces of nature, to which, in our scientific nomenclature, differing names are assigned, such as magnetism, galvanism, etc. These people consider that in vril they have arrived at the unity in natural energetic forces" (XXX, 271).[35] With the help of vril, these underground dwellers have perfected the art of human flight and learned to combat and liquidate both the hostile *or* obstructive forces

[35] Quotations from Edward Bulwer-Lytton, *The Coming Race*, and later citations from Lytton, refer to the "Knebworth Edition" of his works, 32 vols. (Boston, 1891-92).

of nature and the less advanced inhabitants of the subterranean world. Moreover, in accordance with what they think of as the rules that govern a Darwinian struggle for existence, their ancient, somewhat Spencerian mythology prophesies that one day they will reemerge to conquer the upper world.[36]

> Wherever ... goes on that early process in the history of civilization by which life is made to struggle, in which the individual has to put forth all his powers to compete with his fellow, we invariably find this result,—namely, since in the competition a vast number must perish, nature selects for preservation only the strongest specimens. With our race, therefore, even before the discovery of vril, only the highest organizations were preserved; and there is among our ancient books a legend, once popularly believed, that we were driven from a region that seems to denote the world you come from, in order to perfect our condition and attain to the purest elimination of our species by the severity of the struggles our forefathers underwent; and that, when our education shall become finally completed, we are destined to return to the upper world, and supplant all the inferior races now existing therein. (XXX, 306-307)

Though many of the inhabitants of the lower world still believe in this legend,[37] they also regard the struggle for existence among individuals of the same "race" and the resulting domination of the weak by the strong as "the surest and most fatal sign of a race incorrigibly savage." "See you not," urges one philosopher,

> that the primary condition of mortal happiness consists in the extinction of that strife and competition between individuals, which, no matter what forms of government they adopt, render the many subordinate to the few, destroy real liberty to the individual, whatever may be the nominal liberty of the State, and annul that calm of existence without which felicity, mental or bodily, cannot be attained? (XXX, 307)

[36] Compare the world of the Eloi and the Morlocks in H. G. Wells, *The Time Machine*.
[37] Thus Zee, one of the sages of the Vril-ya, "philosophically assumed that the inhabitants [of the 'upper world'] were to be exterminated one day or other by the advent of the Vril-ya" (XXX, 307).

This philosophy sounds strange in the context of the oligarchic society of the Vril-ya, where misfits are liable to be annihilated without notice. But Lytton's American observer does not sojourn long enough to resolve the seeming contradictions. Not being himself one of the "highest organizations," he would have been sacrificed to avert a misalliance had one of the beings of the underground world not guided his escape to the upper regions.

It would be a distortion to imply that *The Coming Race* displays a modern sensibility, especially with regard to science. The nature of vril, despite the fact that Lytton compares it to electricity and magnetism and quotes Farraday to enforce the notion that some such powerful galvanic energy exists, remains mysterious, controlled as it is by the psychic impulses of the human will. Rather than anticipating Einstein's Unified Field Theory, this aspect of Lytton's last romance looks to the ideas about the power of the will deriving from Schopenhauer and popular among Lytton's contemporaries.

The point of bringing up the authenticity of Lytton's science judged by modern standards is not to suggest that the critic should obtrude current conceptions of science to decide what does and does not count as science fiction, instead of recognizing what science was available to the writer and his audience. Rather I mean to stress that the relation of the fiction to contemporary science, or at least to what passes as science, is exactly that which the fiction bears to reality generally: the fantasy, so to speak, regards science as part of the ideological ethos that delimits the concerns of both science and fiction. This point has been implied previously in the discussion of science fiction as a strategy for deflecting reality, and is readily illustrated in *Gulliver's Travels*, where science is at once the means and the object of the satire of Laputa.

But if science itself is also deformed in science fiction, then what finally gives plausibility to the seemingly fantastic state of affairs in the fiction must be redefined. The locus of credibility, as it were, must be extended from the scientific rationale to the entire fictive situation—or, precisely, to its signification. The truth, and hence the credibility (in a meaningful sense), of the fantastic state of affairs can be said to pertain ultimately to the perception in the fantasy of the reality that it displaces, and thereby interprets, rather than to the scientific rationale or the anticipations of the future in that fantasy per se.

Science Fiction as Mythic Displacement

Up to now I have considered science fiction as a rhetorical strategy; that is, as a strategy for bringing about a suspension of disbelief in some fantastic state of affairs by means of some more or less scientific explanation designed to justify the fantasy. I have attempted to examine that strategy both in itself and from the point of view of its development in satiric and utopian fiction making use of it. In relocating the ultimate source of credibility in the science fantasy as displacement, I do not mean to supersede that earlier definition, which in essence distinguishes science fiction from other forms of fantasy; but the relocation does necessitate a shift in emphasis from the technique of the genre to its content.

This transition from technique to content is comprehended in the analysis of still another motive for employing science fiction as a rhetorical strategy: the didactic motive of popularizing scientific theory, whether to favor or oppose it, which enters early into the history of science fiction with Bishop Godwin, Kepler, and Cyrano. In Gabriel Daniel's *Voyage to the World of Cartesius* (1690)—to take a case where the science fictional technique is a mock strategy—the narrator embarks upon an intellectual journey to explore Descartes's philosophy. Daniel explains facetiously that Descartes first discovered "the Secret, not only of the Union of the Soul and the Body, but also how to separate them when I please" (p. 16),[38] through the extraordinary effect of his inhaling a certain snuff.

> [He] concluded it to be the Herb, which he mix'd with the Tobacco, that caused [a] Trance, and took away his Senses; and that the Tobacco at the same Time unharbouring all the Fumes that might benight the Brain, left the Soul with the entire Liberty of knowing and reflecting upon itself. (P. 22)

[38] Gabriel Daniel, *A Voyage,* tr. T. Taylor (London, 1692). Daniel's title is *Voyage du Monde de Descartes* (Paris, 1690).

The author obtains some of this psychedelic substance, and with one tremendous sneeze propels his soul to the outer limits of space. There he encounters the disembodied soul of Descartes, who had not really died but merely separated his soul from his body permanently; and in a series of imaginary conversations with him, and debates between him and other philosophers (chiefly Aristotle), Daniel expounds Cartesian physics and metaphysics—purposely in such a way as to reveal wherein Descartes's theories are inconsistent with one another or undemonstrable in themselves.

What Daniel's *Voyage* illustrates, whether one is willing to admit it as science fiction or not, is the tendency of science fiction, as one kind of fantasy, to transmute an abstract idea into concrete myth. Having "invented" a means for separating the soul from the body that takes their ontological dissociation literally, to the point of parody, Daniel realizes the metaphor of intellectual exploration as the soul's journey through space to the world of Descartes. What is therefore characteristic of science fiction (and other kinds of fantasy) in Daniel's approach is his fictional embodiment of the metaphoric substance of an idea. For science fiction generates its mythic fantasies by taking literally, and dramatizing, the metaphors expressive of those ideas that define, at least in part, the beliefs and nature of the social order.

These metaphors often motivate the form of the myth.[39] In *A Modern Dædalus* (1885), as a simple example, the Irish hero engineers wings which, like those of his mythic eponym, prove to be a "revolutionary invention" (p. 151)[40] and a means of escaping oppression. The scientist, reluctant to aid the cause

---

[39] On the relation of myth and metaphor, compare Ernst Cassirer, *Language and Myth*, tr. Susanne Langer (New York, 1946), pp. 83-99, in which he discusses the derivation of the one from the other; also Roland Barthes, "Le Mythe Aujourd'hui" in *Mythologies* (Paris, 1957) pp. 215-268.

[40] Tom Greer (pseud.?), *A Modern Dædalus* (London, 1885). The Introduction is dated 1887 and signed John O'Halloran; it has obviously been written by this same "Tom Greer"; and this together with the sentiments expressed in the work lead me to suppose that the author has suppressed his real name.

In the Introduction, the author writes of his "invention," that its "reality has been experimentally proved . . . and I publish the following narrative as a vindication of the peculiar method of proof which I was forced by circumstances to adopt" (p. xv). In the correspondence, insinuated here, between revolutions in science and politics, the structural principle of the book resides.

of Irish nationalism at first, is bullied by the English establish-
ment into joining his brothers in opposition to "the Tory mil-
lenium of wealthy landlords and a starving peasantry" (p. 9)—
with the result that his invention proves revolutionary indeed.
The Irish openly rebel, and an airborne contingent of their
forces annihilate the invading English on land and sea, thereby
winning Irish independence.

Although the implications of the "revolutionary invention"
govern the plot, and consequently what the author projects
as the outcome of official English policies in Ireland, the myth
of Dædalus's escape from the Cretan tyrant certainly contributes to the structure of *A Modern Dædalus,* such as it is,
The example is therefore illustrative of how, in addition to
realizing a direct source of myth in metaphor, the writer of
science fiction also mythopoetically creates new myths from
old. *Frankenstein, The Strange Case of Dr. Jekyll and Mr.
Hyde,* and *The Invisible Man* clearly exemplify this process,[41]
as do the interplanetary romances of C. S. Lewis.

In my previous discussion, I implied a distinction between
science fiction critical of the social and moral condition of
man and that which accepts and reflects the status quo. Such
a distinction can be applied, mutatis mutandis, to science fantasies considered as myth. To some extent, all science fiction
draws upon the metaphors inherent in current ideas and transforms them into myth. But the writer of satiric science fiction
is likely to expose the limits of commonly accepted ideas, and
ideals, mainly by dramatizing those ideas as universal principles or by mythicizing their antitheses. In either case, the
mythic fantasy discovers their partiality and incompleteness as
models of reality.[42] The writer of science fiction who intends
no criticism of the prevalent world-views, on the other hand,
is usually unconscious of their limitations.

In fantasies assignable to the subclass of science fiction re-
flecting dominant social values, however, one often finds a

[41] See chap. 4.
[42] I employ the term *model* in a sense analogous to its scientific usage, as a
metaphoric exposition of a theory describing empirical evidence. In this sense,
both Darwin's "struggle for existence" and Marx's dialectical class struggle
exemplify models of reality. Compare C. S. Lewis, *The Discarded Image*
(Cambridge, 1964), pp. 216-223.

curious inconsistency, namely that the overall myth does not correspond to, and sometimes contradicts, the sentiments that the author indicates, generally by intruding commentary in propria persona, to be his own. Emeric Hulme-Beaman's *The Experiment of Doctor Nevill* (1900), for instance, proclaims the respectable Victorian ideals of spiritual love and moral purity, and praises Doctor Nevill for "his simple religious faith. Although he was an advanced man of science, he still retained a belief in God; and there is no denying that this constitutes a very significant anomaly in the present day, when science and atheism usually walk hand in hand" (p. 97).[43] But the main line of Beaman's plot does not substantiate the spiritual ideal at all. On the contrary, it suggests that men are essentially material, that the brain entirely regulates their behavior, and that to postulate the existence of a soul would thus be otiose in accounting for the way a man acts.

The science-fictional experiment of Doctor Nevill suggests these conclusions to the critical reader. The experiment involves the transplanting of part of the brain from one man to another; specifically, the doctor removes the damaged portion of the brain of Wilfrid, Lord Oaklands, and grafts in its place a portion from the brain of a murderer named Warr (lately executed). The basis of Nevill's operation is his

> discovery . . . that transposition of vital tissue from one human organism to another is able to supply the loss of recuperative force consequent upon disease or accident, always assuming the vitalising condition of the extracted tissue to be sufficiently retained in transit; a kind of grafting, you understand . . . the human brain retains the essence of vitality for a certain period after death, [so] that its vital power is communicable by the application of artificial impulse. (Pp. 123-124)

The result "bids fair to prove a Frankenstein" (p. 159)— meaning the monster that Frankenstein animated. But the monster of Nevill's experiment, the body (Wilfrid's) over whose actions part of a criminal's energetic brain gains domi-

[43] Emeric Hulme-Beaman, *The Experiment* . . . (London, 1900). The pagination in parentheses refers to this edition.

nance, only thinks he begins "life afresh with a clean sheet—a man without a past—a man practically born again." For this monster goes on to observe of himself, ominously, that he is "furnished with a certain amount of instinctive common sense, knowledge of men and things, and a suggestion of fairly wide experience, which he knows not how he has come by" (pp. 178-179). As in James Whales's film version of *Frankenstein* (but not as in Mary Shelley's original Gothic romance), the scientist, unwittingly or not, implants in his experimental subject a criminal brain, the material correlative of Original Sin (but not with any discernible intent, ironic or otherwise, on Beaman's part).

Young Wilfrid soon begins to show alarming symptoms of "inheriting a portion, some few idiosyncrasies of Warr's character"; chiefly, an unwonted taste for "painting, music, literature" (pp. 185-186). These interests quickly awaken the latent "criminal instincts," and in a relatively short time he has become a reincarnation of Warr. This unforeseen result Doctor Nevill calls an "inconsistency":

> It is easier to account for inconsistencies after they have been established than before. . . . The transplanted brain tissue carried with it a separate consciousness, a separate identity and separate memories, which swamped the already weakened personality of the brain with which it was forced to assimilate. At the same time, by contributing its own superabundance of vital energy, it restored to the whole brain its normal and original health and vigour. (Pp. 310-311)

Fortunately, this "inconsistency" does not preclude a happy ending. Nevill succeeds in removing the offending brain tissue, and thereby restores Lord Oaklands to his original fox-hunting self.

The inconsistencies in Beaman's romance are not so easily resolved. If one takes Nevill's experiment as another mythic version of Original Sin, the moral is reminiscent of the inverted state of affairs in Erewhon, where no one is held morally or legally accountable for what would ordinarily be called crimes. "It is not . . . your son . . . who commits these follies, these excesses—" Doctor Nevill comforts the Duke, "but the

dead man Warr, whose brain, whose personality, still survives
in Wilfrid. . . . We cannot hold Wilfrid morally responsible
for his mode of life, his habits, his inclinations or his actions!"
(p. 238). This reasoning, which exonerates Wilfrid as a burglar
and an accessory to the fact of murder, resembles in detail the
argument against any man's being held morally accountable
or legally reprehensible for his acts on the grounds that those
acts are determined by forces beyond his control. Since Nevill's
rationalization meets with no contradiction in word or deed—
in fact, it assures the happy ending—one must conclude that
the author's profession of spiritualism compensates for an un-
shakable belief in material causality.

A discordance between the intended moral and the dramatized myth is also difficult to reconcile when it seems that the
author could not very well be unaware of the myth and its
implications. At least two of George Griffith's romances illustrate this difficulty: *The Outlaws of the Air* (1895), for which
Griffith borrows from Jules Verne the *Nautilus* and the *Go
Ahead*;[44] and *The Great Pirate Syndicate* (1899), which is not
strictly the sequel to the earlier work but follows a similar
plot. Both are jingoistic in tone, and the one recapitulates the
myth of the other, so that an analysis of either is sufficient to
make the point.

In *The Great Pirate Syndicate,* fifteen millionaires from
various parts of the British Empire amalgamate their resources
to check the decline of English economic power, which is about
to be depreciated further by the impending loss of trade with
China and of gold mines in the Yukon (this last calamity being
the effect of a map forgery that would move the boundary of
Alaska five degrees east). Proposing to "fight piracy with
piracy" (p. 10),[45] the newly formed Syndicate commissions the
manufacture of several unconventional weapons, including

[44] The *Nautilus* is of course the submarine in *Twenty Thousand Leagues
under the Sea;* the *Go Ahead* is the airship driven by thirty-eight vertical and
horizontal propellers in *Clipper of the Clouds* (also translated as *Robur the
Conqueror,* a literal rendition of the French title).

Griffith takes from Verne the conception of the romantic outlaw also, but
to a large extent he analyzes it into its components so as to have only "good
guys" and "bad guys" (see n. 46).

Possibly another source for Griffith's romances is Frank R. Stockton, *The
Great War Syndicate* (London, 1889).

[45] George C. Griffith, *The Great Pirate Syndicate* (London, 1899).

an unmanned airplane (which operates on an extension cord
and can be modified into a submarine) and a device for para-
lyzing and destroying warships (a device purchased from an
anarchist named Dardo).[46] The latter is

> a simple and yet extraordinarily clever development of what
> is popularly called wireless telegraphy . . . when these rays, or
> whatever they are, which Dardo's apparatus gives out [,] are
> concentrated on an isolated fabric of steel, they have the extra-
> ordinary effect of . . . polarising it. That is, they drive all the
> electricity in it to the poles. (P. 224)

Using these weapons, the Syndicate is able to blockade Europe
and force the rest of the world to come to terms with English
trade. "Foreign sea-borne trade practically disappeared, for no
competition with the enormously wealthy firms of Anglo-
Saxondom was possible by countries which now found their
former selfish methods of taxation and protection turned
against themselves" (p. 296). Henceforth, the world would be
an open market for organized British industry.

To the critical reader, the myth seems virtually self-explana-
tory. Griffith dramatizes in the Syndicate a monopoly capitalism that defines itself as the national interest and wages war to
extend its piratical dominion. Were it not for the justificatory
tone—and the date of publication—this romance of adventure, and exploitation, could be a dramatic presentation of
Lenin's *Imperialism, the Highest Stage of Capitalism*. As it is,
one statement taken out of context provides an ironic commentary on the myth. "I don't think that, morally speaking,
there [is] any more real piracy in our warfare than in anybody
else's," the president of the Syndicate self-righteously remarks
(p. 242).

[46] In both these romances of Griffith's, there is an implicit analogy between
the Syndicate and anarchy. The anarchists in *The Outlaws of the Air* are never
as united in one purpose as the Syndicate, and hence never as effective. But the
members of the Syndicate are like the anarchists in one essential respect: they
too act as if they did not "'owe allegiance to any of the Governments of the
world'" (*Outlaws* [London, 1895], p. 51). In this sense both the anarchists and
the Syndicate members are outlaws; only, the former destroy gratuitously and
unmethodically, whereas the Syndicate, motivated by the desire for economic
profit, is just as ruthless but more thorough. The basic sympathy of the anarchists with the Syndicate is dramatized in their fusion of interests in *The
Great Pirate Syndicate*.

Among the immediate literary precedents for the world holocausts in Griffith's romances of international piracy are the twenty or more versions of "The Battle of Dorking"—accounts of the fictive invasion or attempted invasion of England, usually by Germany or France.[47] Although this battle, which raged in pamphleteering literature for more than thirty years, is now largely a matter of antiquarian interest, many readers are familiar with its transformation as *The War of the Worlds* (1898).[48]

In Wells's early scientific romances, from *The Time Machine* (1895) to *The First Men in the Moon* (1900), science fiction first attains its highest consciousness of myth.[49] These works satirically dramatize accepted ideas and ideals, reducing them to near absurdity by depicting their consequences as cosmic principles or demonstrating their partiality by embodying as myth the "opposite idea."[50] *The War of the Worlds* does both. It deprecates the motive for imperialism as a "missionary enterprise" (III, 213)[51] by exhibiting that imperialism on a

[47] As I. F. Clarke reports, the Battle of Dorking began as an unsigned article (by Sir G. T. Chesney) in *Blackwood's* for May, 1871. "'The number of pamphlets provoked by Chesney's story and the large number of foreign translations indicate the effectiveness of his ominous predictions," writes Clarke in his annotated checklist, *The Tale of the Future* (London, 1961), p. 24. See Clarke, pp. 24-59 *passim*, for a catalogue of such pamphlets up to the eve of the First World War. Of course, in attending to literary precedents or speaking of the effectiveness of Chesney's story in prompting other pamphlets, one should not neglect to mention that there were enough wars going on on the Continent to make English popular writers take note of the portent.

[48] There are some general similarities between Wells's story and Kurd Lasswitz's *Auf Zwei Planeten* (1897)—which does not argue for Lasswitz as Wells's source but does back up the notion that the Battle of Dorking underlies *War of the Worlds*. *Auf Zwei Planeten* is obviously an offshoot of the Dorking controversy. See Hillegas, "The First Invasion from Mars," *Michigan Alumnus Quarterly Review*, LXVI (1959), 109-111.

[49] See chap. 7.

[50] Wells uses this term in "Zoological Retrogression," p. 246.

Kenneth Burke, in *A Grammar of Motives* (New York, 1962), gives a simple illustration of how the "opposite idea" can restore a representative totality: "The man who would postulate an 'instinct to kill' can be asked to round out his dialectic by postulating a contrary 'instinct not to kill.' For there is certainly as much empirical evidence that men let one another live as there is evidence that they kill one another" (p. 49).

[51] Compare Henry Stanley's gospel of capitalism in *The Congo and the Founding of its Free State,* 2 vols. (New York, 1885). Having tried to sell the takeover of the Congo as a business proposition by emphasizing the richness of its resources, Stanley, in a chapter entitled "The Kernel of the Argument," pleads: "Of the 325,000,000 of people [sic] in civilized Europe there must be

universal scale, at the same time describing the effects of colo-
nialization from the point of view of those invaded and
colonized. And it counters the idea that man is the consumma-
tion of the evolutionary process with the myth of an alien
intelligence superior to, and possessing a technology more advanced than, man's own.

The two myths are fused in the opening chapter of *The
War of the Worlds:*

> We men, creatures who inhabit this earth, must be to [the
> Martians] at least as alien and lowly as are the monkeys and
> lemurs to us. The intellectual side of man already admits that
> life is an incessant struggle for existence, and it would seem
> that this too is the belief of the minds upon Mars. Their world
> is far gone in its cooling and this world is still crowded with
> life, but crowded only with what they regard as inferior ani-
> mals. To carry warfare sunward is, indeed, their only escape
> from the destruction that generation after generation creeps
> upon them.
>
> And before we judge them too harshly we must remember
> what ruthless and utter destruction our own species has
> wrought, not only upon animals . . . but upon its own inferior
> races. . . . Are we such apostles of mercy as to complain if the
> Martians warred in the same spirit? (III, 215-216)

What Bernard Bergonzi identifies as the *fin du globe* motif,
the myth of a dying world,[52] is thus transferred from earth to
Mars, and is projected as part of the Darwinian struggle on a
universal scale.[53] The defense mechanism for survival which
such a cosmic struggle provokes is alienation—the dissociation
from reality of the artilleryman on Putney Hill or of the narrator himself. The former dreams up programs that he makes

---

some surely to whom the gospel of enterprise preached in this book . . . will
present a few items of fact . . . capable of inspiring action" (II, 377). The idea
of "missionary capitalism" was of course very much in the air in the 1890's,
and in its various forms is part of the background of *War of the Worlds* and
The First Men in the Moon.

[52] Bernard Bergonzi, *The Early H. G. Wells* (Toronto, 1961), pp. 3-16 *passim*,
131-132.

[53] Compare the self-justificatory speeches of Weston, the scientist in C. S.
Lewis, *Out of the Silent Planet* (New York, 1943), pp. 145-153.

no attempt to carry out for subsisting under a Martian regime; and the narrator develops a similar state of mind: "I suffer from the strangest sense of detachment from myself and the world about me; I seem to watch it all from the outside, from somewhere inconceivably remote, out of time, out of space, out of the stress and tragedy of it all" (III, 248).

The progression of Wells's myth of hostile superior beings, evolving in some remote region to take revenge on man for his imperialistic depredations, can be traced through several of his earlier pieces bearing directly on *War of the Worlds*. Logically the first of these is the essay "Intelligence on Mars," in which he writes: "Granted that there has been evolution of protoplasm upon Mars, there is every reason to think that the creatures on Mars would be very different from creatures on earth, in form and function, in structure and habit, different beyond the most bizarre imaginings of nightmare."[54]

The hint of what this strange form and function might be is the subject of "The Man of the Year Million," reprinted in *Certain Personal Matters* as "Of a Book Unwritten."[55] Here Wells declares: "Clearly, then, man, unless the order of the universe has come to an end, will undergo further modification in the future, and at last cease to be man, giving rise to some other type of animated being" (pp. 162-163).[56] This creature of the future will have a body adapted solely to fulfill the requirements of its brain; and as mechanical devices become extensions of the organism more intimately than they are now, almost all natural appendages will atrophy and in time disappear (pp. 166-169).

The result as it appears in *War of the Worlds*, however, looks less like the "human tadpoles" (p. 171) Wells imagined in "Man of the Year Million" than the intelligent and predatory octopuses envisioned in "The Extinction of Man"

[54] H. G. Wells, "Intelligence on Mars," *Saturday Review*, LXXX (Apr. 4, 1896), 346.
[55] "The Man of the Year Million" first appeared in the *Pall Mall Budget* for November 6, 1893. (See Gordon S. Haight, "H. G. Wells's 'The Man of the Year Million,'" *NCF*, XII [1958], 323-326).
[56] H. G. Wells, *Certain Personal Matters* (London, 1898 [1897]). I have taken the text of this essay and of "The Extinction of Man" from this volume, since neither is collected in Wells's *Works*.

(1894).[57] He had already dramatized the ravages of this strange species, "in shape somewhat resembling an octopus" ("Extinction of Man," p. 176), in "The Sea Raiders (1896);[58] and a similar species, also with "a preferential taste for human nutriment" ("Extinction," p. 176), figures, in form and function, as the nemesis from Mars. As one voice observes of the Martians, "Octopuses . . . that's what I calls em" (III, 259).[59] Thus what Wells originally conceived of as the man of the distant future or the hitherto unknown species from the depths of the sea returns in a later fiction as the monster from Mars.[60]

The genesis of myth in *War of the Worlds* exemplifies how the myths of science fantasies can arise from scientific theory and develop to implicate larger portions of present reality. Such myths can never wholly be explained by referring them to timeless archetypes. To analyze the details of their meaning, one must take into account the relation these myths bear to contemporary science—and, more generally, to prevailing ideas about science and the established social order—as well as to whatever antecedent myths the fantasy may draw upon and recast.

Science fiction, then, can be defined as a strategy of interpreting sectors of historical actuality through mythic displacement. That is to say, the fantastic state of affairs imagined by the writer of science fiction represents a deflection of reality into myth, and especially myth derived by dramatizing the metaphoric substance of various models of reality. To go further than this would be to attempt to determine the nature of fiction generally, which is not the purpose of this essay.[61]

---

[57] This essay first appeared in *The Pall Mall Gazette*. (See Bergonzi, "Another Early Wells Item," *NCF*, XIII [1958], 72-73).

[58] David Y. Hughes, "H. G. Wells: Ironic Romancer," *Extrapolation*, VI (May, 1965), 32-33, provides evidence for a date late in 1895 as being the terminus a quo for Wells's writing of this story. He argues that Wells was inspired by the discovery of some hitherto unknown species of deep-sea cephalopod, and more specifically, by an account of that discovery printed in *Nature* in January, 1896.

[59] Another reference to the Martians as being octopuslike appears at III, 237.

[60] Similarly, the Morlocks, that degenerate species of the distant future, return in *The First Men* transfigured as the Selenites. See chap. 7.

[61] See, for example, Frank Kermode, *The Sense of an Ending* (New York, 1967). It should be noted that Mr. Kermode uses the term "fiction" mostly in the sense that I appropriate the term "model" to convey.

Before concluding these analytical remarks, however, it might be useful to introduce a distinction between two kinds of myth, public and private. In differentiating public from private myth in science fantasy—which I will identify respectively with H. G. Wells and Jules Verne—I begin by considering the received opinion concerning the two writers.

Public Myth and Private

It is often proposed that modern science fiction originates with Verne and Wells. According to this view, Verne, with his interest in technology and his attention to buttressing speculation with solid scientific fact, stands opposed to Wells, who uses pseudo-scientific explanations as a means of transporting the reader into the world of his fantasy.

This notion has a certain heuristic value in classifying science fiction on the basis of its preoccupation with realizable technological advances (Verne) or satiric mythifications of reality (Wells); and aside from that, both Verne and Wells encouraged it. In an interview (1903) a few years before his death, Verne said of Wells's stories that they

> do not repose on very scientific bases. No, there is no *rapport* between his work and mine. I make use of physics. He invents. I go to the moon in a cannonball, discharged from a cannon. Here there is no invention. He goes to Mars in an airship, which he constructs of a metal which does away with the law of gravitation. "Ça c'est très joli," cried Monsieur Verne in an animated way, "but show me this metal. Let him produce it."[62]

Verne was addressing his remarks especially (and no doubt invidiously) at *The First Men in the Moon*. But thirty years later Wells himself agreed that all his science fantasies were essentially different from Verne's in the way that Verne had suggested. Verne's "work dealt almost always with actual possibilities of invention and discovery," Wells wrote in the preface to his *Scientific Romances*, "and he made some remark-

[62] Quoted in Ingvald Raknem, *H. G. Wells and his Critics* (Norway, 1962), p. 406.

able forecasts. . . . But these stories of mine collected here do not pretend to deal with possible things. . . . They are all fantasies. . . . They have to hold the reader to the end by art and illusion and not by proof and argument" (p. vii).

Despite their agreement on the point, however, the artificiality of this particular distinction between them is apparent, as far as Wells is concerned, from his many anticipations of the technological shape of things to come. As for Verne, very few of his extraordinary voyages contain imagined technological innovations and even fewer "actual possibilities of invention."

Looking again at the interview with Verne in *T.P.'s Weekly,* one can detect what may be, unintentionally, an indication that the Frenchman was not always so intransigent to fantastic romances as he later gave himself out to be. Verne mistakenly says that Wells's voyagers go to Mars; perhaps his memory failed him. But possibly he confused Wells's romance with another, for which he himself had written a short but laudatory preface to introduce readers to his "English disciple," Robert Cromie. Cromie's interplanetary travelers do in fact journey to Mars; and the irony, given Verne's disparagement of Wells's approach to science fiction and especially his lack of scientific authenticity in *The First Men,* is that it would have been natural for him to confound Cromie's romance with Wells's: both authors rely on virtually the same principle to get their spacecraft launched. The scientist in Cromie's *A Plunge into Space,* explains that

> The space between the earth and Mars is, as it were, one vast charged wire . . . a body insulated from the Earth's attraction would by it pass almost instantaneously to Mars for the attraction of gravity is inconceivably rapid. . . .
>
> My chief difficulty . . . has been to regulate the speed at which we travel. (P. 60)

In other words, Cromie's scientist, like Cavor (in *The First Men*), has discovered how to make his spherical spaceship "opaque to gravitation" *(FMM,* VI, 18). Apart from this correspondence, Cromie's Martian society is at least as fantastic as the world Bedford and Cavor find in the moon.[63]

But however one accounts for Verne's error of thinking that Bedford and Cavor go to Mars, the most casual reading of those extraordinary voyages of his which can be considered science fiction is sufficient to reveal that Verne sometimes devotes only the most cursory attention to making the impossible situation seem plausible. Occasionally the "invention" (in Wells's sense of a hypothetical situation on which the fantasy is founded) is outright incredible, as when a comet grazes the earth without doing more damage than carrying away a small portion of northern Africa (in *Hector Servadac*);[64] and even when Verne goes to great lengths to substantiate a technological possibility, as in the voyage around the moon by three members of the Baltimore Gun Club, the project is no more convincing, for all his calculations, than Cavor's discovery of a metal impervious to the force of gravitation.[65]

Although this one distinction between Verne and Wells admits of too many exceptions on both sides to be a valid generalization, the difference between the two can be located in the differentiation of public myth from private. In saying that Verne's fantasies, individually and taken together, develop a private myth, I mean that they present a rather personal vision of man in the world. This poetic vision is coherent without recourse to a purely psychoanalytical interpretation of it;[66] nevertheless, the impulse is to think of Verne's fantasies as embodying his own beliefs, rather than displacing, and thus commenting upon, the historical condition of man. This is not to say that Verne disregards history; but usually historical actualities, instead of generating Verne's myths, are subsumed as part of his private and primarily ahistorical vision. What

[63] Cromie's vision of life on Mars is discussed on p. 17.

[64] Compare Wells's short story "The Star" (1897) or *In the Days of the Comet* (1906).

[65] Verne himself later viewed with an ironical eye his early attempts to create mathematical plausibility (see *The Purchase of the North Pole* [London, 190–]).

[66] But see Marcel Moré, *Le Très Curieux Jules Verne* (Paris, 1960). M. Moré argues that several of Verne's romances reveal his *"drame intime et secret"* (p. 15); namely, the conflict between the spiritual father and the natural father which leads to "le triomphe du 'père sublime' sur le 'père naturel' " (p. 25).

the fantasies immediately displace, in other words, are their original psychological determinants; and historical considerations enter in only secondarily, as they affect those determinants.[67]

The idea of private myth that I am trying to get at can be clarified by comparing Verne with Wells. In Wells's fiction, there is an element of private myth also: principally, the dramatization of a destructive impulse to do away with any sort of confinement, ideational or social.[68] But one never loses the awareness that the fantastic state of affairs in Wells's science fiction relates outward to the public world, that it displaces and reflects upon the realities and possibilities of man in society; whereas in most of Verne's fantasies, the private myth is central and moves, as it were, inward on itself.

Verne's private myth is an introverted vision of man seeking self-enclosure. As Roland Barthes observes (*Mythologies*, p. 90), taking *The Mysterious Island* as the paradigm of this vision:

> To shut oneself in and take possession, such is the existential dream of childhood and of Verne. The archetype of this dream is close to perfection in this romance: *The Mysterious Island*. Here the child-man reinvents the world, fills it, encloses it, locks himself in it, and crowns his encyclopedic effort with the bourgeois gesture of appropriation . . . while outside, the storm, that is to say the infinite, rages in vain.

This same myth can be perceived elsewhere: in *Twenty Thousand Leagues under the Sea* (1870), in *Around the Moon* (1870), in *Hector Servadac* (1877), in *Godfrey Morgan* (*L'école des Robinsons:* 1882), and so on. Even when Verne seems to be

---

[67] Thus the private element in Wells, the claustrophobic fear of and consequent rebellion against confinement, can be understood in the context of the world situation prior to the Great War, just as Verne's antithetical fantasy of man seeking self-sufficient enclosure can be seen as his reaction to the chaotic and threatening world about him (see n. 68).

[68] Compare Robert P. Weeks, "Disentanglement as a Theme in H. G. Wells' Fiction," *Papers of the Mich. Acad. of Science, Arts and Letters* XXXIX (1954), 439-444. Whereas in Verne's fiction the characters "are inclined to accept all the restrictions of their environment and to work *within* them," Wells's "central image is of man trapped by his environment" and his heroes try to break out of their situation (pp. 442, 443).

pointing out the vulnerability of self-enclosure, as in *The Begum's Fortune* (1879)—a romance influenced by the belated impact on Verne of the Franco-Prussian War—he is still operating within the confines of his private myth; and his mania for factual detail in itself is intimately connected with that myth. He "scrupulously inventoried the lacunae of the geography of his age," writes Michel Butor, "and filled them with myths inscribed within the extension of the known facts."[69]

On a larger scale, the private myth of self-containment, of taking possession of and filling a world whose limits Verne carefully circumscribes, finds expression in the tendency of Verne's fantasies to be self-referential, that is, to refer to one another. Again *The Mysterious Island* is an apt example, since that trilogy brings together and concludes two earlier extraordinary voyages, *The Children of Captain Grant* (1868) and *Twenty Thousand Leagues*. But in *From the Earth to the Moon* (1865) also, one finds a foreshadowing of its sequel, *Around the Moon*, and of *The Purchase of the North Pole* (1889), in which the Baltimore Gun Club makes another appearance to attempt to right the earth's axis.

Through such interconnections among Verne's romances one becomes aware, as Butor says, that "they organize themselves into a mythology that is uniquely structured" ("Point Suprême," p. 38). Yet this mythology remains a private one; and Verne's motive in relating his fantasies to each other is as much to demarcate the limits of his world as it is to fuse their discrete myths into an inclusive whole.

This discussion of the difference between public and private myth concludes the overview of the various kinds of fantasy to be found in works using a science fictional strategy of presentation. If I have concentrated on private myth in this last section, the reason is that I will be dealing solely with the public element of the myths analyzed in the rest of this essay. In the next chapter, I will take up some of the points made in

---

[69] Michel Butor, "Science Fiction: The Crisis of its Growth" (tr. Richard Howard), *Partisan Review*, XXXIV (1967), 599.

An excellent essay on Verne is Butor's "Le Point Suprême et l'Age d'Or à Travers Quelques Oeuvres de Jules Verne" in *Essais sur les modernes* (Paris, 1960), pp. 35-94.

the foregoing sections of this survey again, detailing them with reference to several of the early voyages to the moon appearing in English.

Lunar Perspectives

2

> In the Moon, is a certain Island
> near by a mighty continent, which small island
> seems to have some affinity to England.
> & what is more extraordinary
> the people are so much alike & their language
> so much the same that you would think
> you was among your friends.
>
> WILLIAM BLAKE

In the argument of my first chapter, I attempted to define science fiction essentially as a rhetorical strategy, and then to suggest where and how works assignable to the class of utopian (or antiutopian) or satiric fiction can and do partake of that strategy. I concluded, in the course of examining the partial coincidence of categories, that the fantasy based on some scientific, or pseudoscientific, hypothesis mythically displaces, and interpretatively deforms, areas of historical reality.

Both the rhetorical strategy of science fiction and the tendency toward displacing models of reality with their mythic, and often satiric equivalents, are incipient in many of the early fictional accounts of voyages, and projects for voyages, to the moon. This idea, mentioned previously, I now intend to detail further, with the general aim of determining how myth can be derived from metaphor. Thus in analyzing a few of the fantasied lunar voyages and related works published in England approximately between 1610 and 1730, I will outline some of the relations science bears to fantasy, particularly those obtaining between the metaphors of science and the myths of fantasy. If I sometimes deviate from the strict order of chronological succession, my reason for doing so is to demonstrate implicitly the emergent consciousness of the process of transforming metaphor into myth.

Lunar Worlds and Lunatics

Giordano Bruno, proclaiming the infiniteness and plenitude of the created universe, supplied the watchword for more than three centuries when he wrote in 1584: "God . . . is glorified . . . not in a single earth, a single world, but in a thousand thousand, I say in an infinity of worlds."[1] It did not take long for the popular imagination, prompted by received opinion about the New Astronomy and about the discoveries of Kepler and Galileo in particular, to begin to speculate concerning other worlds, especially the new world in the moon.[2] That new world did not promise any immediate prospects of colonial aggrandizement in the name of the crown; but it did provide new territory for satire, the more readily because the felicitous derivation of the word *lunatic* suggested at once an appropriate epithet for anyone who was desirous of commerce with the moon or had otherwise come under its influence.

Among the first to exploit some of the satiric possibilities the new world afforded, as one might expect, was John Donne. In *Ignatius his Conclave* (1611), he has Lucifer propose to Ignatius Loyola that he transfer his Jesuits to the moon. Access to that planet will present no problem, for Galileo "shall have made new [perspective] Glasses, and they received a hal-

---

[1] *De l'infinito universo e mondi*, tr. Dorothea Waley Singer in her *Giordano Bruno: His Life and Work* (New York, 1950), p. 246.

A. O. Lovejoy, of course, discusses the evolution of the idea of plenitude in *The Great Chain of Being* (Cambridge, Mass., 1936); but see also Alexandre Koyré, *From the Closed World to the Infinite Universe* (New York, 1957), pp. 39 ff.

[2] See Marjorie Hope Nicolson, *A World in the Moon: A Study of the Changing Attitude toward the Moon in the Seventeenth and Eighteenth Centuries*, Smith Coll. Studies in Mod. Langs., XVII (1936). Since I have selected relatively few lunar voyages and related works to make my point about the derivation of myth from metaphor, readers interested in the tradition of the lunar voyage are referred to this scholarly historical account and to Miss Nicolson's almost exhaustive bibliographical discoveries in *Voyages to the Moon* (New York, 1948).

lowing from the *Pope*," so that Loyola "may draw the *Moone*, like a boate floating upon the water, as neere the earth as he will" (p. 117).[3] Once passage to the Moon has been gained by this means, Loyola can establish his *"Lunatique Church"*; and, the Devil continues,

> without doubt, after the Jesuites have been there a little while, there will soone grow naturally a *Hell* in that world also; over which, you *Ignatius* shall have dominion, and establish your kingdome & dwelling there. And with the same ease as you passe from the earth to the *Moone*, you may passe from the earth to *starrs*, which are also thought to be worlds, & so you may beget and propagate many Hells. (P. 118)

Thus Donne introduces the motif of appropriating the new world in the moon as a convenient location for fanatics, with whom he associates the belief in a plurality of worlds.

For a long time works "Wherein many things are mingled by way of Satyr" and incorporating this motif coexist alongside those arguing seriously about reaching the inhabited, or habitable, world in the moon. Aphra Behn's *The Emperor of the Moon* (1687), a farce relying heavily on Molière for its plot, alludes to some of these serious treatises while dismissing the enthusiasm for "lunatick" excursions with characteristic Restoration skepticism. The dupe of the play, one Doctor Baliardo, is obsessed with the idea of going to the moon, though he has no means of getting there except on flights of a disorddered imagination. Two of the characters analyze the source of his disorder:[4]

> *Scaramouch.* . . . Lunatick we may call him without breaking the Decorum of good Manners; for he is always travelling to the Moon.

[3] John Donne, *Ignatius his Conclave: OR His Inthronisation in a late Election in Hell: Wherein many things are mingled by way of Satyr* . . . Facsimile Text Soc. Pub. No. 53 (New York, 1941). I have made a few minor emendations in this and other quotations from early seventeenth-century texts so that they accord with modern printing conventions.

[4] Aphra Behn, *The Emperor of the Moon. A Farce. As it is Acted by Their Majesties Servants, at the Queens Theatre* . . . (London, 1687).

Elaria.   And so Religiously believes there is a World there, that he discourses as gravely of the People, their Government, Institutions, Laws, Manners, Religion and Constitution, as if he had been bred a *Machiavel* there.

Scaramouch.   How came he then infected first?

Elaria.   With reading foolish Books, *Lucian's Dialogue of the Lofty Traveller,* who flew up to the Moon, and thence to Heaven; an Heroick business called, *The Man in the Moon,* if you'll believe a *Spaniard,* who was carried thither upon an Engine drawn by wild Geese; with another Philosophical Piece, *A Discourse of the World in the Moon;* with a thousand other ridiculous Volumes too hard to name. (P. 4)

Happily the good doctor is finally cured of his quixotic obsession; and his exclamation, "No Emperor of the Moon,—and no Moon World!" is followed by a book-burning amid rejoicings that "I see there's nothing in Philosophy" (p. 67).

Francis Godwin's "Eyewitnesse"

The "Heroick business" Mrs. Behn refers to is *The Man in the Moone: or A Discourse of a Voyage thither* (1638), written by Francis Godwin, Bishop of Hereford, and published pseudonymously (and posthumously) under the name of its hero, Domingo Gonsales.[5] This curious little work, a conjunction of picaresque, moon voyage, and utopia, managed to conceal its English authorship from most of its readers for the better part of three centuries, passing alternately as the original creation of some Spaniard—the said Domingo Gonsales—or

[5] Two of the extant first editions of Godwin's work are listed in Nicolson's *Voyages,* p. 265. A third, which I have consulted, belongs to the Folger Shakespeare Library. A modern edition of the 1638 text, prepared by Grant McColley, is available in Smith Coll. Studies in Mod. Langs., XIX (1937).

No indication of the true authorship appears in the first edition; but the title page of the second edition (1657) reads: *The Man in the Moone . . . by F. G., B. of H.*

There has been some controversy about the possible date of composition of this work (throughout this essay I have given only the dates of publication), but it is now generally agreed to have been written sometime between 1625 and 1630. See McColley, "The Date of Godwin's *Domingo Gonsales,*" *MP,* XXXV (1937), 47-60; and Harold W. Lawton, "Bishop Godwin's *Man in the Moone,*" *RES,* VII (1931), 35-37.

of its French translator, Jean Baudoin.[6] Since Domingo Gonsales for a time attained the sort of mythic status in the popular
imagination that Frankenstein and his monster achieved at a
later date,[7] *The Man in the Moone,* as far as Godwin's hero
was concerned, did prove to be

> a meanes of eternizing my name for ever with all Posteritie,
> (I verily hope) and to the unspeakable good of all mortall men,
> that in succeeding ages the world shall have, if at the leastwise
> it may please God that I doe returne safe home againe into my
> Countrie, to give perfect instructions how those admirable de
> vices, and past all credit of possibilitie, which I have light upon,
> may be imparted unto publique use. You shal then see men to
> flie from place to place in the ayre . . . but that which far sur
> passeth all the rest, you shall have notice of a new World, of
> many most rare and incredible secrets of Nature, that all the
> Philosophers of former ages could never so much as dreame
> off. (Pp. 10-11)

What now seems unusual about Godwin's fiction though is
neither its revelation of "secrets of Nature" nor its Baconian
impulse to reveal them, but rather the way Godwin chose to
convince his readers of the truth of those secrets.

Gonsales's voyage to the moon was not the first such journey in fiction; nor was it the first to disclose in fictional form
the discoveries of the New Astronomy. Lucian's Icaromenippus
had flown to the moon long before Sr. Gonsales began his ascent from Teneriffe, and a strong gale had also carried there
the cosmic argonauts of Lucian's *True History.* More recently,
Duracotus had been transported to the moon by demons in
Kepler's *Somnium* and had found that world to be as Kepler,
rather than Galileo, supposed it.[8] But Godwin's is, somewhat

---

[6] Thus Jules Verne, in *From the Earth to the Moon* (1865), ascribes Godwin's work to Baudoin, whose translation first appeared in 1648; and J. Kagarlitski, *Life and Thought of H. G. Wells,* tr. Moura Budberg (New York, 1966),
among its many errors (not all of which seem to be the fault of the critic) speaks
of "Jean Baudouin, author of the book *Men on the Moon* (1647), whose hero,
Señor Gonsales . . . " (p. 85).

[7] An account of both the serious and the satiric treatment of Gonsales and
his gansas after 1638 can be found in Nicolson, *op. cit.,* pp. 85-108.

[8] For Kepler's differences with Galileo, see Nicolson, *A World in the Moon,*
pp. 37-39.

precociously, the first moon voyage to provide a scientific, or quasi-scientific, rationale for the possibility, however primitive that rationale now appears to be.

Stranded on St. Helena, Gonsales gets hold of some "gansas" and gradually accustoms them to carry weights, regulated according to Galileo's principles of the pulley, from one end of his island to the other. "I fastened about every one of my *Gansas* a little pulley of Cork," he reports,

> and putting a string through it of meetly length, I fastened the one end thereof unto a blocke almost of eight Pound weight, unto the other end of the string I tied a poyse weighing some two Pound, which being done, and causing the signall to be erected, they [the gansas] presently rose all (being 4 in number,) and carried away my blocke into the place appointed. (Pp. 25-26)

This experiment proving a success, he next conceives a contrivance whereon he can be transported by these gansas and makes a trial run with the contraption. On the second attempt, however, he experiences one of those unforeseen catastrophes that seem to have beset aeronautical history, real or fictive; for having elevated him above the danger of imminent murder by Canary Island savages, his gansas continue their upward progress.

> But what then, O Reader? *Arrige aures,* prepare thy selfe unto the hearing of the strangest Chance that ever happened to any mortall man, and that I know thou wilt not have the Grace to beleeve, till thou seest it seconded with Iteration of Experiments in the like, as many a one, I trust, thou mayst in short time. (P. 42)[9]

As Gonsales later concludes, it is the season when these birds of his migrate to the moon, and of course they are taking him along with them.

At some distance from earth, he encounters a feeling of

---

[9] The conjunction here of Grace and experimental proof is reminiscent of *The New Atlantis* and Bacon's insistence on the "Revelation" of nature's secrets.

weightlessness (though it is the cause of no inconvenience) and resorts to Gilbert's theory of magnetism to explain the phenomenon.[10] Finding that his gansas "forbare moving" and that "neither I, nor the Engine moved at all, but abode still as having no manner of weight," he conjectures:

> I found then by this Experience that which no Philosopher ever dreamed of, to wit, that those things which wee call heavie, do not sinke toward the Center of the Earth, as their naturall place, but as drawen by a secret property of the Globe of the Earth, or rather some thing within the same, in like sort as the Loadstone draweth Iron, being within the compasse of the beames attractive. (Pp. 45-47)

He has overcome his initial fright by this time and can now report what he sees.

> Now shall I declare unto you the quality of the place, in which I then was. The Clouds I perceived to be all under me, betweene mee and the earth. The starres, by reason it was alwaies day, I saw at all times alike, not shining bright . . . but of a whitish Colour, like that of the Moone in the day time with us: And such of them as were to be seene (which were not many) . . . shewed farre greater then with us, yea (as I should ghesse) no lesse than ten times so great. As for the Moone being then within two daies of the change, she appeared of a huge and fearefull quantitie. (Pp. 51-52)

He also observes that from where he is the earth appears "like another Moone" (p. 66)—a correlation furnishing the basis for later satiric worlds in the moon.

Reaching that satellite, he finds a lunar utopia that "seemeth to be another Paradise." After a sojourn barely long enough for him to ascertain that the lunar authorities perpetuate a utopian state of affairs by deporting anyone "likely to bee of a wicked or imperfect disposition" to North America,[11] Sr.

---

[10] Gilbert's *De Magnete* had come out in 1600. McColley ("Godwin's *Domingo Gonsales*," pp. 55-56) discusses Godwin's knowledge of Gilbert's work and reports that "the author of the *Gonsales* is definitely more advanced than the Gilbert of *The Magnet*."

[11] I speak of Godwin's lunar utopia in chap. 1, p. 14.

Gonsales takes leave for China. There he relates his adventures to one of the mandarins, who exonerates him from heresy or superstition by recognizing "in all my discourse nothing any way tending to Magique" (p. 124); and so confessing his intent to "reape the glory of my fortunate misfortunes" (p. 126), Domingo Gonsales ends his narrative.

What is noteworthy about this moon voyage is not only the evidence it gives of the extent to which the experimental method had become a habit of thought for the Anglican bishop who imagined it; but also its emphasis throughout on seeing and perceiving the external universe. Indeed, it might be said on the testimony of *The Man in the Moone* that the New Astronomy (together with the printing press), by placing renewed stress on the importance of eyesight, gave a new concreteness to the metaphoric implications of sight and blindness. Thus when Bishop Godwin has his hero remark, "mine eyes have sufficiently informed me there can be no such thing" as a region of fire above "the uppermost Region of the Ayre" (pp. 65-66), or exhort, *"Philosophers* and *Mathematicians* I would should now confesse the wilfulnesse of their owne blindnesse" in believing the earth to have no diurnal motion (p. 58), one has the sense that the words convey a rediscovered, and secular, literalness. Not content to write an academic treatise on astronomy, Godwin demanded "the faithful relation" of an "eyewitnesse, our great discoverer" (sig. A_4ᵛ). The bishop admits the "Fancy" of the lunar voyage, but leaves "the Ingenious Reader" to profit from the "conceite": "Thou hast here an essay of *Fancy,* where *Invention* is shewed with *Judgment.* It was not the *Authors* intention . . . to discourse thee into a beliefe of each particular circumstance. Tis fit to allow him a liberty of conceite; where thou takest to thy selfe a liberty of judgment" (sigs. A_3ʳ-A_3ᵛ). Despite his disclaiming the intention of discoursing his reader into belief, however, Godwin's persistent emphasis that he is presenting exactly what was seen, as it was seen, through the eyes of his witness Domingo Gonsales clearly suggests that he considered such empirical observations, even if fancied, a means of compelling conviction.

Projects and Voyages: The View from the Moon

Godwin did not persuade every reader to take his flying machine seriously. But his *Man in the Moone,* together with the learned arguments of John Wilkins in a work bearing the self-contradictorily defensive title, *The Discovery of a World in the Moone. Or a Discourse Tending to Prove that 'tis Probable there may be another habitable World in that Planet* (1638),[12] and especially Wilkin's addition in 1640 of "A Discourse concerning the possibility of a Passage thither,"[13] directed serious and satiric attention to the means of reaching the moon.

To be sure, such attention to the means of celestial navigation, like the idea of an exploratory journey to the moon, was not completely new. Lucian's *Icaromenippus, The Lofty Traveller* Mrs. Behn alluded to, devised a method of flying to the moon long before Michael Drayton's *Cynthia* raised Endymion "up to those excelling sights."[14] Taking the right wing of an eagle and the left wing of a vulture, "and buckling them

[12] Wilkins's logic in the body of his discourse fulfills what the reader might expect from its title. After citing numerous authorities who deny that the moon or any celestial body other than the earth is a habitable world as examples of how opinion can err, he goes on to say: "Having read *Plutarch, Galileus, Kepler,* with some others, and finding many of mine owne thoughts confirmed by such strong authorities, I then concluded that it was not onely possible there might bee, but probable that there was another habitable world in that planet [i.e., the moon]" *(The Discovery* . . . [London, 1638], pp. 22-23). (For Galileo's real opinion about the possibility that the moon could support life, see the reference at n. 8).

[13] The 1640 edition of Wilkins's treatise, in two parts, was published under the title, *A Discourse concerning a New World and another Planet.*

[14] "The Man in the Moone" (1606) in *Pastorals Contayning Eclogues, With the Man in the Moone* . . . (London, 1619).

The idea of having the moon descend to earth and pick up passengers persisted well into the second half of the eighteenth century. "The Man of the People," Charles Fox, goes to the moon by hanging on to a wart on the Man-in-the-Moon's nose in William Thomson's *The Man in the Moon; or, Travels into the Lunar Regions by the Man of the People,* 2 vols. (London, 1783). "'I brought you to the moon at present not so much with an intention of praising what is right, as pointing out what is wrong,'" says the Man-in-the-Moon, declaring Thomson's didactic purpose and also that of many other celestial voyages of the period. "'The persons whom I attack,'" he continues, "'have no reason to complain; for . . . it is only their public character I correct'" (II, 128-129).

about me, [I] fastned them to my shoulders with thongs of strong leather, and at the ends of the uttermost feathers made mee loopes to put my hands through, and then began to trie what I could do." After a few successful trials, "I thought myselfe a chicken no longer but got me up to the top of *Olympus,* and there furnishing my selfe with victuals as expeditely as I could, from thence took my way directly towards Heaven" (p. 15).[15] Menippus lands on the moon all right, but he cannot see the earth from there until Empedocles, "that tumbled [him] selfe into the tunnells of mount *Ætna,* and was thence cast out againe by the strength of the smoke, and tost up hither" (p. 17), instructs him to remove the vulture's wing—whereupon he sees with the eyes of an eagle. "Adulteries, murthers, treacheries, rapines, perjuries, fears and false-heartednesse towards their friends: thus was I occupied in beholding the affaires of Kings" (p. 19).

Put in lunar perspective, the "affaires of Kings" appear of Lilliputian consequence.

> How little was left for our rich men to be proud of, when the greatest landed man amongst them seemed to possesse scarcely the quantitie of an *Epicurean Atome*: then casting mine eye upon the *Peloponnesus,* and in it beholding the country of *Cynuria,* I remembered how many *Lacedæmonians and Argives* lost their lives in one day for a plott of ground hardly so bigge as an Ægyptian beane. (Pp. 20-21)

After making these observations, Menippus proceeds "directly towards Heaven," where Jupiter greets him with a typically Lucianic harangue against the follies of various philosophers and has him returned, somewhat indecorously, to earth: *"Mercurie* taking hold of my right eare, so carried me dangling downe" (p. 29).

The lunar perspective on earthly affairs, illustrated in *Icaromenippus,* recurs in moon voyages of the seventeenth and eighteenth centuries. Following publication of Godwin's *Man in the Moone,* however, devices for getting to the lunar regions

---

[15] Lucian, *Certaine Select Dialogues of Lucian: Together with his True History,* tr. Francis Hickes (Oxford, 1634).

tended to gain in complexity, if not always in sophistication. David Russen of Hythe, a schoolteacher who claimed Cyrano de Bergerac as the inspiration for his *Iter Lunare* (1703),[16] proposed the construction of a gigantic spring, controlled by pulleys, to extend from the earth to the moon.[17]

> If it be objected, that the Diurnal Revolution of the Earth will carry away the Basis of the Engin[e], and the swift Motion of the Moon Eastwards, will alter the Spring, so that it will be uncertain when [!] it will touch the Moon; I answer, That 'tis less difficulty to overcome this Hazard, than to fly to the Moon, or frame flying Chariots. (P. 45)

There is no indication that Russen, who chooses as his motto *Sic Itur ad Astra*, is being ironic in this procatalepsis. But he does go on to declare—no doubt alluding to the depression of his own genius—that although England can afford the materials and men to build his engine, "Covetousness, Vice, Intemperance, Slothfulness and Ignorance hinder those who have Abilities; and such is the Poverty of those (whose Parts and Ingenuity joyned with Industry, would prompt them to accomplish it) that they cannot perform what their Wills would undertake, if able" (pp. 49-50).

It might be expected that Daniel Defoe also would not fail to share the new enthusiasm for mechanical projects, an enthusiasm given impetus by the simplistic accounts of Newton's principles of celestial mechanics and by the mechanistic psychological theories of John Locke. And, in fact, his journalistic sense of what would have immediate popular appeal led Defoe to turn out his *Consolidator: Or, Memoirs of Sundry Transac-*

---

[16] Hence, David Russen, *Iter Lunare; or, A Voyage to the Moon* (London, 1703), pp. 12 ff., weighs at length the question of whether Cyrano did in fact, as he reports, find the works of Cardano lying open on his desk.

[17] Russen's project many seem exceedingly naive from a scientific point of view, but such naivete is not solely the consequence of the youthfulness of science at the time. *The Conquest of the Moon* (London, 1889), published pseudonymously as the work of A. Laurie, but really an inferior imitation of Verne by Pierre Grousset, hinges on the proposal to use a powerful magnetic force to draw the moon to earth. This being accomplished, the force is cut off; and the "Moon, suddenly freed from her terrestrial attraction, sprang back to her own orbit" (p. 322).

tions from the World in the Moon (1705), a title which could well be concocted by the method Swift suggested in "The Mechanical Operation of the Spirit."[18]

It is obvious that Defoe's "transactions from the world in the moon" are mainly the vehicle for a purportedly satiric review of recent politics. But to avoid any misapprehension of this point, he reports that the Lunarians have invented powerful telescopes through which "they could plainly discover, That *this* World was *their* Moon, and *their* World *our* Moon; and when I came first among them, the People that flockt about me, distinguisht me by the Name of, *the Man that came out of the Moon*" (p. 56).[19] Thus the title of Defoe's work affords an ambiguity that, though not consistently exploited, at least acknowledges the strategy of projecting the satirical reflections pertaining to earthly affairs into a "lunar" fiction.

In addition to illustrating another stage in the development of a strategy of displacing actuality with fantasy—a strategy that by Blake's time had come to be a recognized convention[20] —*The Consolidator* again exemplifies the procedure by which fantasy assimilates science, and also, like Russen's *Iter Lunare,* the increasing distance between the up-to-date understanding of the "natural philosopher" and the somewhat archaic notions of the interested layman. The several hypothetical inventions that Defoe introduces into his "transactions" are not at all practicable; and in fact he has subordinated their scientific plausibility to the design of pointing out that the body politic must be unified to achieve its purposes.

The principal device for enforcing this moral is the Consolidator itself. This Consolidator is "a certain Engine formed in the shape of a Chariot" made of *"Lunar Earth"* and kept "in a most exact and regular Motion," always ascendant, by "Springs and Wheels" energized from the fires of a central furnace (p. 36). The chariot is supposed to get everyone to the moon, but,

---

[18] See "The Mechanical Operation" in *A Tale of a Tub,* ed. A. C. Guthkelch and D. Nichol Smith, 2d ed. (Oxford, 1958), p. 262.

[19] All quotations from Defoe are taken from *The Consolidator* (London, 1705).

[20] Of course, the "eastern tale" too played a part in the development of this strategy. See Mary Lascelles, *"Rasselas* Reconsidered," *Essays and Studies,* n.s., IV (1951), 40-43.

as it turns out, it is also intended to symbolize the English government, or more precisely, the political conjunction of King and Parliament. "The number of Feathers" comprising its two wings "are just 513"; and one "extraordinary Feather . . . placed in the Center" (presumably the King) acts as "Rudder to the whole Machine" (p. 37). Like this contraption, however, the satire is never successfully launched.

The other devices in *The Consolidator*, all of which have the intention of showing a man his right mind and thus bringing about a (Whig) consensus, derive in one way or another from *A Tale of a Tub*. But where Swift is finely (sometimes too finely) ironic, Defoe is grossly didactic, with the result that Defoe's mechanisms appear as vulgar parodies of their originals. There is, for example, the *"Cogitator," "to screw a Man into himself."* When the subject has seated himself in the chair of the machine,

> *certain Screws* . . . draw *direct Lines* from every *Angle of the Engine to the Brain of the Man,* and at the same time, other direct Lines to his Eyes; at the other end of which Lines, there are Glasses which convey or reflect the Objects the Person is desirous to *think upon.*

The operation of a series of springs, screws, and wheels then allows him "to form just ideas of the things" they focus his perception on, so that he can *"think and act like himself,* suitable to the sublime Qualities his Soul was originally blest with" (pp. 96-98). Such a machine might do to caricature Lockean epistemology; but Defoe, having no purpose of that kind, seems rather to accept the notion—always ridiculed by Swift— that ideas correspond to things. He takes at face value the scientific metaphor of mechanism and uses it as the basis of his (would-be) political satire in *The Consolidator*.

Though not influenced by the substance of *The Consolidator*, most of the imaginary celestial flights later on in the eighteenth century do share Defoe's didactic purpose and to some extent his circumstantial technique. Some of these anonymous and pseudonymous voyages—*The Life and Adventures of Peter Wilkins* (1751), for instance, or *The Life and Aston-*

ishing Adventures of John Daniel (1751)—are decidedly imitations, in part, of another work of Defoe's, *Robinson Crusoe* (1719).[21] Others, like the *Voyage to Cacklogallinia* (1727) and *A Trip to the Moon* (1728), attempt to follow the example of *Gulliver's Travels.*

Usually these subsequent imaginary voyages, whatever they may contain by way of satire, consider without any self-regarding irony on their author's part various projects for human flight; and sometimes this can lead to bizarre results like the grotesque creatures in *Peter Wilkins* whose large wings are integral to their anatomy and envelop them like a sheath.[22] The author of *A Trip to the Moon*—perhaps the most eclectic of these later voyages—is virtually alone in reintroducing a Lucianic skepticism regarding the means of celestial navigation.

Murtagh McDermot, the pseudonymous author and quondam hero of the narrative, sets out to sea "against the Will of my Mother" (p. 5).[23] He soon finds himself, the victim of shipwreck, on that same Mount Teneriffe from which Domingo Gonsales had been carried to the moon nearly a century before. But McDermot is destined to get to the moon by another means.

> Whilst I was . . . meditating on my own corrupt Nature, a sudden Whirlwind came, that rais'd me from the Place I stood on . . . it is probable in the last Degree that my Body became then so proportionate to the subadjacent Columns of Air, that it [the air] easily sustain'd me. Or admitting, not granting, that this will not clearly account for it, I can yet have recourse to the storm, which was then the Occasion of the continued Motion of my Body. (Pp. 8-9)

---

[21] *Peter Wilkins* has generally been attributed to Robert Paltock; *John Daniel* to Ralph Morris. For other works influenced strongly by *Crusoe*, see Walter de la Mare, *Desert Islands and Robinson Crusoe* (London, 1932).

[22] *Wilkins* had enough appeal for Leigh Hunt, however, to provoke this rhetorical flight from him: "after all, how founded in nature itself is the human desire to fly! We do so in dreams: we all long for the power when children: we think of it in poetry and sorrow" (*A Book for a Corner; or, Selections in Prose and Verse from Authors Best Suited to that Mode of Enjoyment* [New York, 1857], p. 75).

[23] Murtagh McDermot, *pseud., A Trip to the Moon* . . . (London, 1728). His "Father being dead a little before" the son decides to venture off as a mariner, McDermot cannot (like Crusoe) go against his father's advice.

Now that he is whirling in space, McDermot conceives that he might be taken for a star or a comet,[24] though as for the latter, "I wou'd not be oblig'd to the *Sun* for his Rays, so that I resolv'd to be independent, and model my Course by my own reason" (p. 10). A conspiracy of the elements, however, makes his carrying out of this admirable resolution impossible. Fearing for his life, he grabs hold of "a Cloud full of Hail"; and "putting both my Hands against it, by all Strength, I caus'd it to re-act upon me as much as I acted upon it, so that I was quickly remov'd into the Sphere of the *Moon's* Attraction." By this application of Newton's third law of motion, he rescues himself from his predicament and arrives safely on the moon. There he lands in a fish pond, "which our sharp-sighted Philosophers mistake for a Part of the Sea" (pp. 10-11), and begins a series of adventures suggestive of *Gulliver's Travels,* and especially of the "Voyage to Laputa"; but the details are often so absurd as to make Gulliver's circumstantial narrative, read literally, seem plausible by comparison.[25]

Although McDermot's attitude toward scientific explanations, and fantastic voyages in general, is Lucianic rather than Baconian, he has much in common with Godwin and Defoe. He assumes, in a way that Lucian does not, that the moon is an inhabited world, and further supposes, like Defoe, a satiric correspondence between his lunar world and that on earth. These notions, moreover, are built into the fantasy and are the necessary premises for McDermot's satire.

Regardless of differences in spirit, the various seventeenth- and eighteenth-century lunar voyages, or projects for voyages, discussed so far illustrate how popular ideas about science are assimilated, more or less immediately, in fiction. While these voyages may not be what one thinks of as science fiction—and certainly they cannot be considered modern science fiction— still they exemplify the technique of absorbing science in fiction as metaphor and explanation.

---

[24] Compare Samuel Butler, *Hudibras,* ed. A. R. Waller (Cambridge, 1905), pp. 162-163; and Ludwig Holberg, *A Journey to the World Under-Ground,* trans. anon. (1742), pp. 7-11.

[25] *A Trip to the Moon* is in fact dedicated "to the Worthy, Daring, Adventurous, Thrice-renown'd, and Victorious Captain Lemuel Gulliver" (sig. M₂ᵛ).

But beyond their reliance on explicit scientific explanations or the (usually implicit) metaphors of natural philosophy, some of these voyages can serve as rudimentary examples of how, by extending the range and detail of human experience and enlarging and multiplying the concepts that order that experience, science can influence the form of the fantasy. The metaphors deriving from science, that is to say, can motivate not only the myth, but the fictional technique as well: specifically, in some of the cases already mentioned, the point of view of the fiction. Godwin, for instance, incorporates a telescopic perspective in picturing the earth as it might appear to an observer in outer space; and similarly, the impression of detached objectivity that Defoe tries to create in his *Consolidator* is a telescopic objectivity, a lunar perspective on earthly affairs.

Whereas prior to the New Astronomy such detachment would almost always have been temporal, or atemporal (that is, the world seen from the point of view of eternity), Defoe's objectivity, at least metaphorically, depends on spatial distance between the observer and what is observed. To be sure, this distance is to be found in Lucian's *Icaromenippus,* but there credibility is lacking for the means of attaining it. The sort of perspective assumed in satiric worlds in the moon, moreover, relies on close-up details as well as objective distance; and these seemingly contradictory requirements the telescope, as metaphor for point of view, was uniquely suited to satisfy.

Thus in Defoe, as in Godwin, the transcendental implications of the power of seeing derive by analogy from telescopic sight. Men are resorting to all sorts of "Glasses, to help and assist their *Moonblind Understanding"* to attain the degree of *"Eye-sight"* we call *General Knowledge,"* writes Defoe; yet he wonders whether *"the Great Eye* of the World had no People to whom he had given clearer Eye-sight, or at least, that made a better use of it than we had here" (*Consolidator,* pp. 58-59, 59-60, 61).

The lunar perspective, therefore, originates with a telescopically enhanced power of eyesight by which terrestrial goings on can be detected from the vantage point of the moon. "Make room there for the *Man in the Moon,* that [in] his Nocturnall walkes, hath discovered more *Knavery* then ever (before these prodigious times) was acted by any People under the *Sun*," declares the anonymous author of a series of pamphlets attacking Cromwell and the Commonwealth:[26] this is the simple motif epitomizing the lunar point of view through all its diverse embodiments. The logically subsequent notion that the earth, viewed from its satellite, looks "like another Moone" provides the correspondence necessary for projecting satiric observations about life on this planet into that "other world." And this displacement (ideally) entails a complex irony whereby the lunar fiction is at the same time a true account.

The Elephant in the Moon: Myth as Satiric Measure

A satiric possibility of still greater formal complexity would allow the nature of the projection itself to expose the limited point of view of whoever was responsible for it. Samuel Butler's *Elephant in the Moon,* published posthumously in 1759, does exactly that. The poem opens as a group of virtuosi assemble to direct their telescope at the moon, "When at the Full her radiant Light/And Influence too were at their Height" (ll. 19-20).[27] In language appropriate to the description of a military assault, Butler tells how his virtuosi readied their engine for conquest. Their telescope or "optic tube," becomes a seige ladder, by means of which they can bridge the gap between the earth and their object:

> . . . the lofty Tube, the Scale
> With which they Heav'n itself assail,
> Was mounted full against the *Moon;*
> And all stood ready to fall on,
> Impatient who should have the Honour
> To plant an Ensign first upon her.
>
> (ll. 21-26)

[26] *The Man in the Moon, Discovering a World of Knavery under the Sunne . . .* (n.p., 1649), sig. A²r. For other works of this sort, see above, n. 14, and also chap. 1, n. 14.

[27] Quotations from *The Elephant* follow the facsimile text, in *Three Poems of Samuel Butler,* Augustan Reprint Soc. Pub. No. 88 (1961).

Obviously, they are not engaged in the disinterested pursuit
of science; and their desire for power over nature, as it turns
out, is not identical with the quest for truth.

Having prepared to project themselves onto the moon, they
discover through their telescope what they take to be an epic
battle between the "Privolvans" and the "Subvolvani" (terms
Kepler coined in his *Somnium*); and, more wondrous yet, the
battle is interrupted by the entrance of an elephant. Enthusi-
astic about this new and rare evidence of life in that world, the
most preeminent among these virtuosi speaks for all:

> . . . one, who for his Excellence
> In height'ning Words and shad'wing Sense,
> And magnifying all he writ
> With curious microscopick Wit,
> Was magnify'd himself no less
> In home and foreign Colleges.
>
> (ll. 167-172)

He proclaims to his colleagues that what they have come upon
amounts to a conquest entitling them to try for universal domination:

> . . . by this sole Phænomenon,
> We've gotten Ground upon the *Moon;*
> And gain'd a Pass, to hold dispute
> With all the Planets that stand out;
> To carry this most *virtuous* War,
> Home to the Door of every Star,
> And plant th'Artillery of our Tubes
> Against their proudest Magnitudes;
> To stretch our victories beyond
> Th'extent of planetary Ground.
>
> (ll. 179-188)

This grandiose scheme for power suffers a serious setback, however. For one of the footboys standing by happens to open the
far end of the optic tube, thereby revealing that the participants in the epic battle were nothing but gnats and flies and

that the elephant, alas, was a mouse that somehow had gotten trapped in the telescope.

The virtuosi are thus exposed as victims of their own eyesight, having impaired its accuracy by interpreting what they saw according to their own ulterior motives. The event proves that they *"Hold no Truth worthy to be known,/That is not huge, and over-grown"* (ll. 516-517). They *"In vain strive Nature to suborn"* (l. 519); and their attempt to project a magnified sense of their own importance onto nature only makes them the more ridiculous.

Though only tangentially related to the tradition of science fiction through its allusions to Kepler's *Somnium* and its more profound relevance to certain aspects of *Gulliver's Travels*, *The Elephant in the Moon* nevertheless serves to clarify the nature of the satiric connection between fantasy and reality referred to earlier (pp. 20 ff.). The imaginary epic battle— reminiscent of the war between the solar and lunar forces in Lucian's *True History*—which the virtuosi in Butler's poem project onto the moon discloses what Butler perceives to be the truth about its projectors: that they see not what is "there" but what they want to see, as determined, at least in part, by an exaggerated conception of both their own importance and the value of what they are doing. The metaphor that the *magnified* sense of their own worth and the worth of their discovery suggests is thus expanded into a myth to dramatize the metaphor. The notion that man's measure of himself is the measure of the universe passes in the course of the myth into its contrariety, that man's measure of the universe is in fact merely the measure of himself.

The theme of man as the measure of his own limits and limitations, as it is embodied in various myths and enters into science fiction proper, forms the subject of the next chapter.

3

The Measure of Man

> It is a false assertion that the sense[s] of man
> [are] the measure [mensura] of things.
> On the contrary, all perceptions as well of the sense[s]
> as of the mind are according to the measure
> [analogia] of the individual and not according
> to the measure [analogia] of the universe.
>
> FRANCIS BACON

The allusions often found in later moon voyages to their predecessors indicate one sort of continuity in the development of science fiction by attesting to the writer's cognizance of a tradition.[1] But there are also thematic continuities among works belonging to the history of science fiction.

One prevalent theme, recurring in the guise of a variety of myths, concerns the limits of human knowledge, and of human nature generally. Here the fantasy gauges some given assessment of the human condition by embodying as myth both that assessment and its limitations or consequences. In *The Elephant in the Moon,* for instance, the virtuosi judge that their enterprise will gain them boundless dominion, an aim revealed in the course of the myth to be chimerical: Butler exposes the capacities of these virtuosi as severely limited, and limited, moreover, in part by the very ideal they have set for themselves.

The idea of constructing a fictive model that allows the commonplace ideals or definitions of an age to evaluate themselves, as it were, is a device of much satiric fiction. The theme

[1] A recent work of science fiction which alludes to ideas of other writers in the genre is Fritz Leiber's *The Wanderer* (New York, 1964).

inherent in such a strategy, that of the measure measured, is perennial in science fiction, and naturally so. For by displacing actuality with a state of affairs beyond the boundaries of man's present knowledge, the science fantasy might very well disclose what those boundaries are.

The theme of the measure measured occurs, as I have already implied, in *Gulliver's Travels*, but also in Voltaire's *Micromégas*, Edwin Abbott's *Flatland*, and Wells's *The Time Machine*. In all of these fantasies, someone or other presumes to take the measure of the universe, to ascertain its nature and limits. But, ironically, it always turns out that man's measure of the universe is in some degree the measure of himself: his estimate betrays his own assumptions, capacities, and proclivities.

Lilliput and Brobdingnag:
Telescopic and Microscopic Perspectives

Certainly the complex irony Swift generates in satirizing the satirist Lemuel Gulliver[2] depends upon the interaction in the reader's mind between the imaginary worlds that Gulliver happens upon and the real world that they displace. In reading *Gulliver's Travels*, however, one may be inclined to forget the tradition of voyages, real and extraordinary, to which it belongs,[3] and to grasp immediately at the impalpable "Air of Truth" (*GT*, ed. cit., p. xxxvii) that floats through what purports to be Gulliver's literal account of his experiences. But by perceiving right away the reality that the fiction displaces, one discounts the fact that Gulliver insists his *Travels* is a record of what he has actually seen and undergone (*GT*, pp. 275-276). I do not mean the reader is wrong to think that *Gulliver's Travels* is satire, and particularly that it satirizes man's pride in being what he is. Nor am I making the claim that Swift was unaware of the fiction. I am saying, though, that

[2] See Robert C. Elliott's discussion of "the satirist-satirized" in *The Power of Satire* (Princeton, 1960), pp. 214-220.

[3] For a detailed account of the tradition of real and imaginary voyages see Percy G. Adams, *Travellers and Travel Liars* (Berkeley and Los Angeles, 1962); and Philip Babcock Gove's annotated bibliography, *The Imaginary Voyage in Prose Fiction* (New York, 1941).

Gulliver's pronouncement that what he states is, in the usual sense of the term, literally true, should not be overlooked; for in so doing one may be tempted to conclude that Gulliver is the same sort of satirist Swift is, and further, that the two are virtually identical.

It is necessary to establish, at least in a general way, this difference between Swift and Gulliver in order to appreciate Swift's use of his creature. A large part of Swift's complex irony is bestowed on Gulliver; and it is the result of the measure Gulliver adopts to evaluate his world, namely, himself. By this standard—in context both a physical and a moral one—he undertakes to gauge the extraordinary creatures he chances upon, beings whom he regards as having the same degree of reality he has himself; and finally he applies his self-conception (modified by his stay with the Houyhnhmns) as the criterion by which to judge his fellow men. The structure of Swift's fictive displacement, however, will only permit that in measuring other things Gulliver measures himself as representative of mankind, and in measuring other men, a misanthropic Gulliver again judges, and in this case unwittingly condemns, Lemuel Gulliver.

This scheme—integral to the meaning of *Gulliver's Travels* —whereby he who would judge actually measures himself instead of those whom he thinks he is judging, has other victims in addition to Gulliver. Thus the Lilliputians, imagining that they are taking Gulliver's measure, really disclose their own dimensions and capacities and those of their world. Similarly, the Brobdingnagian sages, who after examining Gulliver and consulting among themselves pronounce him a *lusus naturae*, merely succeed in impugning their own wisdom.

The theme of the measurer-measured introduces another way in which, foreshadowing the techniques of science fiction, *Gulliver's Travels* illustrates how science may be transformed for the purposes of fiction—not in Swift's handling of the "Voyage to Laputa" in this case, but in his presentation of the imaginary worlds of the first two voyages. In the worlds of Lilliput and Brobdingnag, as Professor Nicolson observes, Swift has "shown man . . . 'placed on the isthmus of a middle state,' between the vastness of the cosmic universe, discovered by the telescope, and the new universe of minute life, which the microscope had disclosed."[4] Perhaps the order could be reversed, so that the Brobdingnagians would represent humanity enlarged under the microscope and the Lilliputians men as political animals whose activities are viewed, as if on a distant planet, through a telescope. Either way, the idea remains the same: Swift was using the main scientific instruments of his age to provide the perspective for his satire. From this idea, the measurer-measured theme can again be educed, since the principal instruments that men were utilizing to take the measure of the universe supplied Swift with the perspective that becomes the measure of man.

Swift's turning the measure against the measurer contributes to the general meaning of *Gulliver's Travels,* which, in its hortative aspect, is that man should be seeking self-knowledge rather than knowledge of the external universe. The technique for enforcing this point—having one's response to the fictive situation reflect (partially at least) back on the respondent— broadly resembles Butler's, though there is no evidence, so far as I am aware, that Swift saw a manuscript of *The Elephant in the Moon* while at Moor Park or afterward.

Micromégas and the Limits of Analogy

There is no lack of evidence that Voltaire was well-acquainted with *Gulliver's Travels.* He mentions Swift by name in *Micromégas,* and that short tale itself is saturated with incidents borrowed from the English ironist.[5] Nevertheless, the meaning of *Micromégas* is complementary to, not identical with, that of the *Travels;* and Voltaire signals this complementarity through his divergence from Swift in emphasis and

---

[4] Marjorie Hope Nicolson and Nora Mohler, "Swift's Flying Island, in the *Voyage to Laputa,*" *Annals of Science,* II (1937), 418. The allusion to Pope's *Essay on Man,* while apt, is of course anachronistic.

[5] Ira O. Wade, from whose edition of *Micromégas* (Princeton, 1950) I have quoted the French text whenever the English translation of 1753 misconstrues the original, catalogues Voltaire's borrowings from the *Travels* in his introduction (pp. 82-87). One parallel not cited by Professor Wade is that between the response of the Brobdingnagian sages to Gulliver (see above) and the Saturnian's pronouncement that man is an inexplicable "jeu de la Nature" (Wade, p. 137).

detail. Thus in the first two books of the *Travels,* Swift insists on a strict proportionality. Everything in Lilliput, for example, is as close to one-twelfth the size of its corresponding entity in the "real" world as he could calculate it to be. For Voltaire, on the other hand, everything is approximately proportional but not exactly so. The Sirian and the Saturnian in *Micromégas* are larger than earthlings, for instance, but not larger in exact proportion to the relative size of their respective planets. This disproportion relates to the limits of analogical reasoning, and hence to the signification of Voltaire's fantasy.

Micromégas is a highly allusive work and has on that account become an esoteric one as well. Its most accessible portions are those expressing Voltaire's animadversions on the extent of human knowledge, but these cannot really be detached from the skepticism directed against certain particular arguments from analogy. In outlining these arguments and their relevance to *Micromégas,* I stress their displacement (and consequent deformation) in Voltaire's myth instead of the science fictional characteristics of that myth per se. I should therefore mention at the outset that the myth owes its place in the history of science fiction not to its theme but to the motif it inaugurates of bringing inhabitants from other planets to earth.

The thrust of *Micromégas* is to call into question—not, precisely, to deny—two arguments based on analogy. One of these concerns the possibility of life on other planets; the other involves the problem of whether animals have souls. Both arguments together implicate the whole of Voltaire's myth.

In *Micromégas,* the reasoning on the subject of whether other worlds are inhabited calls attention to itself because of the absurdity of the conclusion arrived at, but also because it turns upside down what had come to be the accepted opinion on the matter. The usual argument—one that Kepler and Wilkins had made commonplace—was the demonstration by analogy in favor of a plurality of worlds. The geography of the moon, for example, can be thought of as similar to that of the earth; ergo, it is probable that the moon is a world like this one, peopled by creatures like men. Voltaire's Saturnian, on the contrary, using the same argument from analogy, concludes there can be no life, certainly no intelligent life, on earth. In contrast to Saturn, the paradigm for this reasoner of an inhabited world, the topography of the earth is too irregular for there to be creatures on it.[6]

The irony of the reasoning here has several aspects. Most obviously, it employs the same sort of analogy cited to prove the plurality of (inhabited) worlds to maintain the contradictory of that proposition. Again, Voltaire puts that argument into the mouth of "the secretary of the academy of Saturn, a man of good understanding, who, though in truth he had invented nothing of his own, enjoyed in peace the reputation of a little poet and great calculator" (pp. 19-20)[7]—a man long ago identified in real life as Bernard le Bovier de Fontenelle, chiefly remembered as the author of *Conversations on the Plurality of Worlds* (1687). Finally, the heading of the chapter preceding that in which the Saturnian propounds this argument refers to him and Micromégas as visitors from *"l'autre Monde,"* an allusion to Cyrano's fantasy about creatures on the moon and sun which many eighteenth-century French readers would not have been likely to miss. By having beings from *l'autre Monde* come to earth, Voltaire reverses Cyrano's procedure and hence points once more to the satiric reversals throughout *Micromégas*.

Attacking the premise of his companion's argument, Micromégas tells him: "Every thing here seems to you irregular, because, you fetch all your comparisons [tiré au cordeau] from Jupiter or Saturn" (p. 20). This criticism does not absolutely condemn all reasoning by analogy; but it is a warning that ethnocentricity makes all such arguments liable to abuse and error.

[6] Ray Bradbury's *Martian Chronicles* (1946) offers a modern example of the ironic use of an argument from analogy, by means of which the reasoner also reaches a paradoxical conclusion. Reversing the usual argument that there can be no animal life on Mars because there is too little oxygen on that planet, Bradbury imagines the following dialogue between two Martians.
"Mr. K turned away. She stopped him with a word. 'Yll?' she called quietly. 'Do you ever wonder if—well, if there *are* people living on the third planet [i.e., earth]?'
"'The third planet is incapable of supporting life,' stated the husband patiently. 'Our scientists have said there's far too much oxygen in [its] atmosphere.'" (*MC* [New York, 1951], p. 4).
[7] Voltaire, *Micromégas: A Comic Romance. Being a Severe Satire upon the Philosophy, Ignorance, and Self-Conceit of Mankind,* tr. anon. (London, 1753). I quote *Micromégas* in English from this translation.

Voltaire again ridicules the absurdities that ethnocentricity can lead to by contrasting the relative magnitude of one of the *philosophes* (whom the voyagers from Sirius and Saturn at last descry) against that philosopher's grandiose design on the universe. Though the beings from other worlds can perceive this man only with the aid of a powerful improvised microscope, that disciple of St. Thomas Aquinas[8] "maintained to their faces, that their persons, their [worlds], their suns and their stars were created solely for the use [of] man" (p. 39).

Connected with the ethnocentric fallacy is another source of error in the analogical approach. When the Sirian and the Saturnian finally focus on the *philosophes'* ship (engaged upon a scientific expedition in the Baltic), the Saturnian, "making a sudden transition, from the most cautious distrust, to the most excessive credulity, imagined he saw them in the . . . work of propagation, and cried aloud, 'I have surprised nature in the very fact.'" "Nevertheless," says an authorial voice, "he was deceived by appearances; a case too common, whether we do, or do not make use of microscopes" (pp. 24-25).

Because appearances and ethnocentric beliefs can be deceiving, and make for specious arguments from analogy, Micromégas remarks, "Nature is like nature, and comparisons are odious [pourquoi lui chercher des comparaisons?]" (p. 7). Yet he himself is an erstwhile maker of comparisons. He has been banished by the Mufti for eight hundred years from the court of Sirius on account of a treatise of his in which he had attempted to determine "whether in the world of Sirius, there was any difference between the substantial forms [la forme substantielle] of a flea and a snail" (p. 4). Although this may seem to be (literally) a small enough matter—one hardly warranting a two hundred and twenty year lawsuit followed by the treatise's being condemned "by judges who had never read it"—the phrase "la forme substantielle" would have evoked for Voltaire's audience the polemics concerning whether animals have souls.[9]

[8] The first English translation says that this *philosophe* knew an "abridgement of St. Thomas"; but actually the French reads: "il sçavoit tout le sécret, que tout cela se trouvoit dans la Somme de Saint Thomas."

[9] On "la forme substantielle," see Wade's note, *op. cit.*, pp. 149-150.

Since the controversy on the matter underlies the final chapters of *Micromégas*—where it is mythically deformed—it is appropriate to rehearse briefly what that controversy entailed.[10] Its basis involves the observation, reinvigorated by Montaigne (particularly in his *Apology for Raymond Sebond*), that there are behavioral similarities between animals and men. From this crucial analogy, if its justness be admitted, an inescapable dilemma follows. If animals are machines, as the Cartesians claimed, then men must also be machines; they cannot have souls. If, on the contrary, men are endowed with souls, then animals must possess souls too. Thus when Voltaire has his celestial travelers speak of men as "ces petites machines" and "animaux" (Wade, pp. 135, 140), these are not mere figures of speech; they recall a dispute having the most serious theological consequences.

Voltaire does not evoke the controversy about the existence and nature of man's soul to take a position one way or the other. It is true that the giants from other worlds, in scrutinizing the little terrestrial animals (the *philosophes*), become aware of their rational behavior; and this would seem to dramatize some such position. But that recognition on the part of the celestial giants is inherently a part of the criticism that the myth directs against arguments from analogy. Micromégas's acknowledgement of man's apparent rationality causes him to ask these philosophers: "since you know so well what is without you, doubtless, you are still more perfectly acquainted with what is within; tell me what is the soul, and how your ideas are framed?" (p. 36). The question, of course, provokes a chaos of opposed assertions; and as none of the contradictions among them is resolved, one is left with a thoroughgoing skepticism concerning the possibility of knowledge about such things.

Indeed, the point of *Micromégas* is that man is not vouchsafed knowledge of ultimate ends. He can attempt to determine

[10] For some idea of the subtle complexities of this controversy, compare Pierre Bayle's article on "Rosarius" in the *Philosophical Dictionary*. Bayle's own position on the subject, somewhat like Voltaire's, is inscrutable; he enjoys playing one side against the other breaking everyone's icons in the process.

the nature of the universe—of the insides or essences of things —only through analogical arguments; but as all arguments of this kind depend for him upon appearances—upon the outsides of things—he is bound to deceive himself in his reasoning. He can measure the outsides of things and calculate their dimensions; he cannot, however, be certain of the inner nature of things. Hence the response to incertitude which meets with general approval is that of the disciple of Locke, who declares: "I revere the eternal power to which it would ill become me to prescribe bounds: I affirm nothing, and am contented to believe, that many more things are possible, than are usually thought so" (p. 39).

Doubt concerning opinions about the nature of the creation is plainly set forth at the close of a myth. In departing, Micromégas gives the terrestrial philosophers a book to "teach them an abundance of admirable sciences, and demonstrate the very essence of things [le bon des choses]." This tome the philosophers carry to the Academy in Paris, whose secretary discovers the pages to be blank—"just what I suspected" (p. 40). Voltaire thereby dramatizes the fact that the condition of incertitude is universal, and that it is the only universal truth about the inner nature of all rational creatures that one can be sure of.

Ultimately, then, *Micromégas* ridicules analogical arguments about the essences of things; it does not attempt to contradict any particular conclusion based on such an argument. Analogies purporting to reveal the essences, or inner selves, of things can have no validity, because man lacks knowledge of his own inner self on which to found any comparison. This ignorance is the one truth which analogical reasoning can disclose.

In the context of the foregoing discussion, W. H. Barber's statement of the meaning of proportionality in Voltaire's myth seems to me adequate:

Man himself can be called "Micromégas"; not only does he stand in the same relationship to some living creatures as the celestial giants do to him; a parallel contrast exists within himself, for while his knowledge of the external world is extensive and accurate, he has no understanding of his own true nature and is incapable of wisdom in human affairs.[11]

Provided that "the external world" means the quantitatively accessible world of appearances, this assessment is judicious enough and points to the complementarity of Voltaire's myth with Swift's. The latter embodies in part the idea that man is seeking the right sort of knowledge, self-knowledge, in the wrong place (outside himself); Voltaire intimates that the epistemological limits man runs up against in trying to ascertain the nature of the external universe will allow him to become self-aware, at least to the extent of discovering his own limits.

Flatland and the Analogy of Limits

By in effect denying Voltaire's premise that the sort of self-knowledge necessary for analogical reasoning about the nature of the universe is unavailable to man, Edwin Abbott created *Flatland* (1884), a fantasy whose implicit argument depends on just such an analogy derived from the nature of the self. Abbott's mathematical fantasy, published pseudonymously as the autobiography of A. Square, tells the story of how an inhabitant of what is geometrically a two-dimensional world is initiated into the concept of three-dimensionality and beyond. Abbott was a dilettante mathematician, and while his fantasy hardly rivals *Through the Looking Glass,* it has its satiric moments and at all points the author remains faithful to the geometry of its situations.

The first part of Abbott's book describes life in Flatland, whose inhabitants are mainly preoccupied with judging the number of sides and the angularity of their fellows and progeny. As it happens, such judgments are indispensable for any upstanding Flatlander since geometrical characteristics constitute class distinctions and determine protocol. In fact, the "political, ecclesiastical, [and] moral" doctrine of Flatland is directed toward "the improvement of individual and collective Configuration—with special reference of course to the Config-

[11] W. H. Barber, "The Genesis of Voltaire's *Micromégas*," *French Studies,* XI (1957), 12.

uration of the Circles, to which all other objects are subordinated" (p. 45).[12] Translated into a three-dimensional world, "Configuration" means external appearances; but then Flatlanders are, by their own nature and the nature of their universe, only able to perceive, and hence solely interested in, external appearances.

Because of the difficulties these two-dimensional beings have in trying to figure out the geometry of other two-dimensional beings in a two-dimensional world, the process of assessing class distinctions has virtually become an end in itself. It is essential for socially upstanding Flatlanders to be thoroughly adept at distinguishing their inferiors and equals from their superiors; so their education is confined to learning about the minutiae of class differences. Higher education at the University of Wentbridge inculcates "the Science and Art of Sight Recognition" (feeling the angles of another Flatlander is considered vulgar, and can sometimes prove fatal). This discipline purposes to familiarize students with the technique of perceiving angularity, so that they can visually differentiate among the various social orders, from the circles, through the several degrees of polygonality, to the lowest scalene triangle. To be able to assign by sight the proper class designation of any Flatlander of course requires practice and consummate skill.

> The meanest mathematician in Spaceland will readily believe me when I assert that the problems of life, which present themselves to the well-educated—when they are themselves in motion, rotating, advancing or retreating, and at the same time attempting to discriminate by the sense of sight between a number of Polygons of high rank moving in different directions, as for example in a ball-room or conversazione—must be of a nature to task the angularity of the most intellectual, and amply justify the rich endowments of the Learned Professors of Geometry, both Static and Kinetic, in the illustrious University of Wentbridge. (P. 25)

[12] Edwin Abbott, *Flatland: A Romance of Many Dimensions*, 2d ed. rev. (London, 1884). The paperback reissue of this edition (New York, 1952) closely follows the pagination of the original but contains a number of textual errors.

Such are "the problems of life" that the elite are daily called upon to deal with.

Social status in Flatland is not entirely and forever fixed. Sometimes a more regular—and hence socially higher—triangle, for instance, derives from a scalene father (all the women in Flatland are straight lines). The procedure for certifying one's exact social status has in fact become an institution, the rationale allowing for advancement in society being that it alleviates discontent among the lower social orders.

> The occasional emergence of an Isosceles from the ranks of his serf-born ancestors is welcomed, not only by the poor serfs themselves, as a gleam of light and hope shed upon the monotonous squalor of their existence, but also by the Aristocracy at large; for all the higher classes are well aware that these rare phenomena, while they do little or nothing to vulgarise their own privileges, serve as a most useful barrier against revolution from below. (P. 10)

Thus in the mythic world of Flatland, which deforms a class-conscious society, the means of avoiding "revolution from below" prefigures the assimilation, in Orwell's *1984*, of potential leaders among the "proles" into the ruling Party.

Mr. Square, who explains these features of Flatland, next goes on to relate his experiences in worlds other than his own and the effect they have had on him. In the second part of Abbott's fantasy, called "Other Worlds," Square recounts first a dream in which he visited Lineland, a linear world whose inhabitants are segments of a single straight line. He had endeavored to convince the king of Lineland of the existence of two-dimensionality; but the king, incapable of perceiving Square as a two-dimensional being, had refused to believe him.

Following this oneiric revelation, Square finds himself in the king of Lineland's position; for he, in turn, is visited by a Sphere. The Sphere, however, by physically taking Square out of the two-dimensional plane of his existence, does finally persuade him that there is such a thing as a three-dimensional world, a world differing radically from Flatland (geometrically speaking, of course). Square proves to be so apt a pupil that he is soon imagining, to the Sphere's horror and indignation,

> some yet more spacious Space, some more dimensionable Dimensionality, from the vantage-ground of which we shall look down together upon the revealed insides of Solid things, and where thine own intestines, and those of thy kindred Spheres, will lie exposed to the view of the poor wandering exile from Flatland. (P. 87)

Ignoring the Sphere's derogation of such an idea, Square propounds an argument in favor of "more dimensionable Dimensionality"—an argument " 'strictly according to Analogy' " (p. 89). That is, there must be a fourth dimension that is to the third dimension what the third is to the second; and so on. When the Sphere in desperation declares that dimensions beyond the third are "visions" that have arisen "from the thought," the buoyant Mr. Square answers:

> if it indeed be so, that this other Space is really Thoughtland, then take me to that blessed Region where I in Thought shall see the insides of all solid things. There, before my ravished eye, a Cube, moving in some altogether new direction, but strictly according to Analogy, so as to make every particle of his interior pass through a new kind of Space with a wake of its own—shall create a still more perfect perfection than himself, with sixteen terminal Extra-solid angles, and Eight solid Cubes for his perimeter. And once there, shall we stay our upward course? In that blessed region of Four Dimensions, shall we linger on the threshold of the Fifth, and not enter therein? (P. 90)

Of course the question is meant to be rhetorical. But Square was not alone in being carried away to Thoughtland; his analogical argument for the existence of a fourth dimension corresponds in detail to that proposed at about the same time by C. H. Hinton in some of his essays and essayistic short stories.[13]

Mr. Square does not fare very well in his attempts to per-

---

[13] See especially "What Is the Fourth Dimension?" (1884) in C. H. Hinton, *Scientific Romances. First Series* (London, 1886).

suade his fellow Flatlanders of the existence of new dimensions few of them have dreamed of. Indeed, the advocating of three-dimensionality has long been deemed heresy in Flatland; and Square is accordingly imprisoned as a heretic and a madman.

The analogy implicit in Abbott's "Romance of Many Dimensions" is obviously one between the limits of a two-dimensional and a three-dimensional universe. Analogical reasoning would suggest—what Square maintains—that there is a fourth dimension from which beings moving in three-dimensionality appear to be like two-dimensional beings seen from the perspective of a third dimension. By a kind of logical ellipsis, therefore, men who deny the possibility of a fourth dimension—at least as a concept—are as foolish as two-dimensional beings dismissing the likelihood of three-dimensionality. Thus Abbot's myth indicates that while ignorance of the spatial confines of one's universe limits thought to those confines, an awareness of them opens up another universe of thought altogether.

The Time Machine; or, The Fourth Dimension as Prophecy

As a satiric commentary on complacency and dogmatism, *Flatland* has certain affinities with *The Time Machine* (1895), which Wells himself described as an "assault on human self-satisfaction" *(Scientific Romances,* p. ix). In the latter, the fourth dimension is temporal rather than spatial; but as in Abbott's fantasy, the possibilities that such a dimension provides are elaborated upon in *The Time Machine* to define the limits man sets for himself. Wells's myth, like Abbott's, imaginatively transcends these limits; *The Time Machine* is in fact structured so as to place in doubt the distinction between the actual and the possible, the real and the fantastic. Since the fantasy thereby arrives at the very postulates of Wells's science fiction, I propose to examine its structure in detail, considering summarily but analytically the components of that structure: the Time Traveller's vision of the future (and the nature of his vision); his own interpretation of it (and his principle for interpreting it); and the reaction of his audience to his prophetic report (and the implications of this response).[14]

To begin then with the Time Traveller's vision, "degeneration" is not, it seeems to me, a precise enough description of the backsliding of the human species into the less and less recognizably anthropomorphic descendants that the Traveller finds in the world of 802,701 and beyond. It is true that Wells used that term himself as early as 1891 in an essay that outlines abstractly the idea behind this vision of the future; but in that same essay, entitled "Zoological Retrogression," he also calls the process of reversion "degradation" (p. 246), which suggests the step-by-step decline from man to beast which he was to take up in *The Island of Doctor Moreau* as well. More accurately still, I think one can term this gradual reduction of Homo sapiens to species lower and lower on the evolutionary scale as a vision of "devolution."

The degenerate species that the Traveller discovers in the "Golden Age" of 802,701, the "ape-like" (I, 59) and predatory Morlocks and the feeble "childlike" Eloi (I, 30) whom they prey upon, are barely recognizable as having human ancestry; and while "modification of the human type" among the Morlocks has been "far more profound than among the Eloi" (I, 65), the process of devolution has by no means reached an equilibrium. Succeeding these creatures—in an episode appearing in an intermediate published draft of *The Time Machine* but subsequently deleted—are a form of animal life the Traveller likens to "rabbits or some breed of kangaroo" and another similar to a gigantic centipede. These two species must have descended in the course of time from the Eloi and the Morlocks; and again the "grey animal, or grey man, whichever it was" is the victim of the carnivorous giant insects.[15]

At the next stop in the distant future, all anthropomorphic life seems to have disappeared, and the Traveller sees instead

[14] All published drafts of *The Time Machine* share these components, though the serialized versions appearing in the *National Observer* (1894) and the *New Review* (1895) differ from the first English edition, published by Heinemann, in many respects—not all of them minor. See Bernard Bergonzi, "The Publication of *The Time Machine* 1894-95," *RES*, n.s. IX (1960), 42-51.

[15] H. G. Wells, *The Time Machine* in the *New Review*, XII (1895), 578-579.

"a thing like a huge white butterfly" and "a monstrous crab-like creature" (I, 106). He continues on into the future aboard his time machine until, thirty million years hence, it appears to him that animal life has devolved out of existence. Plant life has degenerated to "livid green liverworts and lichens" (I, 108). Here he witnesses a solar eclipse that prefigures the end of the world.

> The darkness grew apace; a cold wind began to blow in freshening gusts from the east, and the showering white flakes in the air increased in number. From the edge of the sea came a ripple and whisper. Beyond these lifeless sounds the world was silent. Silent? It would be hard to convey the stillness of it. . . . As the darkness thickened, the eddying flakes grew more abundant . . . and the cold of the air more intense. At last, one by one, swiftly, one after the other, the white peaks of the distant hills vanished into blackness. The breeze rose to a moaning wind. I saw the black central shadow of the eclipse sweeping towards me. In another moment the pale stars alone were visible. All else was rayless obscurity. The sky was absolutely black. (I, 109)

In retrospect, it seems that the unbalanced struggle between the Eloi and the Morlocks prepares for this final vision, that a terrible logic compels the conclusion: "The sky was absolutely black." "People unfamiliar with such speculations as those of the younger Darwin," the Time Traveller had remarked earlier, "forget that the planets must ultimately fall back one by one into the parent body" (I, 58). This is a vision hardly in accord with "Excelsior" optimism; on the contrary, it is precisely calculated, as Wells later admitted, to "run counter to the placid assumption . . . that Evolution was a pro-human force making things better and better for mankind" (*Scientific Romances,* p. ix).

Indeed, the ideas Wells is dealing in are, as he remarked in the early essay on "Zoological Retrogression," an "evolutionary antithesis." He argues in that essay for "the enormous importance of degeneration as a plastic process in nature," for its "parity with evolution" (p. 246); and his conclusion there is especially relevant to his vision of the future in *The Time Machine.*

> There is . . . no guarantee in scientific knowledge of man's permanence or permanent ascendancy. . . . The presumption is that before him lies a long future of profound modification, but whether this will be, according to his present ideals, upward or downward, no one can forecast. Still, so far as any scientist can tell us, it may be that, instead of this, Nature is, in unsuspected obscurity, equipping some now humble creature with wider possibilities of appetite, endurance, or destruction, to rise in the fulness of time and sweep *homo* away into the darkness from which his universe arose. The Coming Beast must certainly be reckoned in any anticipatory calculations regarding the Coming Man. (P. 253)

Clearly Wells is fascinated by this "opposite idea": the vision of man's being swept away "into the darkness from which his universe arose"—of "life that . . . is slowly and remorselessly annihilated," as he says in "On Extinction"[16]—the vision, in other words, of *The Time Machine.*[17]

But the vision of the future as a devolutionary process, in reversing the expectations of "optimistic evolution," is not isolated as an imaginative possibility for its own sake. It implicates man's "present ideals"—his assessment of his condition and direction—as the Time Traveller's theories about the world of 802,701, and particularly the principle underlying those theories, demonstrate.

Although at several points he revises his theories as he learns about the nature of the Morlocks, the Time Traveller temporarily settles on an etiological interpretation of the relationship between the effete (and virtually androgynous) Eloi and their more energetic predators. "The great triumph of Humanity I had dreamed of," he says,

> took a different shape in my mind. It had been no such tri-

---

[16] H. G. Wells, "On Extinction," *Chambers's Journal,* X (Sept. 30, 1893), 623.
[17] This prophecy of "the Coming Beast" also figures in "The Sea Raiders" (1896) and *The War of the Worlds* (1898), (see chap. 1), and in "The Empire of the Ants" (1904), (see chap. 7).

umph of moral education and general co-operation as I had imagined. Instead, I saw a real aristocracy, armed with perfected science and working to a logical conclusion the industrial system of to-day. Its triumph had not been simply a triumph over nature, but a triumph over nature and the fellow-man. (I, 64)

To be sure, he himself reserves a doubt concerning this account of how this future world had come about: "My explanation may be absolutely wrong. I still think it is the most plausible one" (I, 65). But his ambivalence here reminds one, not accidentally, of his subsequent remark as to how the reader may accept this vision of the future. "Take it as a lie—or a prophecy. . . . Consider I have been speculating on the destinies of our race, until I have hatched this fiction" (I, 112). Together these statements suggest that any explanation of the imaginary world of the Eloi and the Morlocks is important only insofar as it makes clear that the world projected in the fiction is "prophecy"; that is, the "working to a logical conclusion" of what can be observed in the world of the present.

The Time Traveller himself makes this point: that he has arrived at his explanation by extrapolating from tendencies existing in "our own age."

At first, proceeding from the problems of our own age, it seemed clear as daylight to me that the gradual widening of the present merely temporary and social difference between the Capitalist and the Labourer, was the key to the whole position. No doubt it will seem grotesque enough to you—and wildly incredible!—and yet even now there are existing circumstances to point that way [i.e., toward 802,701]. (I, 63)

What this passage implies is that the procedure for interpreting the vision of *The Time Machine* recapitulates the process by which the fiction was "hatched"; so that the science fictional method of "prophecy"—of pointing out present-day problems by projecting their consequences as fantasy—is itself "the key to the whole position." On the evidence of the Time Traveller's own interpretation, according to this view, the future that Wells has projected does not, precisely speaking, embody only

the consequences of "the industrial system of to-day," but also
the results of whatever ideal directs the course and uses of
technological advance.

While they summarily describe a world proceeding from
man's present ideals, the Time Traveller's theories also evaluate them. In saying, for example, that "the great triumph of
Humanity . . . had not been simply a triumph over nature [as
T. H. Huxley had urged[18]] but a triumph over nature and the
fellow-man," the Time Traveller makes a negative moral judgment: "moral education and general co-operation" had not
been achieved. And condemnation is again entailed in his observation that the human intellect "had set itself stedfastly
towards comfort and ease, a balanced society with security as
its watchword"; for "Only those animals partake of intelligence
that have to meet a huge variety of needs and dangers." The
ideal (perfect security) therefore undermines the means of
maintaining it (intelligence); and the result, the Traveller
continues, is that "the upper-world man had drifted towards
his feeble prettiness, and the under-world to mere mechanical
industry. But that perfect state had lacked one thing even for
mechanical perfection—absolute permanency" (I, 100-101).
This last interpretation, which elaborates upon and at the same
time supersedes his earlier explanations, accounts more fully
for the world of the Eloi and the Morlocks as it obviously im-
pugns man's "present ideals." The ideal of subjugating man
and nature to realize a state of "comfort and ease" is thus satirically evaluated by projecting its consequences as a vision
of the future.

Both the Traveller's principle for interpreting the vision
and the process by which that vision had been projected assume, therefore, that man's ideals do affect the course of evolution, that the world of 802,701 and beyond is the working to
a logical conclusion of man's striving for comfort and ease. As
far as the Traveller's theories are necessary to understanding
the prophecy, then, it is somewhat misleading to say that the
degeneration of the Eloi and the Morlocks "has occurred because mankind, as Huxley feared, was ultimately unable to

[18] In "Evolution and Ethics" and other essays, Huxley declares that ethical
man can exist only by modifying the "cosmic process."

control the cosmic or evolutionary process."[19] Rather, the Traveller implies, mankind apparently controlled the cosmic process too well, according to an ideal the consequences of which no one could foresee. One of those consequences is that by 802,701 no species has the intelligence any more to set limits on the struggle for existence, in which the defenseless Eloi fall victim to the carnivorous Morlocks. Among these descendants of Homo sapiens, the struggle for survival—which, engendered by "Necessity," makes the "absolute permanency" of "mechanical perfection" impossible—now resumes the character that struggle takes among other animals. "Man," the Traveller reflects, "had been content to live in ease and delight upon the labours of his fellow-man, had taken Necessity as his watchword and excuse, and in the fulness of time Necessity had come home to him" (I, 81). And once this "Necessity" reasserts itself unchecked—once, that is, man's descendants begin reverting to beasts—anthropomorphic life, according to the vision of *The Time Machine,* is irrevocably on the downward path of devolution.

This vision of social disintegration and devolution as a critique of the accepted ideal of striving toward "ease and delight" can exist only in the dimension of "prophecy," that dimension into which the critique can be projected and imaginatively given life—the world, in other words, of science fantasy.[20] The "Fourth Dimension" as a time dimension is thus a metaphor: it is the dimension open to the imagination. "Our mental existences, which are immaterial and have no dimensions, are passing along the Time-dimension" (I, 5), the Traveller had said in introducing his audience to the concept of this new dimension. Hence as a world wherein the consequences of the accepted ideal can be envisioned, the Fourth Dimension provides a critical and comprehensive point of view from which to evaluate the present.

That at the beginning of *The Time Machine* no one except

[19] Mark R. Hillegas, "Cosmic Pessimism in H. G. Wells' Scientific Romances," *Papers of the Mich. Acad.,* XLVI (1961), 657-658.

[20] As late as *Men Like Gods* (1923), the utopian fantasy that takes place in the "F dimension," Wells has one of his characters say of another (neither is a Utopian, as yet): " 'He has always had too much imagination. He thinks that things that don't exist *can* exist. And now he imagines himself in some sort of scientific romance and out of our world altogether" (XXVIII, 21-22).

the Time Traveller has conceived of—or even can conceive of
—this dimension already indicates a lack of imaginative (and
critical) awareness on the part of his audience. His argument
for a Fourth Dimension, prefaced by the caveat that "I shall
have to controvert one or two ideas that are almost universally
accepted" (I, 3), meets with incomprehension and complacent
skepticism. Quite predictably, his audience fails to take seriously—if the point is grasped at all—the relevance of the Time
Traveller's vision. No one else seems to connect the vision of
"The two species that had resulted from the evolution of man
. . . sliding down towards, or . . . already arrived at, an altogether new relationship" (I, 74) with his preconception of an
"inevitable tendency to higher and better things" ("Retrogression," p. 247). Perhaps no one in the audience takes this
vision seriously because, as Wells speculated elsewhere, "It is
part of the excessive egotism of the human animal that the bare
idea of its extinction seems incredible to it" ("Extinction of
Man," p. 172). Certainly there is no sign that anyone among
the listeners sees how, or that, this vision implicates his "present ideals," which are responsible for the shape of things to
come. On the contrary, the reactions typifying the attitude of
the audience are the skepticism of the Medical Man, who
wants to analyze the flowers that the Traveller has brought
back with him, and the arrant disbelief of the Editor, who
thinks the Traveller's account a "gaudy lie"; only the unidenti-
fied narrator of the entire *Time Machine* lies "awake most
of the night thinking about it." (I, 114).

In fact, the Time Traveller himself does not seem to be
wholly cognizant of the implications of his theories. If his eti-
ology is correct, the cause of the degeneration he discovers
exists in the present. Therefore, the burden of what he calls
"moral education" remains here and now; and his return to
the world of 802,701 would appear to be either a romantic
evasion of a piece with his sentimental "squirms of idyllic
petting" that V. S. Pritchett finds embarrassing,[21] or a pessi-
mistic retreat from a world "that must inevitably fall back
upon and destroy its makers" (I, 117). In any case, the Time

[21] V. S. Pritchett, *The Living Novel* (London, 1946), p. 119.

Traveller's point of view, though more comprehensive than that of any of the other characters, is still limited; and this limitation finds its structural correlative in the fact that his narrative is related secondhand, as it were, three years after his disappearance, and comprises only a part—albeit a large part —of the fiction.

That the structure of *The Time Machine* encompasses, and thereby defines the limits of, the Traveller's point of view indicates that the romance follows an inner logic of its own, a logic, like that governing the Time Traveller's vision, which compels ultimate consequences from a given premise. Accordingly, the logic that necessitates the Traveller's vanishing into the world of his vision derives from how he accepts that vision. His insistence that "The story I told you was true" (I, 114) suggests that he takes his vision literally, that he allows it the same ontological status he himself has. Hence to dramatize the assertion that he has told the literal truth, he must go back into the world of the future: since he cannot accept it as prophecy, as an invented metaphor, he must disappear into the dimension where his vision "exists." The demand that his vision be literally true, in other words, requires the Traveller be no more real than it is; and his return to the future fulfills this demand.

In being subsumed in his vision, however, he also renders it no less real than any member of his fictive audience; so the reader, though he is not of course persuaded to take *The Time Machine* as fact, is nevertheless forced to allow the same degree of credibility to the futuristic fantasy as to the contemporary scene in which the Traveller relates his story. What the reader is left with, then, is the "prophecy," the metaphorical truth that relates the blind and complacent optimism evidenced by the fictive audience to the resultant devolution envisioned by the Time Traveller.

Far from vitiating the impact of *The Time Machine,* therefore, the Traveller's return to the world of 802,701 reinforces its claim to integrity: by having the Time Traveller act out the ultimate consequence of taking a "prophetic" myth literally, Wells illustrates the rigor that he submitted himself to in satirizing certain "present ideals." The myth of devolution as measure of those ideals derives from them and at the same time contradicts the expectations they foster; and the response of the fictive audience to that myth corroborates its "prophetic" accuracy. Thus this last illustration of the theme, myth as measure of some given assessment of the nature of man and the human condition, signifies that the truth, and credibility, of science fiction pertains to the mythic displacement of "existing circumstances" and tendencies as they are projected into the dimension of "prophecy."

Having indicated the variety of myths that can embody one general theme, I will now go on to analyze some thematic variations of one basic myth: the myth of Faust.

4

Old Myths And New:
Or, Faustus Redivivus

> I will do such things—
> What they are, yet I know not, but they shall be
> The terrors of the earth.
> KING LEAR

The myth of the Faustian magus who, in seeking godlike power over the external world, liberates the hellish impulses within him and thus surrenders control of his destiny to the forces of unreason expresses the fears and uncertainties of an age to which the models of the past seem inapplicable and for which no new system of concepts and values has been formulated. The Victorians themselves articulated the belief that theirs was such a period of transition;[1] and while they did not usually describe their predicament in Faustian terms, the documents suggest that the central paradox of the age could be put in those terms. Though the evidence of cumulative advances in science and technology gave impetus to a belief in material progress, and though one effect of Darwinism was to encourage in some people the idea such progress must be inevitable,[2] there was also disturbing evidence that the accelerated rate of technological change was far exceeding human capacities to comprehend and direct the social transformations such technology was bringing about. Man's power over his environment

---

[1] See Walter E. Houghton, *The Victorian Frame of Mind* (New Haven, 1957), pp. 8-23.

[2] Compare J. B. Bury, *The Idea of Progress* (London, 1928), pp. 209-212, 334-347; and also Houghton, pp. 32-38.

was increasing out of all proportion to the range of his foresight and understanding; so that the unanticipated consequences of that augmented power were becoming more and
more a source of bewilderment about his destiny and a cause
for alienation from his future.[3] In striving for Faustian power
over nature, man was losing control of himself and the forces
of history; the threat of nemesis for his presumption came
from the irrational impulses within him, not from any gods
without.[4]

The apocalyptic belief that self-destructive impulses, gen-
erated, paradoxically, by a rational estimate of the human
condition, might usurp control of the mind, and the future—
this nightmare is the subject of Robert Cromie's *The Crack
of Doom* (1895). The mad scientist in Cromie's romance, one
Herbert Brande, refuses to accept a universe whose purpose he
cannot understand and a future that man cannot rationally
ordain. For him, the eternal motive of the universe is the
ceaseless infliction of suffering, an evil virtually identical with
the processes of nature itself. Nature "has no system," he says,

> unless it be the *reductio ad absurdum,* which only blunders
> on the right way after fruitlessly trying every other conceivable
> path. . . . The theory of evolution—her gospel—reeks with ruf-
> fianism, nature-patented and promoted. The whole scheme of
> the universe, all material existence . . . is founded upon and be-
> gotten of a system of everlasting suffering as hideous as the fan-
> tastic nightmares of religious maniacs . . . the atrocities of the
> Inquisitors . . . have their prototypes in every cubic inch of
> stagnant water, or ounce of diseased tissue. And stagnant water
> is as natural as sterilised water; and diseased tissue is as natural
> as healthy tissue. Wholesale murder is Nature's first law. She
> creates only to kill, and applies the rule as remorselessly to the
> units in a star-drift as to the tadpoles in a horse-pond. (Pp.
> 85-86)[5]

Such suffering, moreover, is meaningless: it has no ultimate

---

[3] For an analysis of this syndrome and its continuity, see Michael Harrington, *The Accidental Century* (New York, 1965), esp. pp. 145-178.
[4] Perhaps the epic expression of the theme is Wagner's Ring Cycle.
[5] Robert Cromie, *The Crack of Doom* (London, 1895).

end. Creation itself, according to this argument, is a perversion, for the only purpose of birth is agony and death. The cyclical recurrence of universal destruction makes the world a hell of unending torment.

> Every atom of every living being will be present in some form at that final impact in which the solar system will be ended in a blazing whirlwind which will melt the earth with its fervent heat. There is not a molecule or cell in any creature alive this day which will not in its ultimate constituents endure the long agony, lasting countless æons of centuries, wherein the solid mass of this great globe will be represented by a rush of incandescent gas, stupendous in itself, but trivial in comparison with the hurricane of flame in which it will be swallowed up and lost.
>
> And when from that hell a new star emerges, and new planets in their season are born of him, and he and they repeat, as they must repeat, the ceaseless, changeless, remorseless story of the universe, every atom in this earth will take its place and fill again the functions identical with those which it, or its fellow, fills now. . . . And so on for ever. (P. 91)

Because the "ultimate constituents" will continue to exist after the universal holocaust, Brande is telling his audience (members of the *Cui bono?* society), life will begin anew. But this is no cause for rejoicing: "the hypothesis of the indestructibility of the atom" threatens that because the integrity of the atom persists through the destruction of the cosmos, apocalyptic convulsions will recur perpetually (p. 116).

To disrupt what he regards as a meaningless cycle, Brande proposes to split the atom.

> If you will consult a common text-book on the physics of the ether [he explains], you will find that one grain of matter contains sufficient energy, if etherised, to raise a hundred thousand tons nearly two miles. In [the] face of such potentiality it is not wise to wreck incautiously even the atoms of a molecule. (P. 20)

The caution does not concern him, though. Reasoning that only by self-destruction can man exert (preemptive) power over the cosmic process, Brande intends to set off an atomic explosion of a magnitude great enough to reduce the world to its "elemental ether" (p. 49). His investigations "into the origin of the Universe" (p. 38) have made him callous to all moral compunction, have in fact alienated him from nature and from life itself.

In many respects, he is typically a modern Faust. His arcane researches into the secrets of nature set him apart from other men and force him to abandon the traditional conception of the universe of values. He is at once isolated from humanity and predestined to fall victim to the conflict in his own nature as a man; he aspires to be a god, and fails through human weakness.

A dialectic of conflict therefore structures the myth of Faust as scientist. In the pursuit of power, the modern Faust employs his reason; but the will to power being unreasonable, an irrational impulse directs his design, and often eventuates in the form of an antagonist to whom Faust reacts ambivalently. Although, as I have tried to indicate, this myth ultimately relates to an attitude toward history, I will only explore its thematic transmutations: in *Frankenstein* (1818), *The Strange Case of Dr. Jekyll and Mr. Hyde* (1886), and *The Invisible Man* (1897).

Frankenstein; or, Faust's Promethean Rebellion Against Nature

Frankenstein, engaged in the Faustian quest of seeking "the cause of generation and life" (p. 45)[6] so that he can animate lifeless matter, desires (as he later ruefully admits) "to become greater than his nature will allow" (p. 46). He strives for power that is inhuman because more than human, and having attained that power creates a being in his own image: a monster subordinating its reason to the carrying out of its irrational purposes.

The experiments leading to the creation of the monster are obscured in shadowy detail and mystery. Although Mary Shel-

[6] Mary Shelley, *Frankenstein; or, The Modern Prometheus* (London, 1960). All quotations from Mrs. Shelley's Gothic romance follow the text of this edition, which is based on the second edition of *Frankenstein*.

ley speaks vaguely in her introduction to the revised edition of *Frankenstein* (1831) of Erasmus Darwin and galvanism and "conversations between Byron and Shelley" concerning "the nature of the principle of life" (p. viii),[7] no statement of any sort on this subject actually appears in the text of her romance. But however much the absence of a detailed theoretical discussion may be a necessity dictated by ignorance, attention is thereby focused on Frankenstein himself and on the consequences of his act.

Shelley emphasizes the same point in his own way, both in the preface he supplied for the original edition of his wife's work and in a review appearing posthumously in the *Athenæum* for November 10, 1832. The preface begins with the cursory remark that "The event on which this fiction is founded has been supposed, by Dr. Darwin, and some of the physiological writers of Germany, as not of impossible occurrence"; but Shelley immediately abandons this line of defense and goes on to say that "however impossible as a physical fact, [the situation] affords a point of view to the imagination for the delineating of human passions more comprehensive and commanding than any which the ordinary relations of existing events can yield."[8] And again, in his review, he writes:

The novel rests its claim on being a source of powerful and profound emotion. The elementary feelings of the human mind are exposed to view; and those who are accustomed to reason deeply on their origin and tendency will, perhaps, be the only persons who can sympathize to the full extent in the interest of the actions which are their result.[9]

His emphasis thus falls (predictably) on *Frankenstein* as a

[7] James Rieger points out that much of what Mrs. Shelley says in her introduction is doubtlessly incorrect, probably because she had lost the diary entries she had made for the period during which *Frankenstein* was conceived and had to rely, fifteen years after the fact, on her own imperfect memory. He conjectures, for example, that Dr. Polidori, who was interested in galvanism at the time and acquainted with the latest discoveries, must surely have taken the principal part in any discussion of that subject. See "Dr. Polidori and the Genesis of *Frankenstein*," *SEL, III* (1963), 461-472.

[8] Shelley's Preface to *Frankenstein*, p. 1.

[9] *The Complete Works of Percy Bysshe Shelley*, ed. Roger Lugpen and Walter E. Peck, 10 vols. (New York, 1965), VI, 263.

novelistic analogue of Romantic closet drama: the objective representation of the workings of the mind.

Certainly the claim that *Frankenstein* is a "source of powerful and profound emotion" helps to explain the creakiness of the narrative machinery and the annoying penchant Mrs. Shelley has for glancing about everywhere for scenes to inspire emotion while leaving the plot in abeyance for pages, and even chapters, at a time. The result, in Muriel Spark's words, is that "Impatience is evoked where suspense was intended."[10] Unfortunately, this defect is likely to detract from the force of the plot, which structurally proceeds from the effects of disillusionment on the modern Faust and his monster.

The monster is, as it were, born of Frankenstein, who works himself into a feverish state before creating it and almost dies in giving it life. Together, Frankenstein and his creature comprise "the modern Prometheus."[11] The scientist, after daring to discover the vital fire and endowing an inanimate body with it, becomes disillusioned with power. The monster, disillusioned by injustice, rebels against the god who gave him life. These two most important instances of disillusionment actuate the plot.

Disenchanted by the success of his experiment, Frankenstein abnegates the use of his power; and just at the time when it seems that he has obtained control over the forces of life and death, he loses control over himself. Karl Mannheim, speaking specifically of the possible consequences that could follow the realization of utopian dreams and the subsequent loss of ideals and direction, describes Frankenstein's situation exactly. "The disappearance of utopia," Mannheim writes,

> brings about a static state of affairs in which man himself becomes no more than a thing. We would be faced then with the greatest paradox imaginable, namely, that man, who has achieved the highest degree of rational mastery of existence, left without any ideals, becomes a mere creature of impulses. Thus, after a long tortuous, but heroic development, just at the highest stage of awareness, when history is ceasing to be blind

---

[10] Muriel Spark. *Child of Light* (Hadleigh, 1951), p. 144.
[11] Compare Spark, *op cit.,* pp. 134-135.

fate, and is becoming more and more man's own creation, with the relinquishment of utopias, man would lose his will to shape history and therewith his ability to understand it.[12]

If one substitutes for the utopian ideal that of animating life-less matter, and for man himself Frankenstein, this passage delineates what happens to Frankenstein once the ideal is within his power. Having forsaken his role as an immanent god for that of a *deus absconditus,* he in effect relinquishes power over the course of events to the monster whose coming into being had coincided with its creator's final loss of self-control. Thereafter, Frankenstein cannot act; he can only react. He is without direction or orientation, led this way and that by the vagaries of emotion that nature and his monster inspire. "Through the whole of the period during which I was the slave of my creature," he reflects, "I allowed myself to be governed by the impulses of the moment" (p. 163).

Following the murder of his brother William and the unjust condemnation of the servant Justine for the crime, "I was seized by remorse and the sense of guilt, which hurried me away to a hell of intense tortures" (p. 90). He seeks to elude the accusing eye of morbid introspection by absorbing him-self in the contemplation of nature.

> The very winds whispered soothing accents, and maternal nature bade me weep no more. Then again the kindly influ-ence ceased to act—I found myself fettered again to grief, and indulging in all the misery of reflection. Then I . . . [strove] . . . to forget the world, my fears, and, most of all, myself. (P. 96)

But it is precisely in attempting to escape a responsibility he recognizes—to flee from himself—that is his undoing; for he thereby gives up his freedom and his power.

The passage describing Frankenstein's flight from the Ork-neys, after he has incited his monster to further acts of venge-ance by renouncing his intention to create an Eve for this Adam, dramatizes his predicament.

---

[12] Karl Mannheim, *Ideology and Utopia,* tr. Louis Wirth and Edward Shils (New York, 1936), pp. 262-263.

The wind was high, and the waves continually threatened the safety of my little skiff. I found that the wind was northeast, and must have driven me far from the coast from which I had embarked. I endeavoured to change my course, but quickly found that, if I again made the attempt, the boat would instantly be filled with water. Thus situated, my only resource was to drive before the wind. I confess that I felt a few sensations of terror. I had no compass with me, and was so slenderly acquainted with the geography of this part of the world, that the sun was of little benefit to me. I might be driven into the wide Atlantic, and feel all the tortures of starvation, or be swallowed up in the immeasurable waters that roared and buffeted around me. I had already been out many hours, and felt the torment of a burning thirst, a prelude to my other sufferings. I looked on the heavens, which were covered with clouds that flew before the wind, only to be replaced by others: I looked upon the sea, it was to be my grave. (Pp. 183-184)

Here Frankenstein's situation is the objective correlative of his state of mind. Alone, disoriented, and impelled by forces of nature over which he is now completely powerless, he finally drifts to shore—and discovers that his escape from the monster has been an illusion. The tides which carried Frankenstein ashore had but a short time previously washed up the body of his murdered friend Clerval. Apparently the monster is omniscient as well as omnipresent.

The monster's grievances against Frankenstein derive from its recognition that he has created it an isolated being and abandoned it to a solitary, and hence unhappy, existence. Although the murders it commits may seem as gratuitously impulsive as Frankenstein's own vacillating behavior, they are really the logical consequence of its refusing to accept the injustice of such a miserable life. In this sense, it is true, as Shelley protests, "The crimes and malevolence of the single Being, though indeed withering and tremendous," are not "the offspring of any unaccountable propensity to evil, but flow irresistibly from certain causes fully adequate to their production" (*Works*, VI, 264). The irony behind the "crimes and malevolence," however, is the perverse logic that produces them.

Having first tried to gain human companionship through acts of benevolence, and then charging Frankenstein to create a female counterpart for it, the monster by the logic of experience arrives at the conclusion that murder is the only recourse it has to relieve its loneliness. The justice of the demand that it should be allowed to be happy Frankenstein himself admits: "For the first time, . . . I felt what the duties of a creator towards his creature were, and that I ought to render him happy before I complained of his wickedness" (p. 103). And the revenge that follows Frankenstein's failure to live up to what he admits is his obligation is satanically consistent with the monster's desire for human sympathy: if it cannot be happy, then Frankenstein must share its misery.

The further irony of this solution is that it is consonant with, and at the same time the reductio ad absurdum of, the ethical theory enunciated by Mary Shelley's father, William Godwin, to whom *Frankenstein* is dedicated.[13] Godwin, rejecting traditional religious sanctions, attempts to establish morality on the psychology of human nature. For him, any ethic must be grounded on the fact that man is essentially a social being: "No being can be either virtuous, or vicious, who has no opportunity of influencing the happiness of others."[14] The monster syllogistically exploits Godwin's principle according to a satanic logic: by generating unhappiness in others, he becomes a moral agent and therefore "a social being."

The clue to the Faustian nature of the conflict between Frankenstein and his monster lies in their being necessarily dependent on one another in their relation as creator-and-destroyer and in their seesawing roles as master-and-slave, pursuer-and-pursued. The monster hints that together they represent man's potential: "Was man, indeed, at once so powerful, so virtuous and magnificent, yet so vicious and base? He appeared at one time a mere scion of the evil principle, and at another as all that can be conceived of noble and godlike" (p.

[13] Without substantiating the allegation, Mrs. Spark suggested that *Frankenstein* was an "unconscious satire" of Godwin. See Muriel Spark, "Mary Shelley: A Prophetic Novelist," *The Listener*, XLV (Feb. 22, 1951), 305.

[14] William Godwin, *Enquiry concerning Political Justice and its Influence on Morals and Happiness*, ed. F. E. L. Priestly, 3 vols. (Toronto, 1946), II, 325.

124). But the contrast between them is not so striking as the impulse that involves each in the destiny of the other and points to an unconscious sympathy of creator and creature. Frankenstein himself, by failing to act decisively or effectively, vicariously shares in the monster's acts of destruction, as if the monster itself were some essential part of his own nature—an active "evil principle" that has been separated from him in bringing the monster to life—a principle corresponding to that part of him which attracts him to death and has led him "to examine the cause and progress of decay, and forced him to spend days and nights in vaults and charnel-houses" (p. 45). In fact, his own sensations of guilt come from the feeling that somehow he has willed the murders. "I felt as if I was about the commission of a dreadful crime, and avoided with shuddering anxiety any encounter with my fellow-creatures," he says before fleeing to discover that his monster has strangled Clerval (pp. 182-183). And after the event he reflects that "Clerval, my friend and dearest companion, had fallen a victim to me and the monster of my creation" (p. 197).

Yet self-knowledge is something that Frankenstein is always fleeing from. He seeks to lose himself in the external world; and along with Robert Walton, the mariner who intends to reach the North Pole and to whom he confides his story, Frankenstein too might have said,

> There is something at work in my soul which I do not understand. I am practically industrious—painstaking;—a workman to execute with perseverance and labour:—but besides this, there is a love for the marvellous, a belief in the marvellous, intertwined in all my projects, which hurries me out of the common pathways of men, even to the wild sea and unvisited regions I am about to explore. (P. 10)

For Frankenstein, the impulse to go beyond the recognized limits of human power points to his Faustian desire to transcend the limits of human nature, in this instance by overcoming death. And his creature is the "monstrous Image" (p. 197) of himself because it shares the same rebellious impulse against the conditions of its existence.

This similarity of impulse also indicates a profound dialectical involvement of creature and creator. That Frankenstein should repeatedly identify himself with his monster, that he should accuse himself, almost proudly, of being responsible for the murders that it commits—"I, not in deed, but in effect, was the true murderer" (p. 93)—all this implies that the monster is the agent of his own clandestine wishes. His desire is not only what he confesses it to be, to learn "the secrets of heaven and earth" (p. 28), but also, in so doing, to attain power over the lives of his fellow creatures. The creation of the monster does not satisfy that desire, because the monster soon shows signs of having a consciousness and will of its own, and refuses to submit to its creator. The acts of the monster, however, represent an alternative access to the power Frankenstein has been seeking; and the monster is in no way constrained to repress the destructive impulses that give it power over human life and allow it to possess the imagination of its creator. Thus the dialectic of power that Frankenstein submits to when he undertakes his Faustian purpose leads to the diabolical conclusion that murder is a means of dominating absolutely the life of another creature.

Toward some such conclusion Frankenstein himself is impelled, for when he finds out that his creature will not obey him, he becomes enraged, possessed by the desire to destroy it. The monster is therefore logically as well as causally an extension of Frankenstein; and the murderous impulse most prominent in one is also present in the other and is inseparable from the Faustian will to power. The monster emerges from an inner struggle that releases impulses Frankenstein himself hardly dares to acknowledge (though they dominate his imagination); and if that monster haunts his creator everywhere and seems preternaturally able to find him out, that only attaches the monster more surely to the secret self from which Frankenstein is perpetually trying to escape. "I felt as if my soul were grappling with a palpable enemy," he says, recalling his response to the idea that scientists "have acquired new and almost unlimited powers"; and the result of this inner conflict is that "my mind was filled with one thought, one conception, one purpose" (p. 40). The issue of his monomaniacal intent is of course the monster, an objectification of the "palpable enemy" within Frankenstein's "soul."

But complete self-recognition of this intimate connection with his monster is withheld from Frankenstein. It remains for Elizabeth Lavenza, later Frankenstein's wife and consequently the monster's (last) victim, to say: "now misery has come home, and men appear to me as monsters thirsting for each other's blood" (p. 93).

Jekyll and Hyde: A Faustian Mystery

There is more than a passing resemblance between *Frankenstein* and *The Strange Case of Dr. Jekyll and Mr. Hyde* (1886). Jekyll's "double," Edward Hyde, like Frankenstein's monster, is the Mephistopheles called forth by the Faustian impulse that obsesses Jekyll to transcend his own nature. For Stevenson's scientist, though, that impulse is not to acquire power over the forces of life and death, but to separate the moral components of his being. The irony of Frankenstein's triumph over death is that it leads to a creature who attains power over life through murder; the irony of Jekyll's achievement in purifying his moral nature is that in so doing he frees a monster of evil who finally dominates him.

Jekyll and Hyde is probably Stevenson's most intricately structured narrative. G. K. Chesterton hints at the source of its complexity in his summary of its theme: "The real stab of the story is not in the discovery that the one man is two men, but in the discovery that two men are one man. . . . The point . . . is not that a man *can* cut himself off from his conscience, but that he cannot."[15] The crucial word here is *discovery;* that Stevenson gives *Jekyll and Hyde* the form of a mystery is essential to its meaning.

The mystery is not, strictly speaking, about a "split personality"; it is literally about the splitting of a personality. This distinction may seem a quibble, but it shifts emphasis from psychoanalysis to literary analysis and from stasis to process. From the point of view of psychoanalysis only the last

---

[15] G. K. Chesterton, *Robert Louis Stevenson* (London, n.d.), pp. 72-73.

chapter—Jekyll's own account of the results of his experiment
—is necessary to the meaning of *Jekyll and Hyde;* the rest is by
and large superfluous. But Jekyll's stating of his case is in-
complete. He does not achieve anything like total self-
knowledge. Thus the mystery cannot be fully solved by considering Jekyll-and-Hyde alone, for that mystery implicates all
of the characters in the "strange case." And as no one of them
comprehends the whole truth of the mystery—none of them
having achieved complete self-awareness—so all of the participants in the mystery must be brought in and the significance
of their testimony examined if one is to identify the real
mystery.

In regard to this fragmenting of the truth—whereby all the
characters in the drama partake of the central mystery of
human nature—a possible influence on Stevenson's conception
is Edward Bulwer-Lytton's *A Strange Story* (1861).[16] The
principal characters in Lytton's romance are, in the order he
describes them in his preface: Margrave, Dr. Allen Fenwick,
and Lillian Lloyd. "Firstly," writes Lytton,

> the image of sensuous, soulless Nature, such as the Material-
> ist had conceived it; secondly, the image of Intellect, obstinate-
> ly separating all its inquiries from the belief in the spiritual
> essence and destiny of man, and incurring all kinds of perplex-
> ity and resorting to all kinds of visionary speculation before it
> settles at last into the simple faith which unites the philosopher
> and the infant; and thirdly, the image of the erring but pure-
> thoughted visionary, seeking over-much on this earth to sepa-
> rate the soul from the mind. *(Works,* XXIV, ix)

Fenwick, in other words, "the image of Intellect," stands between the brutal Margrave and the spiritual Lillian, both of
whom draw him to them and each of whom represents a single
element in his own personality separated out of his nature and
purified. The plot concerns Fenwick's involvement, through

---

[16] Edwin M. Eigner, *Robert Louis Stevenson and the Romantic Tradition*
(Princeton, 1966), p. 28, says that *"A Strange Story* is worth pausing over . . .
because it was an influence on Stevenson"; but he offers no evidence for Stevenson's familiarity with it. (Eigner, pp. 201-202, argues that the impact of this
work of Lytton's is to be found principally in Stevenson's "Olalla.")

Lillian, in Margrave's desperate search for the elixir of life; and in the course of that plot Fenwick, first drawn to and then repelled by Margrave's animality, must release himself from Margrave's power to attain finally the "simple faith" that brings him peace of mind. Thus as one critic of *A Strange Story* has noted, "Margrave is an 'image' as 'conceived' by Fenwick; that is, allegorically, something within Fenwick, and the novel may be read as an allegory of conflicting forces within the human personality."[17]

The Margrave in himself Jekyll never succeeds in exorcising; and the spiritual component, represented by Lillian in *A Strange Story*, does not take possession of Stevenson's scientist, though he had intended for his experiment to cast out the Margrave (Hyde) in his nature and leave him a purely spiritual being. "Had I approached my discovery in a more noble spirit . . . all must have been otherwise," he sorrowfully reflects, "and from these agonies of death and birth, I had come forth an angel instead of a fiend." Indeed, the drug which effects his transformation "had no discriminating action; it was neither diabolical nor divine; it but shook the doors of the prisonhouse of my disposition" *(J&H, VII, 435).*[18] Hence his attitude toward his experiment entirely determines its result; and if Jekyll has affinities with Dr. Fenwick, the imprisoned fiend within him whom Jekyll liberates is certainly related to Margrave, whose mind

> had lost all sympathy in the past [sic], because it had lost all conception of a future beyond the grave; it had lost conscience, it had lost remorse. . . . The azure light [denoting soulless animal energy] was even more vivid in certain organs useful to the conservation of existence, as in those organs I had observed it more vivid among some of the inferior animals than it is in man,—secretiveness, destructiveness, and the ready perception of things immediate to the wants of the day. (SS, XXIV, 170)

---

[17] Joseph I. Fradin, " 'The Absorbing Tyranny of Every-day Life'; Bulwer-Lytton's *A Strange Story*," *NCF*, XVI (1961), 9.

[18] Citations from *The Strange Case of Dr. Jekyll and Mr. Hyde* and from other works of Robert Louis Stevenson refer to the "Vailima Edition" of his works, 26 vols. (London, 1922-1923).

Such animality is of course characteristic of Hyde, and he too shows a disregard for the value of human life and takes pleasure in the power of cruelty.[19] "I was often plunged into a kind of wonder," Jekyll admits,

> at my vicarious depravity. This familiar that I called out of my own soul, and sent forth alone to do his good pleasure, was a being inherently malign and villainous; his every act and thought centred on self; drinking pleasure with bestial avidity from any degree of torture to another. (*J&H*, VII, 437)

Thus Stevenson makes it quite explicit that Hyde is an element in Jekyll's "own soul"; and although an elixir transmogrifies the aging doctor into the youthful Hyde, the two remain doubles—Hyde an essential part of him, and he an essential part of Hyde.[20]

The irony of Jekyll's experiment is that he had wished to banish the Hyde in him so that his good acts might be unadulterated by evil. He recognizes the duality of man's moral nature, but refuses to accept it.

> It was on the moral side, and in my own person, that I learned to recognize the thorough and primitive duality of man; I saw that, of the two natures that contended in the field of my consciousness, even if I could rightly be said to be either, it was only because I was radically both; and from an early date, even before the course of my scientific discoveries had begun to suggest the most naked possibility of such a miracle, I had learned to dwell with pleasure, as a beloved day-dream, on the thought of the separation of these elements. If each, I told myself, could but be housed in separate identities, life would be

[19] There is some correspondence of detail between Lytton's portrayal of Margrave and Stevenson's of Hyde. Hyde directly and Margrave through an agent under the influence of his magical powers commit murders witnessed by romantically inclined maidservants. Also, both Margrave and Hyde easily give way to their murderous impulses. Compare, for instance, Margrave's killing of a squirrel—"every feature quivering with rage, [he] was stamping his foot on his victim again and again!" (XXIV, 116)—and Hyde's assault on Sir Danvers—Hyde "broke out of all bounds and clubbed him to the earth. And next moment, with ape-like fury, he was trampling his victim under foot" (VII, 375).

[20] For a further discussion of the psychology of the double in the literature of the second half of the nineteenth century, see Eigner, *op. cit.*, pp. 20-33.

relieved of all that was unbearable; the unjust might go his way, delivered from the aspirations and remorse of his more upright twin; and the just could walk stedfastly and securely on his upward path . . . no longer exposed to disgrace and penitence by the hands of his extraneous evil. (VII, 430)

In the face of his own contradiction (he says that he was "radically both" good and evil and that the evil was "extraneous"), Jekyll had hoped to relieve life of all that was unbearable *to him,* to free action, that is, from the sting of remorse. Instead, he finds himself gradually dominated by Hyde, though not completely absorbed by this agent of evil; so that finally enough of Jekyll reasserts himself in Hyde to cause the latter to commit suicide rather than confront discovery by others. If, as Stevenson wrote, "The Hypocrite let out the beast of Hyde,"[21] the hypocrite also destroyed it.

Jekyll never really abolishes the "thorough and primitive duality of man." Although he tries to keep Hyde hidden,[22] a creature of the night, his own hypocrisy evokes the Hyde in him at unexpected moments, especially at times when he fancies himself to be better than other men.

It was a fine, clear, January day, wet under foot where the frost had melted, but cloudless overhead; and the Regent's Park was full of winter chirruppings and sweet with spring odours. I sat in the sun on a bench; the animal within me licking the chops of memory; the spiritual side a little drowsed. . . . After all, I reflected, I was like my neighbours; and then I smiled, comparing myself with other men, comparing my active goodwill with the lazy cruelty of their neglect. And at the very moment of that vainglorious thought a qualm came over me, a horrid nausea and the most deadly shuddering. (VII, 446-447)

Hyde is therefore an objectification of Jekyll's own destructive animal instincts—the beast in man—and his emergence in Jekyll is a judgment that what the experiment has actually

---

[21] Letter to J. P. Bocock (1887), quoted in George S. Hellman, *The True Stevenson: A Study in Clarification* (Boston, 1925), pp. 129-130.

[22] The pun here is Stevenson's. Compare Utterson's remark: "If he be Mr. Hyde . . . I shall be Mr. Seek" (VII, 362).

accomplished is the replacing of "the lazy cruelty of . . . neglect" with the active commission of cruelty. Jekyll finds that he has been mistaken in thinking that the beast in his nature ceases to conflict with his "spirit" once it has been given an identity of its own and thus has been liberated from moral compunction and restraint. Hyde still shares "some of the phenomena of [Jekyll's] consciousness" (VII, 451-452) and struggles to dominate that consciousness completely.

The compulsion to resolve the contradictions inherent in his nature motivates Jekyll's experiment; but, as evidenced in his own statement of his purpose, the theoretical basis of the experiment contains "a profound duplicity," since Jekyll at once acknowledges and denies that duality is an essential part of man's nature. To some extent he is aware of his own hypocrisy: "I concealed my pleasures; and . . . when I reached years of reflection, and began to look around me and take stock of my progress and position in the world, I stood already committed to a profound duplicity of life" (VII, 428). His analytical mind cannot accept this deception, arising from the disparity between appearance and reality; and Hyde is born of Jekyll's intellectual urge to purify both parts of what he conceives of as an essential dichotomy of beast and spirit, to separate the one from the other in fact as well as in theory and thus have appearance and reality coincide. But not only is the theory self-contradictory; the desire also is self-opposed; for Jekyll is equally concerned with his "progress and position in the world," and his attempt to seek out his purely altruistic self conflicts with this self-seeking wish for repute. Moreover, his Faustian rejection of his own nature leads him to separate "the moral and the intellectual" elements of his mind (VII, 429), so that he becomes even further divided against himself.

Jekyll's impulse to purify himself, to purge himself of evil, is therefore self-defeating. His analysis of the dichotomies in his own nature only accentuates his essential duality, his essential contradictoriness; and the researches meant to transform that nature assume clearly the character of a strategy for self-deception. He thus becomes a victim of his own duplicity—a victim of both his own "doubleness" and his own deceit. A Hyde distinct from Jekyll still brings out the residue of Hyde remaining in Jekyll; for if "nothing lived in [Hyde] but fear and hatred," "I still hated and feared the thought of the brute that slept within me" (VII, 449, 450). Once the monster has been set loose, in Jekyll, as in Frankenstein, that monster inspires impulses identical with its own except that they are turned against it.

If the contradictions in Jekyll are essential to man's nature, so is self-deception. Dr. Lanyon, for example, who is Jekyll's friend until his colleague reveals to him his secret, is horrified to learn that Jekyll and Hyde are doubles. Lanyon had never permitted himself to imagine that the same man is capable of extremes of good and evil, and he finds this knowledge so strange and terrible that it soon kills him. Utterson, too, personifies an alternative response: unlike Jekyll, he chooses to make the nature of man a subject for external, rather than introspective, investigation; and consequently he is never shown to be aware of himself as a subject—aware, that is, of how the mystery of Jekyll-and-Hyde touches his own self. He comes to suspect that all is not what it seems, but he discovers evidence for the duality of man in others, and not, like Jekyll, "in my own person." His preoccupation with what is external to him makes him slow to appreciate the meaning of the fact that Jekyll and Hyde partake of one consciousness; yet by embodying an approach to the mystery of human nature antithetical to Jekyll's, Utterson serves to underscore the point that either approach is possible in arriving at the truth of human nature.

The polarity of Jekyll versus Utterson, introversion versus extroversion, is established by Stevenson's narrative technique, and that technique is inseparable from the meaning of *Jekyll and Hyde*. The various points of view which Stevenson introduces represent, at least in part, one or the other side of the polarity. Utterson, acting as detective; the maid-servant who witnesses the Carew murder; the handwriting analyst, Mr. Guest, who identifies Jekyll's hand with Hyde's—all of these observers report on Jekyll-and-Hyde from a behavioristic point of view; whereas Dr. Lanyon, Richard Enfield (Utterson's nephew) and, of course, Jekyll himself are directly aware, in varying degrees, that Hyde somehow bears upon their own selves. To be sure, any such schematizing can never be wholly satisfactory. It is also true, for example, that Jekyll sometimes looks upon Hyde as something "extraneous" to him and considers Hyde's cruelty to be his own *"vicarious* depravity," as if Hyde were not even an accidental element of his own being. What the polarity of inside and outside, the individual and society, clarifies, however, is that no purely objective investigation, or purely subjective experiment, can solve the mystery of Jekyll-and-Hyde. Jekyll's process of self-discovery coincides structurally with the process by which Utterson finds him out; but Jekyll would never be completely found out were it not for his own intimate statement of the case *and* the outside evidence to check that self-assessment against. The outside point of view is necessary for delineating social appearances; it is insufficient for explaining the Jekyll-and-Hyde mystery altogether.

The limits of objective inquiry are indicated by the maidservant's report of the Carew murder. Here Stevenson does not allow the reader an internal view of the events, so that the murder itself appears totally wanton and unmotivated. Sir Danvers encounters Hyde in a moonlit lane; he speaks to him; and suddenly Hyde is bludgeoning him with a cane. Yet before being attacked, Sir Danvers seemed undaunted by Hyde's appearance; unlike everyone else who sees Hyde, Sir Danvers apparently was not repelled by his hideousness. According to the witness,

> When they had come within speech (which was just under the maid's eyes) the older man bowed and accosted the other with a very pretty manner of politeness. It did not *seem* as if the subject of his address were of great importance; indeed, from his pointing, it sometimes *appeared* as if he were only inquiring his way; but the moon shone on his face as he spoke, and the girl was pleased to watch it, it *seemed* to breathe such an innocent and old-world kindness of disposition, yet with something high too, as of a well-founded self-content. (VII, 375; my emphasis)

This account is confined entirely to appearances. What business the civilized Sir Danvers might have had with the unconstrainedly brutal Hyde is not revealed. What he might have said to Hyde and what he had written in his letter to Utterson —a letter found on Carew's person after his death—these details remain unknown. Whether his pointing had been to punctuate a threat to Hyde's reputation—a threat to which the Jekyll in Hyde certainly would have responded—is a matter of groundless speculation. Gratuitous cruelty is not inconsistent with what the reader knows of Hyde; and the virtual pantomime of the scene gets across the gratuitousness of Hyde's act. The unanswerable question is what Sir Danvers should have had to do with him; and about such questions of motive, and consciousness generally, the outside point of view must necessarily be inconclusive.[23]

The integrity of Jekyll-and-Hyde is therefore grasped only in the fusion of the internal and external points of view; and this fusion in turn discovers that the identity of Jekyll-and-Hyde is ultimately a mystery analogous to the combination of two chemicals into an effervescent potion having the characteristics of neither which transmogrifies Jekyll into Hyde. In one or both of these chemicals is an impurity Jekyll cannot analyze; and this detail again points to the futility of Jekyll's attempt to analyze himself, "on the moral side," into components of pure good and pure evil. The apparent mystery that Jekyll and Hyde share the same being, in other words, leads to the real mystery: that the nature of man is inexplicably and unalterably dual.

Thus "the machinery" of the narrative (Stevenson's term) is integral to the meaning of Jekyll and Hyde; and that it should be so accords with what Stevenson himself stated in his essay "On Lord Lytton's 'Fables in Song,'" which first appeared in the Fortnightly Review (1874) more than a decade before Stevenson conceived of Jekyll and Hyde. In that essay he declared that in the modern fable—and an "ought" is implied—"There will be . . . a logical nexus between the moral

[23] The dehumanizing effect of Utterson's objectivity in investigation instigates Jekyll-Hyde's suicide. When Jekyll, in his laboratory, begs Utterson not to come in and find out that he can no longer rid himself of the physical appearance of Hyde, Utterson judges the voice, and not what is being said, decides that the pleading voice belongs to Hyde, and proceeds to break down the door to the laboratory (VII, 409).

expressed and the machinery employed to express it" (XXXIV, 51). What necessitates such a nexus, he says, is that "men learn to suspect some serious analogy underneath" the "purely fantastic" tale—for example, "a comical story of an ape touches us quite differently after the proposition of Mr. Darwin's theory" (XXIV, 50).

The particular illustration is appropriate to *Jekyll and Hyde*, for on several occasions Stevenson likens Hyde's natural and atavistic "energy of life" (VII, 452) to that of an ape or monkey.[24] Stevenson knew a good deal more about science than Mrs. Shelley,[25] and considering his own statements about fables one should, I think, interpret the similarity of Hyde and ape as an allusion to "Mr. Darwin's theory." In that case the universality of the mystery of Jekyll-and-Hyde takes on another aspect. "The thorough and primitive duality of man" gains biological sanction, and at the same time the mystery remains as to what unknown factor makes man better or worse than—but anyway incommensurate with—other animals.

The moral conflict in Jekyll subsumes that between instinct and reason, between impulses deriving from man's biological origins and the demands of civilized society. Through his Faustian quest for power to transcend his nature, Jekyll precipitates the Hyde in him and thereby brings out the potential antagonism of the good and evil inherent in man. But if the science of this modern Faust gives him power sufficient to liberate his evil instincts, it does not afford him control over himself; and his experiment finally cuts him off from all human sympathy and damns him to perish because he cannot command the forces he has set loose except by destroying himself. Thus the myth of Faust is explored in *Jekyll and Hyde* to determine the psychology of the Faustian impulse and to discover the mystery of human nature that necessarily renders that impulse self-contradictory.

[24] Hyde is spoken of as a "thing like a monkey" (VII, 407); and Jekyll recalls "the apelike tricks that he would play me" (VII, 452) and Hyde's "apelike spite" (VII, 454).

[25] See R. B. Strathdee, "Robert Louis Stevenson as a Scientist," *Aberdeen University Review*, XXXVI (1956), 268-275.

The Invisible Man: New Myth for Old

Another victim of the obsessive desire for knowledge and the power that knowledge confers is Griffin, the Invisible Man. In *The Invisible Man* (1897), however, Wells focuses on a different thematic aspect of the myth of Faust, emphasizing the relation between the modern Faust and a society intolerant of the innovative, and eccentric, scientist, rather than the self-destructive nature of Faust himself. Griffin's own attitude provokes others to vengeance, for having attained unusual power through his scientific researches, he thinks he can act with impunity, ignoring the ethical restraints imposed by society on individual behavior; but Wells stresses the societal matrix of Griffin's action much more than the effect of those actions on Griffin's being apart from their social context. Specifically, then, the theme of *The Invisible Man* concerns the dissociation of personal ambition from social responsibility, of scientific pursuits from moral and socially acceptable objectives; and the Faustian myth of the romance embodies the notion that scientific discoveries, so far from being good in themselves, can actually be utilized for immoral, even diabolical, purposes.

Although Wells's use of the motif of invisibility has made it almost commonplace in modern science fiction, neither that motif nor the theme it attaches to is original with him. The best-known example of a prototype of Griffin is Marlowe's Faustus, who asks Mephistopheles to make him invisible so that he can play blasphemous tricks at the papal court:

> Sweet *Mephasto:* so charme me here,
> That I may walke invisible to all,
> And doe what ere I please, unseene of any.[26]

A much earlier instance of an invisible man who acts without restraint is alluded to in *The Republic*. There Glaucon, desiring Socrates to explain why a man should behave ethically if he can escape punishment for immoral deeds, brings up the

---

[26] Christopher Marlowe, *The Tragical History of Doctor Faustus*, B-Text (1616), ed. W. W. Greg (Oxford, 1950), ll.1025-1027.

myth of Gyges' ring—a ring that confers invisibility on whoever wears it and enables Gyges to get away with adultery and
regicide.[27] Still another case where the possibility of becoming
invisible invokes the question of why an invisible man should
not violate the norms of moral behavior is to be found in Godwin's *Man in the Moone*. Domingo Gonsales asks the inhabitants of the lunar utopia

> whether they had not any kind of Jewell or other meanes to
> make a man invisible, which mee thought had beene a thing of
> great and extraordinary use. . . . They answered that if it were
> a thing faisible, yet they assured themselves that God would
> not suffer it to be revealed to us creatures subject to so many
> imperfections, being a thing so apt to be abused to ill purposes.
> (Pp. 100-101)

The recurrence of the motif, and its conjunction with the
question of right conduct, are sufficiently in evidence in these
examples to obviate multiplying instances from folklore and
medieval romances.

Since Wells could have gotten the general idea for *The
Invisible Man* from any of a number of sources, an assessment
of his own success with the motif of invisibility begins with the
fact that he attempts to make it scientifically plausible. He
himself singled out this contribution of his to fantasy in the
preface to his *Scientific Romances*; and though he is not speaking particularly of *The Invisible Man,* what he says is especially
applicable to it.

> Hitherto, except in exploration fantasies, the fantastic ele-
> ment was brought in by magic. Frankenstein even, used some
> jiggery-pokery magic to animate his artificial monster. There
> was trouble about the thing's soul. But by the end of the last
> century it had become difficult to squeeze even a momentary
> belief out of magic any longer. It occurred to me that instead
> of the usual interview with the devil or a magician, an in-
> genious use of scientific patter might with advantage be sub-

[27] Plato, *The Republic*, 359c-d.

stituted. That was no great discovery. I simply brought the fetish stuff up to date, and made it as near actual theory as possible. (P. viii)

In *The Invisible Man*, the "scientific patter" Griffin uses to account for his invisibility amounts to the argument that a body could become invisible "if its refractive index could be made the same as that of air" (III, 122).

Clearly the explanation by itself does not alter the reader's attitude toward Wells's story. But together with the fact that the Invisible Man is a scientist, it does give Wells's myth a contemporaneity it would not have if the "fantastic element" were "brought in by magic." Moreover, Wells's myth of invisibility, like that of Gyges' ring as cited by Glaucon, is paradigmatic: it raises the question of why a man with certain powers should not traduce conventional moral standards. More particularly, however, Wells delineates the case of the scientist who, having discovered something that could give him extraordinary power over the lives of his fellow creatures, feels no compunction against employing that discovery to "establish a Reign of Terror" (III, 169) to satisfy his own ambition at the expense of the common good. The details of the myth, in other words, stipulate that it displaces certain realities of modern life; and Wells was being less than fair to his achievement in deprecating his "discovery" of how the contemporary relevance of science fantasy might be brought home by "an ingenious use of scientific patter."

Wells's Invisible Man resembles Jekyll and Frankenstein in that he too is possessed by a Faustian impulse to deny and to transcend the limits of his humanity. But in his negation of all human ties he goes further than either of these Faustian predecessors. He not only brings his own father to ruin and suicide by stealing from him the money he (Griffin) requires to carry on his scientific research; he in effect repudiates any connection with his father by refusing to recognize any responsibility for his death (III, 125-127). Thereafter Griffin thinks himself to be above other men and beyond good and evil; and once he determines the secret of invisibility, he desires the godlike power that consists with his godlike conception. The emblem of this desire, Mrs. Hall, the innkeeper's wife, unwittingly perceives when she unexpectedly enters Griffin's room on the day after his arrival in Iping: "for a second it seemed to her that the man she looked at had an enormous mouth wide open,—a vast and incredible mouth that swallowed the whole of the lower portion of his face" (III, 12). Indeed, Griffin has an insatiable desire for power, and he gives no indication that he desires it for anything other than its own sake and for the license it would give him. "I beheld, unclouded by doubt," he says, "a magnificent vision of all that invisibility might mean to a man,—the mystery, the power, the freedom" (III, 124).

One irony of Griffin's grandiose plan for becoming invisible ruler of the world is that in attempting to transcend his nature he manages, like Jekyll, to enslave himself to it. He is so caught up by his "fixed idea" (III, 132) of making himself invisible and thereby unburdening himself of the impediment to freedom his opaque body presents, that he fails to take account of his bodily needs in transforming himself into "the Unseen" (III, 171, 199). The result of his lack of foresight in practical matters—he neglects to make his clothes invisible—is literally fatal. Instead of obtaining complete freedom for godly or diabolical—at any rate, superhuman—purposes, he immediately finds himself more preoccupied than other men in seeing to quotidian necessities. His criminal acts of murder, robbery, and assault are all causally related to this banal oversight.

While Griffin's actions are consequent upon his failure to consider the pragmatic aspects of invisibility, the motives for his actions proceed through three stages: the will to stay alive, the hope of restoring himself to visible normality, and the wish to get revenge on Dr. Kemp and mankind generally for betraying him and frustrating that hope. At all points, however, he abandons himself to the indiscriminate and impetuous use of force. It is ironic that his violent temper, like his impracticality, humanizes him.

None of the other characters, not even Kemp, can really understand Griffin's scientific theories; but the possibilities for acting criminally afforded by invisibility they can all imagine. Thus a mariner at Port Stowe divulges to the disquieted

Thomas Marvel, who has been forcibly engaged in the service
of the Invisible God Griffin,[28] that if—as the newspapers are
claiming—there is an Invisible Man, he would be virtually
immune to the usual social sanctions against criminality. "It
makes me regular uncomfortable," says the mariner,

> the bare thought of that chap running about the country!
> He is at present At Large . . . just think of the things he might
> do! Where'd you be, if he took a drop over and above, and had
> a fancy to go for you? Suppose he wants to rob—who can pre-
> vent him? He can trespass, he can burgle, he could walk
> through a cordon of policemen as easy as me or you could give
> the slip to a blind man! Easier! (III, 87-88)

The mariner's speculation of course reflects on his own moral
integrity; but what he envisions is exactly what Griffin does
with his power—if one adds murder to the list. The further
irony here is that Griffin, who thinks himself exceptional,
really has no more imagination than the next man when it
comes to conceiving of evil uses for his power and putting
that power to those uses.

The crimes of the Invisible Man therefore make him under-
standable and familiar. Contrary to his intention, they actually
mitigate the fear and mystery he thinks to inspire by them, for
they translate the mystery and strangeness of his being into
terms that the pedestrian minds of Iping can comprehend. His
acts of violence render him visible, as it were, not only because
they provide evidence of his presence and whereabouts, but
because they seem to establish his nature. They call for action,
not intellection, to combat his power.

An illustration of this sense in which the Invisible Man becomes visible figures in the reaction of Mr. Heelas, who, caught

---

[28] Warrant for speaking of Griffin as a god is to be found in the chapter in
which he first encounters Thomas Marvel, who receives the Call to do what
Griffin wills (the following dialogue alternates between Marvel and Griffin):
 " 'A voice out of heaven! And stones! And a fist—Lord!'
 " 'Pull yourself together,' said the Voice, 'for you have to do the job I've
chosen for you.'
 " 'All I want to do is help you—just tell me what I got to do. (Lord!) What-
ever you want done, that I'm most willing to do.' " (III, 63)

napping during Griffin's siege of Kemp's, awakens to see his neighbor's house in a shambles.

> He [Heelas] slept through the smashing of the windows, and then woke up suddenly with a curious persuasion of something wrong. He looked across at Kemp's house, rubbed his eyes and looked again. . . . He said he was damned, and still *the strange thing was visible*. The house looked as though it had been deserted for weeks—after a violent riot. Every window was broken, and every window, save those of the belvedere study, was blinded by the internal shutters. (III, 194; my emphasis)

What is going on is at once "visible" and "blinded"; but Mr. Heelas has no occasion to ponder the invisible meaning of the scene. His attention is immediately arrested by Kemp running toward him—from which he concludes that there is an Invisible Man after all and that he is headed this way. "With Mr. Heelas to think things like that was to act": he sets to work right away barricading himself in.

As long as the villagers can locate an object or direction for their fear, they can react instinctively. Hence by resorting to violence, Griffin loses what advantage his intelligence and superior knowledge might have given him, and by abandoning all self-control, he betrays himself and his ambitions for the sake of indulging the meanest whims. His blindness to the error of his strategy justifies Wells's choice in treating this aspect of "Griffin *contra mundum*" (III, 183) as farce.

But the absurdity of the Invisible Man's fate is tragic as well as farcical. If his own statement of his case partially substantiates Kemp's charge that "He has cut himself off from his own kind" (III, 175), if Griffin himself confirms his alienation from the rest of humanity, still his moral and intellectual isolation is not all his own doing. His researches, like Moreau's, are frustrated and misunderstood, and his intolerance of petty annoyances, the intrusions of people who can only think of their everyday concerns, is at least matched by society's intolerance of him. Indeed, Griffin's uncompromising perseverance in trying to carry out his outrageous aims attains a kind of tragic nobility in contrast to the narrow-mindedness of those who would betray him and hunt him down as if he were a rabid animal. Though he is not admirable in himself and though his intent is hardly laudable, compared with the mean provinciality of those whom he is forced to depend upon the Invisible Man has heroic stature. His antagonists, including Kemp, cannot imagine any but perverse uses for the power of invisibility either; and none of them can resist succumbing to the rules of the game that Griffin imposes—which for them means contradicting the moral position they act to defend.

The one who compromises his principles most is Kemp. Like the mariner at Port Stowe, he can only conceive of the evil an Invisible Man might do. Before he hears anything of Griffin's own story, he reflects with horror: "He is invisible! . . . And it reads like a rage growing to mania! The things he may do! The things he may do! And he's upstairs free as the air" (III, 116). It seems that Kemp has no impulse to imagine any good coming of invisibility—which presumably means that he could see himself doing what Griffin does if he were invisible.

The potential similarity of Kemp and Griffin is not purely conjectural. Kemp, for example, says that he recognizes moral responsibility no more than Griffin does. When the latter asks Kemp for absolution, the question and response are:

> "You don't blame me, do you? You don't blame me?"
> "I never blame anyone," said Kemp. "It's quite out of fashion." (III, 161)

The reply might be appropriate coming from Lord Henry in *The Picture of Dorian Gray*. But from Kemp the remark is compromising. Of course, Kemp is merely trying to keep Griffin talking until the police arrive, and he does not want to risk his life by antagonizing Griffin. The circumstances, however, merely reinforce the point that Kemp, like Griffin, is willing to employ any means necessary to achieve his end, regardless of whether the means, in Kemp's case, subverts the principles he is trying to safeguard. In summoning the police, he has broken his promise, and to compound the offense he plays the hypocrite to accommodate Griffin. When Griffin relates the incident of his robbery of a shop in Drury Lane and his assault on its proprietor, Kemp first reacts with controlled indignation. The Invisible Man demands that he say what he means: "Kemp's face grew a trifle hard. He was about to speak and checked himself. 'I suppose, after all,' he said with a sudden change of manner, 'the thing had to be done. You were in a fix. But still——' " (III, 161). Kemp, unlike Griffin, is amenable to self-restraint and the restraint of social convention, even if he is thereby made a time-server.

In this last respect, Kemp and Griffin stand in a Jekyll-and-Hyde relationship to one another: Griffin, the scientist without intellectual or emotional or moral constraint, who in attempting to acquire unlimited freedom and power alienates himself from his fellow men, shares a dialectical involvement with Kemp, the pragmatic and accommodating scientist who ruthlessly sets out to confine and destroy the Invisible Man and afterward tries to seek out the secret of his invisibility (III, 205).

This example concludes my survey of thematic variations on the myth of Faust as the scientist who comes to be dominated by the irrational element within him in his quest for power to escape the confines of his nature. As the myth of the modern Faust takes in a larger and larger social scene, until in *The Invisible Man* the entire social order seems to be motivated by irrational impulses, it comes to represent a view of history in an age of science—the view of a technological society continuously redefining its goals and limits, but also a society governed by man's irrationality and directing the discoveries of reason toward irrational ends. Some other myths, displacing the dreams of reason with nightmares that negate them, will be discussed in the following chapter.

5

Charles Darwin and the Utopian Nightmare: Science and Metaphysics

> What is a man without desire, without free will
> and without choice if not a stop in an organ?
> What do you think? Let us consider the probability—
> can such a thing happen or not?
>
> I admit that
> two times two makes four is an excellent thing,
> but if we are going to praise everything,
> two times two makes five is sometimes also
> a very charming little thing.
>
> FËDOR DOSTOEVSKI

I have traced, in the preceding two chapters, certain paradigmatic continuities of theme and myth subsisting between romances that are not, strictly speaking, science fiction—at least not modern science fiction in their relative lack of conversance with the sophistications of scientific theory—and those that are. Of the fantasies considered up to now, only *The Time Machine* exemplifies clearly the translation of science into the totality of the myth. Starting from the premise that evolutionary progress is contingent, and not at all inexorable, Wells has imagined a mythic world embodying the "opposite idea," that of biological degradation.

The devolutionary world of 802,701 and beyond is one of

the many myths suggested by Darwin's theory of evolution.[1]
I have already discussed some of the others, but I will presently
use still other examples to illustrate what may happen to a
scientific hypothesis when it is adapted to the purposes of
science fantasy.

As implied in my analysis of *The Time Machine,* the effect
of redirecting scientific theory to account for a fantastic, instead
of a real, state of affairs sometimes transforms that theory,
according to Hans Vaihinger's distinction, from a "hypothesis"
into a "fiction."[2] By its being subsumed in the fantasy as a rationale for the fantastic state of affairs, the scientific theory appears as part of the fantasy—that is, it appears to be as much an
invention as the fantasy itself. Within that fantasy, the theory
does ultimately regain the character of a "hypothesis," of a
discovery about the real world; but it does so only indirectly,
only by participating in the fantasy and thus in the interpretation of whatever reality the fantasy displaces. In other words,
the scientific theory becomes absorbed in an invented "as if"
(the science fantasy) which "states an impossible case and draws
from it the necessary conclusions";[3] so that insofar as the "impossible case" (the initial fantastic situation) displaces elements
of reality and "the necessary conclusions" (the consequences
adduced from the fantastic situation in the course of the plot)
apply to that reality, the scientific theory, through its translation into an "invention," shares in the "discovery" about the
real world that the mythic fantasy arrives at.

To clarify this rather abstract formulation of the process
that a scientific theory undergoes in being translated into
fiction, I will consider the status of theories of evolution in
two kinds of fantasy written by Samuel Butler (1835-1902).
Where he expounds his own theory of evolution, his exposition
is virtually devoid of prophetic content (in the Wellsian sense;
see chap. 3, p. 73), so that his alternative answer to Darwin's
evolutionary hypothesis never attains credibility as discovery.

---

[1] It might be noted that tales of the prehistoric past, of which Wells's "A
Story of the Stone Age" (1897) is the prototype, comprise one subclass of science fiction deriving from Darwinian theory.
[2] See Hans Vaihinger, *The Philosophy of "As If,"* tr. C. K. Ogden (New
York, 1924), p. 88: "The hypothesis tries to discover, the fiction, to invent."
[3] *Ibid.,* p. 262.

His fantasies concerning the Darwinian evolution of machines, on the contrary—though their immediate effect is to impugn the veridical nature of Darwin's theory through satire—restore some degree of empirical validity to Darwinism by offering it up as the explanation of the origin of an automaton-dominated universe.

The diversion of Darwinian theory observable in Butler can also be seen in *The Island of Doctor Moreau* (1896). There again Darwinism supplies the theoretical basis of the fiction: scientific theory wrenched from a scientific context is once more a source of imaginative fantasy and receives meaning from the prophetic myth developed in the fantasy. But Wells, like Butler, confers on evolutionary theory a meaning not originally intended, for in the case of *Moreau* that theory participates in a discovery about the moral, rather than the biological, nature of man.

Samuel Butler on Evolution: Darwin Among the Machines

Samuel Butler sailed from London for New Zealand the year Darwin's *Origin of Species* was published (1859). On December 20, 1862, the New Zealand *Press* printed a dialogue of Butler's in which he explained and argued in favor of Darwin's theory. In January of the next year, *The Press* editorially insinuated that that theory was fallacious. Butler, signing himself "A. M.," responded that the question of its truth or falsity ought to be left for the naturalists to decide. Someone calling himself the "Savoyard" and later claiming to be the writer of the editorial attacking Darwin answered, irrelevantly, that Erasmus Darwin, in anticipating his grandson's theory, had "forestalled Mr. C. Darwin" (I, 203).[4] Granting this, A. M. "would still ask, has the theory of natural development of species ever been placed in anything approaching its present clear and connected form before the appearance of Mr. [Charles] Darwin's book?" (I, 204). The Savoyard repeated his position, adding the name of Buffon alongside that of Erasmus Darwin. A. M. chose to ignore the allusion and instead, in his

⁴ The references in parentheses in this section are to "The Shrewsbury Edition" of *The Works of Samuel Butler*, ed. Henry Festing Jones and A. T. Bartholomew, 20 vols. (London, 1923-24).

final letter to this antagonist, cited recent evidence confirming Darwin's theory.

A month later, "Cellarius"—another of Butler's pseudonyms —subscribed his name to "Darwin Among the Machines," a prophetic account of the evolution of machines by natural selection that concludes with the warning "war to the death should be instantly proclaimed against them" lest they enslave their masters and take over the world (I, 212). Two years passed, during which time Butler returned to England. Finally, in July of 1865, "Lucubratio Ebria" appeared in *The Press*. The anonymous author of this essay took issue with "Cellarius" and asserted that "It is a mistake to take the view adopted by a previous correspondent of this paper, to consider the machines as identities, to animalize them and to anticipate their final triumph over mankind" (I, 217). Denying Cellarius's premises and controverting his Luddite program, this opponent maintained that, on the contrary, civilized men must invent better machines; for "the full complement of [mechanical] limbs" is an index of evolutionary superiority.

It is known that Butler wrote both "Darwin Among the Machines" and the essay that contradicts the basis of that prophecy to reach an antithetical conclusion. Unfortunately, the evidence seems to be against the supposition that A. M. and his antagonist, the Savoyard, both conceal Butler also, an identity that would reveal further his divided attitude toward Darwin at the time; it is certain only that Butler was responsible for the letters signed "A. M." Later, however, Butler did adopt the opinions of "Savoyard" about the priority of Buffon, Erasmus Darwin, and others over Charles Darwin as part of his own theory of evolution.

In one respect, Butler's teleological theory of evolution is related to his prophetic fantasies concerning the evolution of machines. Both the theory and his prophecies, that is, originate in a critique of Darwin—specifically, in Butler's objection to the paradoxical notion of evolution as mechanical and at the same time fortuitous. But since the teleological theory of evolution and the prophetic fantasies about machines occur in separate works, it is possible, and desirable, to consider them distinct from one another.

Butler thoroughly outlines his theory of evolution in *Life and Habit* (1877)—detailing various points made in that treatise subsequently in *Evolution, Old and New* (1879), *Unconscious Memory* (1880), and *Luck or Cunning?* (1886); and although the theory may seem unfounded and extravagant, if not willful and absurd, the critique of Darwin from which it arises is nevertheless most perspicacious. Butler clearly detected the flaw in Darwin's theory: the latter's inability to explain the origin of "variation" among species; and without some consistent and plausible accounting for variations, Darwin's assertion that they come about by accident and perpetuate themselves through the random mechanical process of natural selection might well appear improbable to a critical mind like Butler's. Thus he records in *Life and Habit*:

> To me it seems that the "Origin of Variation," whatever it is, is the only true "Origin of Species," and that this must, as Lamarck insisted, be looked for in the needs and experiences of the creatures varying. Unless we can explain the origin of variations, we are met by the unexplained *at every step* in the progress of a creature from its original homogeneous condition to its differentiation, we will say, as an elephant; so that to say that an elephant has become an elephant through the accumulation of a vast number of small, fortuitous, but unexplained variations in some lower creatures, is really to say that it has become an elephant owing to a series of causes about which we know nothing whatever, or, in other words, that one does not know how it came to be an elephant. (IV, 215)

As for Butler's allusion to Lamarck's theory of use and disuse, it should be mentioned that at some points in the *Origin of Species* Darwin seems to favor the idea himself. The important difference is that whereas Darwin understands by use and disuse the mechanical influence of the environment on variations, Butler emphasizes the concept of a teleological will in Lamarck's hypothesis.

Apart from the critique of Darwin, Butler's teleological theory of evolution sounds more like an invention than a discovery. His theory claims that evolution results from willed deviations from unconscious memory. An egg becomes a chicken because it remembers, without being aware of remembering, that countless generations of eggs before it have become chickens. If instead, the egg of a chicken hatches, say, a peacock, it is because the egg wills itself to become a peacock. The panpsychism inherent in this theory may be an indirect attack on the implications of Darwinian evolution—that is, if man is biologically continuous with lower forms of life and those forms with inorganic matter, then either everything has consciousness or nothing has—but Butler never explicitly says this much in any of his early tracts on evolution.[5]

Any such teleological theory of evolution is of course anathema to modern biologists,[6] and Butler has accordingly been censured and ridiculed in various scientific quarters.[7] But perhaps Butler's theory that the essence of heredity is unconscious memory does not seem quite as absurd as it did until a few years ago, especially now that geneticists speak metaphorically of DNA and RNA, the chemical carriers of heredity, as substances encoding the memory of genetic attributes.

Just how seriously Butler took his own theory is a moot point. He continually protested that he was serious about it; and his having written four volumes to explain and defend it would make the theory, if it is a joke, an elaborate one, time-consuming for writer and reader alike. Still, it is difficult to imagine that it is entirely serious; and Butler, after declaring at the end of *Life and Habit* that it is, goes on to state its fascination for him principally as an invented philosophy of "as if":

> I admit that when I began to write upon my subject I did not seriously believe in it. I saw, as it were, a pebble upon the ground, with a sheen that pleased me; taking it up, I turned it over and over for my amusement, and found it always grow brighter and brighter the more I examined it. At length I be-

---

[5] The chapters on "The Rights of Animals" and "The Rights of Vegetables" in *Erewhon*, however, do present the deduction, along these lines, that it is impossible to differentiate the nature of other forms of life from the nature of man.

[6] Evidence that the antipathy is reciprocated can be found in Arthur Koestler, *The Ghost in the Machine* (New York, 1968), wherein Koestler sets his own teleological view of evolution against what he deems to be the mechanistic theory of scientific orthodoxy.

[7] See, for example, George Gaylord Simpson, "'Lamarck, Darwin, and Butler," *American Scholar*, XXX (1961), 238-249.

came fascinated, and gave loose rein to self-illusion. The aspect of the world seemed changed; the trifle I had picked up idly proved to be a talisman of inestimable value, and had opened a door through which I caught glimpses of a strange and interesting transformation. (IV, 249-250)

No doubt his attitude toward his theory changed dramatically the more he thought about it; it came to strike him, according to his own metaphor, as an aesthetic object. But for all that, he did not succeed in redeeming it as a hypothesis concerning reality.

P. N. Furbank attributes to Butler's conception of evolution the character of "a theory at once ingenious, plausible, and useless, [that] has the effect of discrediting the whole business of scientific theorizing."[8] This seems to me more apt as a description of Butler's prophetic myth of the evolution of machinery, which—as related most successfully in "The Mechanical Creation" and again in the chapters in *Erewhon* called "The Book of the Machine"—satirizes both Darwin's *Origin of Species* and the tendency in modern society to rely increasingly on machines of greater and greater complexity.

Writing to Darwin to rationalize what seemed to be a parody of that scientist's theory, Butler claimed that "The Book of the Machine" attacked Bishop Butler's analogy of the universe as a mechanism set in motion by God.

I developed and introduced it ["The Book of the Machine"] into Erewhon with the intention of implying: "See how easy it is to be plausible, and what absurd propositions can be defended by a little ingenuity and distortion and departure from scientific methods," and I had Butler's *Analogy* in my head as the book at which it should be aimed, but preferred to conceal my aim for many reasons. Firstly, the book was already as heavily weighted with heterodoxy as it would bear . . . ; secondly, it would have interfered with the plausibility of the argument, and I looked to this plausibility as a valuable aid to the general acceptance of the book; thirdly, it is more amus-

[8] P. N. Furbank, *Samuel Butler (1835-1902)* (Cambridge, 1948), p. 56.

ing without any sort of explanation . . . and also the more enig-
matic a thing of this sort is, the more people think for themselves about it.[9]

However all this may be, it is certain that any satirical thrust
at that other Butler (to whom he was not related) is very well
concealed indeed—at least in the particular chapters of *Erewhon* he is referring to in this letter. What is patent in "The
Book of the Machine," and in "The Mechanical Creation" as
well, is that the author has applied the concepts of Darwinian
evolution to machines and has departed "from scientific methods" only in adapting the terminology and mechanism of
Darwin's theory to something it was not intended to explain.

Thus in "The Mechanical Creation," for example, published in *The Reasoner* (1865), Butler argues that

> although we grant that hardly any mistake would be more
> puerile than to individualize and animalize the at present
> existing machines—or to endow them with human sympathies,
> yet we can see no *a priori* objection to the gradual develop-
> ment of mechanical life, though that life shall be so different
> from ours that it is only by a severe discipline that we can think
> of it as life at all. (I, 232-233)

Having conceded something to the afterthoughts that had
prompted him to follow "Darwin Among the Machines" with
"Lucubratio Ebria," he proceeds to outline the evolution of
machines from the simplest tools to highly complicated mechanisms. The steam engine, being relatively far up on the scale
of mechanical evolution, already has many of man's abilities.

> It eats its own food for itself; it consumes it by inhaling the
> very air which we ourselves breathe; it rejects what it cannot
> digest as man rejects it; it has a very considerable power of self-
> regulation and adaptability to contingency. It cannot be said
> to be conscious, but the strides which it has made are made in

---

[9] Quoted in Henry Festing Jones, *Samuel Butler*, 2 vols. (London, 1919),
I, 156-157.

the direction of consciousness . . . in [the] reproduction of machinery we seem to catch a glimpse of the extraordinary vicarious arrangement whereby it is not impossible that the reproductive system of the mechanical world will be always carried on. (I, 233)

On the basis of the analogy between man and the machine, it is predicted that "allowing for the increasing ratio at which mechanical progress advances," machines "may be more alive than man" in a million years (I, 234).

"The Mechanical Creation" attends somewhat to how natural selection operates in the case of machinery to insure survival of the fittest;[10] but Butler is much more explicit in his use of Darwinian concepts in *Erewhon* (1872). There, speaking of the evolution of machines through cumulative variation, he points out that man

> spends an incalculable amount of labour and time and thought in making machines breed always better and better; he has already succeeded in effecting much that at one time appeared impossible, and there seem no limits to the results of accumulated improvements if they are allowed to descend with modification from generation to generation. (II, 190)

The theory that evolution is the result of fortuitous changes mechanically perpetuated, Butler seems to be saying, had best be confined to explaining the progress of actual mechanisms: for a theory that regards man as a machine is no less absurd than one that supposes machines to be animate.

Although Butler's myth of the mechanical creation, in its application of Darwin's theory to machines, deflects and thereby satirizes that theory as a fiction, the prophetic aspect of the myth redeems the theory as a hypothesis—albeit a hypothesis about a historical tendency it was not intended to account for. The myth, that is, appropriates Darwin's theory to dramatize the fact that the machine is coming to dominate its creators.

[10] See Butler, *op. cit.*, I, 234-236; and also "Darwin Among the Machines," I, 209-210, where Butler argues for the evolution of machines on the evidence of vestigial "organs" found in some of them.

The Erewhonians, whose fantastic world is often the reverse of the state of affairs in the real world, have responded to the threat of machines encroaching on their pastoral existence by destroying them. That plan is also put forward in "Darwin Among the Machines." But "The Mechanical Creation" advocates no such destruction. Foreseeing sufficient reason why machines will not be abolished, and hence foreshadowing the cybernetic nightmares of a machine-regulated world as portrayed in much antiutopian fiction and science fiction of the twentieth century, Butler explains why man will submit to being a "machine-tickling aphid" (II, 183) rather than give up relying on machines.

The first reason is that man "is committed hopelessly to machines"; he is as dependent upon them as they are on him; and he is becoming more dependent while they are beginning to emerge as independent beings. More ironic than the fact that man has brought this situation about, however, is the second reason: "man's interests may not really be opposed to his becoming a lower creature." Indeed, "the interests of the two races"—man and machine—

> may continue in the same direction, notwithstanding the change in their relative situations, and man is not generally sentimental when his material interests are concerned. It is true that here and there some ardent soul may "look upon himself and curse his fate" that he was not born a steam engine, but the insensate mass will readily acquiesce in any arrangement which gives them cheaper comforts. (I, 236-237)[11]

Such an arrangement of asymmetrical dependence would probably exist for an indefinite period: "it would hardly suit" the interest of machines "to exterminate us [any more] than it would ours to do the like by them" (I, 237). Thus mechanical evolution as a philosophy of "as if" eventuates in a vision of a future when men will be subservient to machines.

[11] Compare Herbert Marcuse, *One-Dimensional Man* (Boston, 1964), pp. 2-12, 23-27, 32-33, 48-50.

The Island of Doctor Moreau: Ape and Essence

In one respect *The Island of Doctor Moreau* comes closer to fulfilling what Butler declared to be his intention in "The Book of the Machine" than those chapters from *Erewhon* do. Wells's romance does not deal with the notion of the universe as a mechanism and God as its mechanic, but it posits a God who takes an immanent part in the cosmic process and "draws . . . the necessary conclusions" from the postulate of the fiction. Certainly it was his recollection of Dr. Moreau as the God of Special Creation, rather than the Swiftian satire of humanity in the myth of the Beast People, that later inspired Wells to refer to Moreau as a "theological grotesque" (*IDM*, II, ix) and a "vision of the aimless torture in creation" (*Scientific Romances,* p. ix).

The "as if it were" dramatized in the myth of Moreau's creating Beast People from various animals by means of some sort of plastic surgery is not Darwin's theory of evolution precisely, but the attempt to reconcile that theory with traditional Christian theology. The synthesis proposed was that the human species has evolved from lower forms of life through natural selection, but God alone creates and animates every individual human being. Wells's response to any such synthesis, it would appear from *Moreau,* is that to reinstate God in the tortuous process of evolution—a process from the standpoint of which many creatures and sometimes whole species are only instrumental to the evolution of fitter species and are occasionally dead ends altogether[12]—exacerbates the problem of theodicy to the degree that God becomes Moreau, a vivisectionist insensitive beyond all humanity to the pain of his creatures.

Moreau is just such a god meddling in the cosmic process. He has undertaken a number of operations to transform beasts into men. Of his first victim, a gorilla, he tells Prendick, a castaway on his island: "All the week, night and day, I moulded him," and on the seventh day "I rested" (II, 95, 96).

---

[12] See H. G. Wells's essay, "Bye-Products in Evolution," *Saturday Review,* LXXIX (Feb. 2, 1895), 155. Speaking abstractly about evolution, he writes: "an end A can only be attained by a process that simultaneously produces B, C, and D, results not needed and yet inevitably involved."

But the gorilla did not satisfy Moreau's longing for perfection. Other experiments followed, concerning which Prendick asks Moreau if he felt no compunction. "To this day," Moreau replies, "I have never troubled about the ethics of the matter. The study of Nature makes a man at last as remorseless as Nature. I have gone on, not heeding anything but the question I was pursuing, and the material has . . . dripped into the huts yonder" (II, 94). Moreau is obviously as apathetic to social responsibility and utilitarian values as the Invisible Man in Wells's romance published the year after *Moreau*.[13]

Wells described the theoretical basis of Moreau's fantastic experiments as god of his island in one of his essays for the *Saturday Review:* "The Limits of Individual Plasticity." "It is a possible thing," he concludes,

> to transplant tissue from one part of an animal to another, or from one animal to another, to alter its chemical reactions and methods of growth, to modify the articulation of its limbs, and indeed to change it in its most intimate structure. . . . If we concede the justifications of vivisection, we may imagine as possible in the future, operators, armed with antiseptic surgery and a growing perfection in the knowledge of the laws of growth, taking living creatures and moulding them into the most amazing forms.[14]

Moreau means to perform such miracles with "individual plasticity." But his efforts, like the workings of the cosmic process, are still subject to chance. He in fact tells Prendick that the decision to take the human form as the model for his experiments was itself purely accidental (II, 91). Thus even on his island the design Moreau takes as his pattern is the result of random selection among many possible designs.[15]

Although Moreau has been able to operate on beasts suc-

---

[13] Moreau has also been ostracized; his vivisectionist activities have caused him to be "howled out of the country" (II, 40), a procedure whose ferocity is relevant to the satiric significance of the Beast People (see below).

[14] Wells, "The Limits of Individual Plasticity," *Saturday Rev.,* LXXIX (Jan. 19, 1895), 90.

[15] For further discussion of the idea of chance in *Moreau*, see Bernard Bergonzi, *The Early H. G. Wells* (Toronto, 1961), pp. 100-109.

cessfully enough to allow them to pass for a time as men—at
least to someone whose only experience of human society in a
long while has been aboard the *Ipecacuanha*—they "somehow
drift back again, the stubborn beast flesh grows, day by day,
back again" (II, 96). To retard the inevitable regression,
Moreau has given the Beast People the Law, which they hyp-
notically chant as a ritual, "a mad litany" (II, 72).

> Not to go on all-Fours; *that* is the Law. Are we not Men?
> Not to suck up Drink; *that* is the Law. Are we not Men?
> Not to eat Flesh or Fish; *that* is the Law. Are we not Men?
> Not to claw Bark of Trees; *that* is the Law. Are we not Men?
> Not to chase other Men; *that* is the Law. Are we not Men?
>
> (II, 72-73)

And to impress upon themselves the power of Him who gave
them these commandments and the punishment that will be-
fall whoever breaks the Law, the Beast People chant:

> His is the House of Pain
> His is the Hand that makes.
> His is the Hand that wounds.
> His is the Hand that heals.
>
> (II, 73)

The first of these ceremonies Prendick witnesses causes him to
conjecture that Moreau "had inflected [the] dwarfed brains"
of the Beast People "with a kind of deification of himself," but
also to imagine the reverse of what is going on on the island:
that the doctor is "animalising . . . men."

As a source for the chanting of the Law, Kipling's *Jungle
Book* (1894) has been cited. But Wells's Beast People have
exactly the opposite signficance of Kipling's animals. *The
Jungle Book* implies that animals are like men; Kipling de-
picts his docile beasts, those obliging servants of the boy
Mowgli, anthropomorphically; he projects onto them crude
human feelings and responses, as if they were lower forms of
human life like (for him) Indian natives. *The Island of Doctor*

Moreau, on the contrary, likens men to animals in certain respects. Its point is not that animals have some of the virtues of men, but that men have bestial traits. The difference between Kipling's animals-like-men and Wells's men-like-animals, in other words, is analogous to that between the humanized animals of a Walt Disney African safari and the Yahoos in *Gulliver's Travels.*

The "as if" of Moreau as (Old Testament) God—as Creator and Law-Giver—provides the given for what can be thought of as an experimental inquiry into the limits of humanity. The hypothesis that Wells dramatizes in the myth of *Moreau* is that civilized man incorporates an uneasy balance between natural man ("the culminating ape") and artificial man ("the highly plastic creature of tradition, suggestion, and reasoned thought");[16] and further, that "what we call Morality becomes the padding of suggested emotional habits necessary to keep the round Paleolithic savage in the square hole of the civilised state" ("Human Evolution," p. 594). By anthropomorphizing beasts and instilling in them the Law and a fear of their Creator, Moreau brings about a parody of "the civilised state"; and in the course of the reversion of that state back into a state of nature, Wells explores the connection between man and beast—revealing that the essence of the one is continuous with that of the other.

The Beast People, Moreau is distressed to perceive, are actuated by fear and desire—fear of pain and desire for pleasure—rather than by the dictates of reason. Pain and pleasure, he tells Prendick, are for men "the mark of the beast from which they came. . . . Pain and Pleasure—they are for us only so long as we wriggle in the dust" (II, 93). His aim is to purify his creature of all bestial impulses of fear and desire: "Each time I dip a living creature into the bath of burning pain, I say: this time I will burn out all the animal, this time I will make a rational creature of my own" (II, 98-99).

Prendick, however, takes a different view of the matter. He too believes that fear and desire are passions common to man

[16] H. G. Wells, "Human Evolution, An Artificial Process," *Fortnightly Review,* LXVI (1896), 590-595.

and beast, but consequently he regards them as humanizing traits. To him the crying of the puma—Moreau's final victim and the one that kills him—sounds "as if all the pain in the world had found a voice" (II, 45). The hunting of the Leopard Man is for Prendick like the hunting of any other dangerous animal; yet once he has it at bay, its bestial attitude is the very thing that strikes him as human: "seeing the creature there in a perfectly animal attitude, with the light gleaming in its eyes, and its imperfectly human face distorted with terror, I realised again the fact of its humanity" (II, 120).

If fear and desire are common to man and beast—if Moreau himself, though relatively free from fear, is ruled "by his passion for research" (II, 123), his monomaniacal desire to shape a rational being—the attempts of the Beast People to reason and imitate the ways of civilized men are sheer caricature. The Ape Man, for instance, "had an idea . . . that to gabble about names that meant nothing was the proper use of speech."

> He called it "big thinks," to distinguish it from "little thinks" —the sane everyday interests of life. If ever I made a remark he did not understand, he would praise it very much, ask me to say it again, learn it by heart, and go off repeating it, with a word wrong here or there, to all the milder of the Beast People. He thought nothing of what was plain and comprehensible. (II, 159-160)

On Moreau's island, though, the sanity of the "everyday interests of life" is put in doubt.

After Moreau's death, the disciplined regime of the island, which had been breaking down gradually since the time Prendick went among the Beast People, begins to come to an end. Fear continues to reign, but this fear attaches to natural law, not to Moreau's Law. From here on, Wells explores the ulterior limits separating man and beast.

The Beast People, of course, slowly start to regress. Their human traits disappear, to be replaced by "a kind of generalised animalism." Nevertheless, Prendick reports, "The dwindling shreds of their humanity still startled me every now and then, a momentary recrudescence of speech perhaps, an unexpected dexterity of the fore feet, a pitiful attempt to walk erect" (II, 162). These are all bare tokens, the outward signs of humanity. But divergence from the outward forms and rituals he is used to has been Prendick's criterion all along for determining the "mark of the beast" in these creatures. Thus of the three swine-men perceived when he had reconnoitered the island earlier he had observed: "Each . . . , despite its human form, its rag of clothing, and rough humanity of its bodily form, had woven into it, into its movements, into the expression of its countenance, into its whole presence, some now irresistible suggestion of the hog, a swinish taint, the unmistakable mark of the beast" (II, 50-51).

Eventually such peculiarities of form alone distinguish Prendick from the Beast People, for he too slowly reverts to a kind of animal savagery. His first step backward is to cut himself off from the one human being remaining on the island—Moreau's assistant, Montgomery. "I felt that for Montgomery there was no help; that he was in truth half akin to these Beast Folk" (II, 141), he says by way of justification for abandoning his fellow. At this point Prendick, though he is an initiate in the secret of the island, thinks his nature is different from that of the rest of the inhabitants; he refuses to recognize he too is "in truth half akin" to the Beast People. Sometime after Montgomery is murdered, however, Prendick finds himself of necessity forced to live with the Beast Men. He does not behave exactly as they do; but on more than one occasion he exhibits a capacity for "anger, hate, or fear"—fear above all—which Moreau at one time had declared to be man's bestial potential (II, 98).

The excuse Prendick gives for having forsaken Montgomery actually rationalizes his own instinct for survival. Indeed, the instinct for self-preservation becomes the law of the island. Overt instead of threatened violence takes over as the logic of the struggle for existence brutalizes Prendick.

> "Presently you will slay them all," said the Dog Man.
> "Presently," I answered, "I will slay them all—after certain days and certain things have come to pass. Every one of them save those you spare, every one of them shall be slain." (II, 155)

A generalized form of the fear that 'if I did not kill [the] brute he would kill me" (II, 151) may be what motivates Prendick to adopt a reign of terror as his final solution, but clearly conditions on the island are dehumanizing him.

In fact, as the Beast People revert to type, Prendick himself becomes bestial in aspect. "I, too, must have undergone strange changes," he recalls. "My clothes hung about me as yellow rags, through whose rents glowed the tan skin. My hair grew long and became matted together. I am told that even now my eyes have a strange brightness, a swift alertness of movement" (II, 162-163). The feeling of fear and terror he had perceived in the eyes of the Leopard Man parallels his own: the same animal fear that shone in the Leopard Man's eyes continues to shine in his years after he has contrived to leave Moreau's island.

Once Prendick has escaped, the persuasion that had overwhelmed Gulliver haunts him. "I felt no desire to return to mankind" (II, 169). Both he and Gulliver share the same response for a similar reason, but the dread of being exposed to the bestialities of man derives from opposite experiences. Gulliver, having spent most of his time on the island of the Houyhnhnms among perfectly rational beings, disdains men for the contrast they present to those creatures; Prendick, who has, as it were, sojourned for almost a year among the Yahoos, comes to fear man's similarity to them. The sight of men, once he has returned to human society, often reminds him of the Beast People, inspiring him again with "the two inconsistent and conflicting impressions of utter strangeness and yet of the strangest familiarity" (II, 50). When at times "a memory and a faint distrust" comes back to him,

I look about me at my fellow men. And I go in fear. I see faces keen and bright, others dull or dangerous, others unsteady, insincere; none that have the calm authority of a reasonable soul. I feel as though the animal was surging up through them; that presently the degradation of the islanders will be played over again on a larger scale. I know this is an illusion, that these seeming men and women about me are indeed men and women, men and women for ever, perfectly reasonable creatures full of human desires and tender solicitude, emancipated from instinct and the slaves of no fantastic Law—beings altogether different from the Beast Folk. (II, 171)[17]

Prendick, unlike Gulliver, may be aware of the illusion, but he still longs "to be away . . . and alone."

Prendick ends his tale with the consolatory hope that "whatever is more than animal within us" will find its vindication in the "vast and eternal laws of matter" (I, 172)—presumably in the future evolution of a more purified race. But the prophetic myth of man's partial animality as an irrational creature motivated by fear and desire is what Wells has substantiated in *Moreau*. That myth, like Stevenson's in *Jekyll and Hyde*, deflects Darwin's theory of evolution to explain not man's origin but his nature at present, so that the theory of man's descent is transformed in the fiction into a hypothesis about his essence.

Similarly, Moreau's endeavor to anthropomorphize beasts and create a perfectly rational being loses its "as if" character as a "theological grotesque" in being assimilated by the larger hypothesis Wells expresses in *Moreau*. As part of the larger experiment of surveying the boundaries of man's nature, Moreau's failure has the effect of denying that any millennial dreams will be realized through man's meddling in the cosmic process. Man's fate, like that of the four survivors of the wreck of the *Lady Vain*, is a matter of chance; even his apparently most rational intentions are not exempt from the interference of this cosmic principle. The regime that Moreau tries to impose on his islanders does not completely abrogate the laws of nature; nor does it mitigate "the painful disorder" of the island (II, 123); it only aggravates "the aimless torture in creation" and turns the island into a nightmarish antiutopia.

By adapting Darwinian theory as the basis for their prophetic if nightmarish fictions about the nature and future of man, Butler and Wells indirectly claim its validity as discovery about a sector of reality it was not originally meant to describe.

---

[17] Compare Daphne du Maurier's short story "The Blue Lenses" in *The Breaking Point* (1959).

But also, the myth of the Beast People as a "travesty of humanity" (II, 99) or of the mechanical evolution as a parody of Darwinism both adduce what might be called the metaphysical implications of the theory of evolution. It is true that neither Butler nor Wells presents a total vision of the metaphysical nature of things; yet such a vision remains a possibility for science fiction. One attempt to describe a metaphysics of "as if," I will argue in the following chapter, is to be found in Cyrano de Bergerac's *L'Autre Monde*.

6

A Flight of the Imagination:
Science as Metaphysics

> The fact that any philosophical system
> is bound in advance to be a dialectical game,
> a *Philosophie des Als Ob,* means that systems abound,
> unbelievable systems, beautifully constructed
> or else sensational in effect.
> The metaphysicians of Tlön are not looking for truth,
> nor even for an approximation of it;
> they are after a kind of amazement.
> They consider metaphysics a branch of fantastic literature.
> They know that a system is nothing more
> than the subordination of all the aspects
> of the universe to some one of them.
>
> JORGE LUIS BORGES

L'Autre Monde, which comprises *The States and Empires of the Moon and of the Sun,* is decidedly an eclectic fantasy, drawing as it does upon various philosophies from Epicurus and Lucretius through Gassendi and Descartes. The two principal schools of thought concerning it are in many respects diametrically opposed. What until recently has been the prevalent view goes back to Cyrano's first editor, his friend Le Bret, who polemically imposed on his bowdlerized version of *The States and Empires of the Moon*—published in 1657—the title of "comical history." The tendency to read the fantasy as a series of comic episodes, discrete from one another, endured Frédéric Lachèvre's restoration of part of Cyrano's original text, largely because Lachèvre reinforced that opinion from another direction. Apart from the service he performed in locating and collating the manuscripts of *The States and Empires of the Moon,* Lachèvre obliquely attacked the work's integrity by attempting to make Cyrano out to be a plagiarist. Since Cyrano himself names or explicitly alludes to all but a few of the sources and analogues Lachèvre cites in the notes to his *texte intégrale,* that attempt is misleading at best and is otherwise downright perverse. Nonetheless, what Lachèvre seems to be implying complements the notion that *L'Autre Monde* is not to be taken seriously; as Richard Aldington expresses the idea in the introduction to his too literal and sometimes obscure translation based on Lachèvre's edition:

> As soon as [Cyrano] begins to discourse of atoms, or attraction, or the magnet, his language becomes vague, involved and hesitating; he is metaphorical at the moment when he should not be, and the thought obviously is not his own; the lack of clarity in his speech suggests that he failed to comprehend the ideas he pretends to expound, that he did not think them for himself but was indoctrinated with them by others.

Aldington accordingly charges Cyrano with "a certain lack of commonsense" which "often precipitates him into absurdity" and grotesqueness.[1]

Other critics have lately challenged the view that *L'Autre Monde* is incoherent in either or both senses of the word—that it is completely chaotic or partially incomprehensible. While admitting that "It would be idle to suggest that Cyrano submits his thinking to rigorous scientific discipline," J. S. Spink nevertheless maintains that Cyrano's "speculation is far from aimless; it is coherent and purposeful."[2] And A. Lavers, after pointing out that more than half of the first part of *L'Autre Monde* "is devoted to discussions of philosophy or pure science," goes on to identify in Cyrano a syncretic impulse

> to unify, willy-nilly, several incompatible philosophies on the grounds of an unshakable belief in the unity of knowledge

---

[1] Savinien Cyrano de Bergerac, *Voyages to the Moon and the Sun,* tr. Richard Aldington (London, n.d.), p. 40.
[2] J. S. Spink, *French Free-Thought from Gassendi to Voltaire* (London, 1960), pp. 65-66.

and in a reality which is perhaps unknowable but in which all diverse phenomena are finally identified with one another, all the contradictory characteristics of experience and of human systems finally harmonized.[3]

The syncretism that Lavers ascribes to Cyrano and that Lachèvre in effect substantiates by indicating the range of Cyrano's allusions perhaps has its parallel in Descartes's epistemological enterprise. In placing *L'Autre Monde* in the context of seventeenth-century thought,[4] however, what has not been emphasized is the influence of certain Renaissance thinkers on Cyrano's habit of mind: the attempt to unify and harmonize theories about the universe also characterizes the Renaissance magus; and although the ideas Cyrano expounds—whether or not he seriously believed in them—bear some resemblance to those professed by his contemporaries, particularly Gassendi, there is a great deal of internal evidence that the occult tradition inspired Cyrano's manner of concealing his theories in myth and allegory. He mentions, for example, the names of Agrippa von Nettesheim and Paracelsus (Faustus); his lunar Eden and his conception of an Adamic universal language point to his awareness of gnostic and cabalistic interpretations of the Bible; and the centrality of the moon and the sun in his fantastic scheme of things suggests a conversance with the doctrines of hermeticism and alchemy.[5]

Apparently the allusion to occult theories in *L'Autre Monde* at one time was recognized, for the 1662 edition of *The States and Empires of the Moon and of the Sun* titles them *"visions et romans cabalistiques."*[6] Indeed an early episode in *The States and Empires of the Sun* seems to dramatize Cyrano's

[3] A. Lavers, "La Croyance à l'Unité de la Science dans 'L'Autre Monde' de Cyrano de Bergerac," *Cahiers du Sud,* no. 349 (1959), pp. 409, 410.
[4] The most thorough account is Spink, *op. it.,* pp. 48-50, 62-64.
[5] Eugène Canseliet's endeavor to prove Cyrano to be a *philosophe hermétique* ("Cyrano de Bergerac, Philosophe Hermétique," *Cahiers d'Hermès,* no. 1 [1947], pp. 65-82) unfortunately presents no arguments that can be taken seriously—as M. Lavers diplomatically phrases it, Canseliet's essay is "unconvincing."
I refer below to discussions of the occult tradition relevant to the possible sources of some of the ideas brought up in *L'Autre Monde.*
[6] See Cyrano de Bergerac, *Voyages,* tr. Aldington, p. 325.

fear that his fantasies might be misunderstood to be treatises on magic. In the episode in question, Dyrcona (an anagram for Cyrano) is being persecuted as the author of a blasphemous work about his voyage to the moon; and the superstitious rabble, finding Descartes's *Principia* in his possession, construes that to be an exposition of the art of black magic. Despite a superficial similarity to occult writings, this episode implies, Dyrcona's own work is no more a discourse on sorcery than Descartes's.

Thus while the influence of the occult tradition affords both a source and a motive for the prima facie incoherence of Cyrano's fantasies, it would be misguided to suppose that Cyrano has slavishly adhered to the doctrines of his Medieval and Renaissance precursors any more than he has to classical philosophies or the systems of his contemporaries. As Lachèvre demonstrates in partially documenting his borrowings, Cyrano took ideas from an astounding number of sources and in most cases transfigured them so that they at best bear only a remote likeness to their originals. Moreover, by associating his own effort with Descartes's, Cyrano would seem to be indicating that the significance of the ideas propounded in *L'Autre Monde* is modern and scientific.

To say that there is a kind of logic operative in *L'Autre Monde*—principally a logic of association—and that the mostly explicit arguments set forth in Dyrcona's voyage to the moon prepare for, and help to elucidate, their allegorical counterparts in the voyage to the sun does not contradict the view that *L'Autre Monde* is satiric fantasy. On the contrary, Cyrano's cosmological theories provide the judgmental basis for the satire and, conversely, the satire establishes the "as if" nature of the physics and metaphysics. Detached from the cosmology, the satire of man's pride and ignorance has little substance or coherence, and much of the fantasy becomes simply pointless. The satire, however, gives Cyrano's theories of physics and metaphysics the complexion of heuristic "as ifs" in the same way that it does in *Erewhon* (some of the arguments in *L'Autre Monde* in fact anticipate the Erewhonian philosophies outlined in Butler's chapters on "The Rights of Animals" and

"The Rights of Vegetables"). Since the presence of a fairly consistent *Philosophie des Als Ob* is less readily perceived than the general drift of the satire, I propose mainly to clarify some of the details of that philosophy.

In *The States and Empires of the Moon,* the voyage to the moon is defined at the outset as an intellectual quest. The fantasy opens with Dyrcona attempting to defend the idea that the moon is also a world, an idea that his friends think ridiculous. Returning to his lodgings, Dyrcona finds a volume of Cardano's works lying on his desk. How it got there he does not know, but it becomes for him a *Book of Changes;* for opening it at random, he hits upon a passage wherein the Italian philosopher relates how he was visited by two beings claiming to come from the moon. The "revelation" reinforces Dyrcona's "fanciful belief" that "the moon is a world" (p. 4),[7] and he determines to investigate firsthand what truth there might be in such an idea. He fastens to himself vials of dew and is thereby drawn upward toward the sun, "that great animus of the universe" (p. 139).

His first flight does not take Dyrcona to the moon; he is forced to reduce altitude and lands in New France instead. There he converses at length with the governor of the province about Copernican astronomy and advances the theory that the universe is infinite and contains a plurality of worlds. When he finally does arrive on the moon—after he is expelled from a lunar Eden—and comes among the Selenians, theories about the nature of the universe are taken up again.

The Demon of Socrates, who acts as Dyrcona's tutor and cicerone during most of his sojourn, proposes many of these theories. He informs Dyrcona that spirits have bodies, but not like those of human beings, "nor like anything which we considered" to be bodily,

---

[7] Savinien Cyrano de Bergerac, *Other Worlds,* tr. Geoffrey Strachan (London, 1965). Mr. Strachan's translation omits a few of the phrases found in the manuscript version of *The States and Empires of the Moon,* but it has the virtue of being free of the obscurities that plague Aldington's attempt to render Cyrano's fantasies into English. Wherever necessary, I have supplied the French text from the first volume of *Les Oeuvres Libertines,* ed. Frédéric Lachèvre, 2 vols. (Paris, 1921).

because we commonly only call a body what we can touch.
There was, in any case, nothing in nature which was not material; and although they themselves were, when they wanted
to make themselves visible to us, they were forced to assume
shapes commensurate with what our senses are capable of perceiving. . . . He added that as they were obliged to be hasty in
manufacturing themselves the bodies they had to use, they very
often lacked the time to make them perceptible to more than
one of the senses. (P. 35)

This explanation illustrates the irreverent tone characteristic
of *L'Autre Monde,* but the notion that everything in nature
is material also anticipates the arguments that the Demon, Sr.
Gonsales, and some of the Selenian philosophers subsequently
put forward.

Following his introduction to the Demon, Dyrcona, whom
the orthodox Selenian sages take to be "the female of the
Queen's 'little animal' " (p. 43) is placed in the cage of Domingo Gonsales in the hope that they will mate. In this absurd
situation, the Spaniard takes the occasion to discuss with his
fellow captive his own ideas about the nature of things. "From
a serious investigation [à pénétrer sérieusement] of matter,"
he tells Dyrcona,

you would discover that it is all one, but that, like an excellent actor, it plays all kinds of roles in this life, in all kinds of
disguises. Otherwise you would be forced to admit that there
are as many elements as there are kinds of body. And if you ask
me why fire burns and water cools, seeing that it is all merely a
single substance, I reply to you that this substance behaves sym-
pathetically according to the situation in which it finds itself at
the time of its activity. Fire, which is nothing but earth even
more rarefied than when it constitutes air, tries to transform
into itself by sympathy everything it encounters. (Pp. 45-46)

This reasoning looks back to the Demon's disclosure that what
men call by various names—oracles, specters, incubi, and the
like—is really a single substance; however, it also provides a
theoretical basis for Dyrcona's becoming translucent as he

approaches the sun, and for the allegorical struggle between the Salamander and the Remora, in the second book of Cyrano's fantasy.

There exists, Gonsales continues, a "perfect cycle and subtle interconnection of the elements" (p. 49). After proceeding to explain this cycle, he concludes:

> Thus we observe the four elements all suffering the same fate and returning to the state they were in. . . . Therefore one can say that there is everything in a man that it takes to make a tree, and everything in a tree that it takes to make a man. In this way all things ultimately meet in everything, but we lack a Prometheus to draw from the bosom of nature and make perceptible to us what I would call *primary matter*. (P. 52)

The idea of a "primary matter" is one of the fundamental principles of the physics underlying the hypothetical metaphysics in *L'Autre Monde,* but it is not by itself sufficient to compel the conclusion that "all things ultimately meet in everything." The consequence that matter can present itself in a multiplicity of interchangeable forms only follows if that matter has freedom of movement.

For that reason, Gonsales has argued for an absence of primary matter as well as for its presence. "You may say it is incomprehensible," he concedes,

> that there should be nothingness in the universe, that we should be partly composed of nothing. Well, why ever not? Is not the whole universe surrounded by nothingness? And since you grant me this much, confess, then, that it is just as easy for the universe to have nothingness within it as around it. (P. 48)

Dyrcona had in fact maintained earlier a supposition contrary to the premise implied in this analogy; he had asserted that the universe was infinite. Yet he does not contest Gonsales's propositions; and later on one of the Selenian philosophers, who in effect resumes the Spaniard's argument, reinstates the theory of an infinite cosmos.

It remains for me to prove that there are infinite worlds
within an infinite world. Picture the universe, therefore, as a
vast organism [un grand animal]. Within this vast organism the
stars, which are worlds, are like a further series of vast organisms, each serving inversely as the worlds of lesser populations
such as ourselves, our horses, etc. We, in our turn, are also
worlds from the point of view of certain organisms incompar-
ably smaller than ourselves, like certain worms, lice, and mites.
They are the earths of others, yet more imperceptible.[8]

Up to this point, the analogy sounds like a variation of Pascal's
conception of man as a creature suspended between the infinite
and the infinitesimal. But here the argument goes further;
"So," says the Selenian, glossing over a transition in the focus
of the reasoning,

just as each single one of us seems to this tiny people to be a
great world, perhaps our flesh, our blood, and our minds are
nothing but a tissue of little animals, nourishing themselves,
lending us their movement, allowing themselves to be driven
blindly by our will . . . carrying us about, and all together pro-
ducing that activity which we call life. (P. 75)

Primary matter, in other words, is revealed to be made up of
aggregates of "little animals," the "primary and indivisible
atoms" (p. 83) that, as Dyrcona subsequently discovers, inhabit
the solar regions.

Although Dyrcona says of this discourse that "the nuance
between parody and seriousness was too subtle for it to be
possible to imitate it" (p. 75), the following arguments proceed
in developing a rudimentary atomic theory. One of the Selenians attempting to enlighten the "little animal" (p. 80) explains
to Dyrcona that the behavior of atoms operates according to
the law of probability. The philosopher likens the movement
of atoms to throws of the dice, and points out that no intelligent being would call it a miracle if two out of three dice come
up with the same number. "Yet," he says,

[8] As Lachèvre points out (I, 71 n.), the metaphor of the universe as an animal
can be found in the writings of Giordano Bruno.

you are still astonished at the way this matter, mixed up pell-mell at the whim of chance, could have produced a man, seeing how many things were necessary for the construction of his person. Are you not aware that this matter has stopped a million times on its way towards the formation of a man, sometimes to make a stone, sometimes a lump of lead, sometimes coral, sometimes a flower, sometimes a comet? All this happened because there were more or less of certain shapes, which were necessary, or certain shapes, which were superfluous to the design of man. Hence it is no marvel that they should have come together, from among an infinity of substances which are shifting and changing incessantly, to make the few animals, vegetables, and minerals which we see, any more than it is a marvel for a triple number to come up in a hundred throws of the dice, since it is impossible for this movement not to produce something. (P. 82)

The idea that man is the result of the chance association of atoms does not shock Dyrcona, but at least one consequence of that hypothesis does; namely, the notion that men cannot therefore possess immortal souls "to the exclusion of the beasts" (p. 94).

Since Dyrcona cannot refute the Selenian's arguments, he asks the Demon's opinion on the subject. The Demon professes to take Dyrcona's side, assuring him that because "all things in nature tend towards perfection, they all aspire to become men"; yet the Demon's reasoning, which is quite consistent with the Selenian's conclusion, prepares for the "consolation" that the birds offer Dyrcona after they have sentenced him to be eaten by flies for belonging to a species that does not respect the lives of other creatures. Outlining the process by which the plum tree absorbs the turf, a pig the plums, and a man the pig, the Demon suggests that "the great pontiff you see with a mitre on his head was perhaps sixty years ago a tuft of grass in my garden." The remark that a man, by devouring a pig, "makes the animal live again, as a more noble species" (p. 95) becomes, by a simple substitution, the reassurance that the birds give to the condemned Dyrcona. Once the flies have assimilated Dyrcona into the substance of their being, he "will have the honour of contributing, however blindly, to their intellectual operations . . . and—though you cannot think for yourself—

you will at least share in the glory of helping them to think!" (pp. 184-185).

The Demon's argument, while lending itself to the ambivalent satire of man's pride in his reason and of the consolation philosophy affords, stops short of, but clearly implies, a cycle of life analogous to the cycle of the elements Sr. Gonsales propounds. The premise that the substance creatures partake of to sustain their being is re-animated as part of their being, moreover, is common not only to the Demon's logic and that of the birds, but also to the Selenian's refutation of the theological concept of immortality (pp. 99-100).

At one point during Dyrcona's stay among the Selenians, the Demon gives him a book entitled *"The States and Empires of the Sun,* together with the *History of the Spark"* (p. 87).[9] *The States and Empires of the Sun*—that is, the second book of Cyrano's fantasy—seems to dramatize symbolically many of the ideas Dyrcona is exposed to while he is on the moon. In one of the kingdoms of the sun, for example, Dyrcona perceives a bejewelled tree with a nightingale perched in its branches. This tree in time disintegrates and before his eyes takes the shape of a man—all at the command of one of the myriad of little animals that had first formed the marvelous tree. The king of these diminutive solar beings then explains to Dyrcona the meaning of what he has just witnessed.

It is us whom you in the world of the earth call "spirits," and your presumptuous stupidity has given us this name, because, not being able to imagine animals more perfect than man and seeing certain beings which do things beyond human power, you have presumed these animals to be spirits. You are nevertheless mistaken: we are animals like you. For although, when we choose, we can give our substance the essential appearance and shape of anything we want to turn into, as you have just seen, this does not prove that we are spirits.

But listen, and I will explain how all these metamorphoses, which seem to you to be so many miracles, are nothing but simple natural phenomena. You must know that being inhabitants of the pellucid part of this great world, where the principle of

[9] The *History of the Spark* has not been found, nor has any manuscript of *The States and Empires of the Sun.*

matter is to be in action, we are bound to have much more active imaginations than those of the opaque regions, and bodies composed of a much more fluid [déliée; i.e., rarefied] substance.

Once one supposes this, it inevitably follows that our imagination, encountering no resistance in the matter of which we are composed, can arrange it at will, and, having become the complete master of our bodies, manoeuvres them, by moving all their particles, into the arrangements necessary to constitute the objects it has pictured in miniature. Thus each one of us imagined the place and the part of this precious tree into which he would change. By this effort of imagination, we excited in our substance the movements necessary to produce them and so changed ourselves into them. (P. 164)

J. S. Spink glosses this episode, culminating in the explanation of the mysterious metamorphoses effected by the movement of these animated particles, as Cyrano's attempt "to express in narrative form the very abstract conception of 'pure act.' "

He applies his corpuscular principle to all the dualism current in his time ("form" and "matter" in the schools, "mind" and "matter' in Descartes's *Meditations,* "heat" and "cold," "contraction" and "expansion," the notions used by the "chemists" and the Italian philosophers) and aims at a thoroughgoing monism. The forms which the solar beings take on must not be separate from their matter, otherwise Cyrano is as far as ever from realizing the perfect unity of nature. Their form must be an arrangement of atoms and at the same time a spontaneous act, not imposed from without; its psychical and physical aspects must be identical; mobility and consciousness must be one and the same function. (*Op. cit.,* pp. 60, 61)

But while the episode brings together many of the ideas expressed in *The States and Empires of the Moon*—the theories of atomic physics, of the interchangeability of material forms, of the analogy between the smallest constituents of being and the largest structures in nature, and so forth—there may well be a skeptical and satiric aspect to the unification of opposites. When the Demon gave Dyrcona a copy of *The States and Empires of the Sun,* he also entrusted him with *The Great Works of the Philosophers,* a tome "composed by one of the best brains upon the sun."

> In it he proves that all things are true and states how the truths of all contradictions may be reconciled physically, such as for example that white is black and black is white; that one can be and not be at the same time . . . that nothingness is something and that everything, which is, is not. (Pp. 87-88)

This passage of course reminds the modern reader of the Houyhnhnms's definition of saying *"the Thing which was not"* in Book Four of *Gulliver's Travels* (p. 224); and indeed there seems to be the suggestion on Cyrano's part that anything can be proved on the authority of philosophers and theologians. Moreover, while the philosophy of "as if" in *L'Autre Monde* would allow that the imaginative penetration of matter reveals a monism underlying the appearance of duality, much of the allegory in the latter part of *The States and Empires of the Sun* concentrates on the conflict inherent in the cosmic process: life versus death, heat versus cold, movement versus stasis, imaginative freedom versus material constraint.

If Cyrano believes in anything, he believes in the power of the free imagination to transcend the restraints imposed on the mind by material existence and repressive authority.[10] He expounds a materialistic monism as a physics and metaphysics of "as if"; but he does so, as Christian Liger observes, "in order to deny matter and praise its absence."[11]

The sequence of Dyrcona's voyages in itself partially dramatizes a movement away from gross earthbound customs and concerns and toward more enlightened, more imaginatively "rarefied" forms of existence. The progress of Dyrcona's flights, from that first voyage to Canada to his landing on the sun, represents a gradual abandoning of all semblance of mundane appearances and orthodox beliefs in favor of worlds that are more and more fantastic and ideas that are more and more idiosyncratic. This movement seems to be dramatized also in an early

---

[10] Compare Frances Yates's discussion of Bruno's belief "in the primacy of the imagination as the instrument for reaching the truth" in her *Giordano Bruno and the Hermetic Tradition* (Chicago, 1964), pp. 334 ff.

[11] Christian Liger, "Les Cinq Envols de Cyrano," *NRF,* XIII (1965), 435.

episode in *The States and Empires of the Sun,* wherein Dyrcona, after being incarcerated by the stultifying forces of authority and superstition, invents a contrivance to fly out of his
prison and rise to the kingdoms of the sun—symbolizing the
idea that the imagination can escape any constraint through
its power of fantastic invention.[12] Similarly, Campanella tells
Dyrcona that darkness and matter hinder the imagination even
in the solar regions; when the philosophers of the sun "wish to
communicate their thoughts, their flights of imagination purge
them of the sombre vapour, beneath which they generally keep
their ideas hidden" (p. 223).

The myth of a lost Eden where Adam had conversed with
other creatures in a secret and forgotten universal language[13]
dominates Cyrano's imaginative vision. That Eden is, of
course, localized as the lunar garden where Dyrcona finds
Enoch and Elijah. But it is implicit also throughout *The States
and Empires of the Sun,* where even the atomistic animals can
speak to Dyrcona in the "original language" of Adam. "That
nature has implanted a secret desire in birds, whichever world
they are in, to fly to" the sun (pp. 168-169), just as Elijah is
advised that if he wishes to acquire perfect knowledge he must
go to the moon and partake of the Tree of Knowledge (p. 22),
suggests a further correspondence between Eden and the world
of the sun as places where beings are "enlightened with all the
truth which one of God's creatures is capable of comprehending."

Cyrano treats satirically, however, the conception of Eden as
a realizable ideal. With Lucianic skepticism, he relates how
Enoch got to the lunar Paradise by attaching to himself vessels
filled with the vapors from sacrificial offerings, and how Elijah
flew there by means of an iron chariot propelled upward by a
loadstone. Equally ridiculous is Dyrcona's experience of par-
taking of one of the apples of knowledge: "hardly had my saliva
moistened it when I was enveloped by universal philosophy"
(pp. 25-26). Complementarily, the Demon of Socrates employs

---

[12] Miss Yates speaks of "an inner movement of the imagination towards the
Sun" (p. 153) and the sun's metaphorical significance as a symbol of epistemo-
logical unity (p. 289) in connection with the occult tradition of mnemotechny
(*The Art of Memory* [Chicago, 1966]).

[13] *Ibid.,* p. 385.

the Edenic myth in his satiric argument about "intellectual cabbages." Moses, he says, "doubtless wanted to teach us, by means of this enigma [of the Tree of Knowledge] that plants are in possession of the perfect philosophy, to the exclusion of ourselves [privativement]" (p. 73).

The lunar Eden, then, together with the possibility of confirming any "universal philosophy," stands for a cosmic unity about which any certainty is not vouchsafed to lapsarian man.[14] As an unattainable ideal that can yet be imagined, however, it can still be a standard for assessing man's ignorance and the fallibility of his reason.

In accordance with this view, *The States and Empires of the Sun* gives an idea of what the empirical corroboration of the metaphysical unity of man and nature would be like. The transformations that the little solar animals perform, for instance, exemplify above all the participation in various forms of being through an act of the imagination. The philosophers of the sun, also, assume other forms of existence: "We all die more than once," Campanella explains, "and, as we are only parts of the universe, we change our shape in order to go and take up life elsewhere—which . . . is a way to perfect one's being and to arrive at an infinite amount of knowledge [connoissances]" (p. 222). However, the cognitive apprehension of the constituents of being in their pure form, Cyrano seems to imply, is only possible within the realm of the sun, defined in *L'Autre Monde* as the source and embodiment of pure imaginative intellection (pp. 211-212).

The irony, in other words, is precisely that the communion of man with nature, whereby his theories about nature might be corroborated, exceeds the limits of man's nature as man— birds and trees can communicate with man in fantasy and in fantasy alone. Thus any metaphysical system of cosmological unity must be a philosophy of "as if," incapable of empirical verification outside the world of fantasy that the imagination can construct.

---

[14] Concerning Cornelius Agrippa's conception of an orderly universe whose unity is "beyond the power of human comprehension" as a result of the Fall, see Charles G. Nauert, Jr., *Agrippa and the Crisis of Renaissance Thought* (Urbana, 1965), pp. 306-309.

7

The First Men in the Moon

> They learned to use machines and numbers,
> and it has become clear that that
> is sufficient for them to master the earth.
> They have omitted from human civilization
> everything that was without purpose, diverting, fantastic,
> or ancient; in this way they have left out all that is human,
> and have taken over only the portion
> that is practical, technical, and utilitarian.
> And this doleful caricature of human civilization
> makes colossal progress; it builds technical marvels,
> renovates our planet, and finally
> begins to fascinate mankind itself.
> From his disciple and servant Faust will learn
> the secret of success, and mediocrity.
> Either mankind will come to close quarters
> with the Newts in a historic conflict of life and death,
> or it will inevitably become salamanderized.
>
> KAREL ČAPEK

Since Cyrano's fantastic myth about the nature of the universe derives from his principles of physics, it provides an occasion to question the extent to which the advance of scientific knowledge encroaches on artistic freedom. Here the view of W. S. Lach-Szyrma, in the preface to his romance *Aleriel; or A Voyage to Other Worlds* (1883), would appear to be a sensible one:

> In the following tale or speculation (as you choose to take it), although apparently I have given . . . rein to the imagination, yet I have endeavoured to avoid so much as possible any

141

conflict with established scientific discoveries; and, indeed, have based my speculations on the known facts of astronomy, only allowing the fancy to have full play where science is, and must be, unable, in its present state, to answer the questions here considered. (Pp. vii-viii)[1]

But even this negative restriction is not, in practice, absolute, for it has been violated deliberately as well as in ignorance.

One of the most flagrant examples of its violation—the instance that seems to have thrown Jules Verne into a fit of contemptuous indignation (see chap. 1, p. 32)—is Wells's last great scientific romance, *The First Men in the Moon* (1901). In the science fiction of his which precedes *The First Men,* Wells had pursued the consequences of scientific theories further than scientists (at least as scientists) were willing to do, or had otherwise adapted such theories for the purposes of his fantasies—usually to give those fantasies some degree of literal plausibility. He had even entertained for their imaginative possibilities quasi-scientific or pseudoscientific hypotheses, without, however, contradicting the evidence of science. But in *The First Men* he chose to disregard known facts and contemporary theories about the moon in favor of the more poetic— and by 1900 pretty thoroughly disproved—conjectures of Johan Kepler.[2]

Wells's choice of poetic fiction over scientific fact in *The First Men*—he was too well acquainted with the sciences not to have had a choice—points to an essential tension in that romance between science and poetry. These Victorian antinomies he still manages to hold together for most of the fiction, but the structure of the romance suggests that they are about

---

[1] *Aleriel* (London, 1883). The actual text reads, "I have given no rein . . ."; but in the context of Lach-Szyrma's remarks the negation makes no sense.

[2] Wells has Cavor specifically mention Kepler (*FMM*, VI, 110), to whose *Somnium* he was indebted (see Marjorie Nicolson, *Voyages*, pp. 248-250).

The Atlantic Edition cited in this chapter represents a revision of the text of the first edition. Most of the changes are insignificant improvements in the writing; but occasionally Wells has deleted poetic (and archaic) words and constructions in favor of a modern equivalent—"burden" replaces "burthen," for example. It is not, of course, within my scope here to examine the textual variants in detail.

to break apart. Indeed, poetry and science in *The First Men* are, as it were, merely juxtaposed, whereas in his earlier science fiction Wells had succeeded in fusing the two.

As if in recognition of these earlier triumphs of the fusing of science and poetry, *The First Men* in effect provides a partial synopsis of much of Wells's previous science fiction. His moon voyage recapitulates a large number of scenes and situations found in his preceding fantasies, from *The Chronic Argonauts,* an apprentice fragment that appeared in *The Science Schools Journal* between April and June of 1888,[3] through *The War of the Worlds* and "The Man Who Could Work Miracles" (1898).

But *The First Men* is not only synoptic; the motif of the voyage to the moon, for instance, is not repeated in any of Wells's other fantasies, early or late; and Bedford and Cavor are his sole human interplanetary travelers. Furthermore, although this cosmic voyage rehearses some of the myths of the previous romances, it also embodies a prophetic myth of its own. Wells said of this myth, more than thirty years after the fact, that he had sent Bedford and Cavor to the moon "in order to look at mankind from a distance and burlesque the effects of specialisation" *(Scientific Romances,* p. ix).

This last observation seems a fair enough assessment of the general meaning of the fantastic world of the Selenites; yet it leaves out the details of the myth and does not touch at all on the other two aspects of its meaning outlined above. I propose therefore to examine the three points I have made about *The First Men* at greater length and in reverse order, considering first the myth of a world in the moon, next the synoptic qualities of that myth, and finally the dichotomy between science and poetry inherent in the structure of the romance.

The Prophetic Myth of the Formicary

To appreciate the nature of the antlike Selenites and their highly organized society in *The First Men in the Moon,* it is

---

[3] The text of *The Chronic Argonauts* is reprinted as an appendix to Bernard Bergonzi, *The Early H. G. Wells,* (Toronto, 1961), pp. 187-214.

relevant to compare them with what in some respects they are not—the conquering ants of Wells's short story, "The Empire of the Ants"—and thereby to determine what in *The First Men* is mythically new for Wells. Though the short story was not published until 1905, it is conceivable that it dates from about the period in which he wrote *War of the Worlds*.[4] At any rate, "The Empire of the Ants" belongs thematically with the short stories, essays, and romances depicting "the Coming Beast"—stories, that is, of strange creatures from the unknown which emerge to threaten man's hegemony in the world.

In "The Empire of the Ants," an Englishman named Holroyd finds himself aboard a South American gunboat assigned to patrol a Brazilian river to investigate some mysterious goings on having to do with ants. Having come to South America fresh from England, Holroyd discovers the experience of the jungle itself to be unsettling, though not exactly the way it is to Marlow and Kurtz in the Congo.

> He was a young man, this was his first sight of the tropics, he came straight from England, where Nature is hedged, ditched, and drained into the perfection of submission, and he had suddenly discovered the insignificance of man. . . . He began to perceive that man is indeed a rare animal, having but a precarious hold upon this land. (X, 492-493))

Even more disquieting, however, are the ants, whose intelligence and discipline have already enabled them to overcome and annihilate or drive out the inhabitants of several villages along the river.

> There can be little doubt that [these ants] are far more reasonable and with a far better social organisation than any previously known ant species; instead of being in dispersed societies they are organised into what is in effect a single nation; but their peculiar and immediate formidableness lies not

---

[4] Wells's source for "The Empire of the Ants" (a book on the Amazon published in 1861 by the naturalist H. W. Bates), as identified by David Y. Hughes, "H. G. Wells; Ironic Romances," *Extrapolation*, VI (May, 1965), 34-35, does not in this case provide a terminus a quo for the date of composition.

so much in this as in the intelligent use they make of poison against their larger enemies. (X, 512)

Indeed, they almost overwhelm the crew of the gunboat, which, like the French man-of-war in *Heart of Darkness*, can do no more than irrationally fire shells into the impenetrable jungle. It is suggested at the end of Wells's story that by the middle of the twentieth century these ants will have reached Europe.

The First Men gives a good deal more detail about the "social organisation" that "The Empire of the Ants" adumbrates. A high degree of specialization characterizes what is structurally the formicary of Selenite society. The antlike creatures who inhabit the moon—who live both on its surface and underground—are often literally molded to fulfill a specific function in the social order. "Quite recently," Cavor relates in one of his messages radioed to earth,

> I came upon a number of young Selenites confined in jars from which only the fore-limbs protruded, who were being compressed to become machine-minders of a special sort. The extended "hand" in this highly developed system of technical education is stimulated by irritants and nourished by injection while the rest of the body is starved. (VI, 240-241)

All these creatures, moreover, regardless of social function, are psychologically as well as physiologically prepared for their roles. Their psychological preparation anticipates the process of conditioning in Aldous Huxley's *Brave New World*.

> In the moon [says Cavor] every citizen knows his place. He is born to that place, and the elaborate discipline of training and surgery he undergoes fits him at last so completely to it that he has neither ideas nor organs for any purpose beyond it. . . .
> A Selenite appointed to be a minder of mooncalves is from his earliest years induced to think and live mooncalf, to find his pleasure in mooncalf lore, his exercise in their tending and pursuit. . . . He takes at last no interest in the deeper part of the moon; he regards all Selenites not equally versed in mooncalves with indifference, derision, or hostility. . . . So also he loves his work, and discharges in perfect happiness the duty

that justifies his being. And so it is with all sorts and conditions
of Selenites. (VI, 236-237)

Here Wells has envisioned the society wherein creatures give
up freedom for the sake of happiness; and he has foreshadowed
Huxley's antiutopia almost in exact detail. Instead of *soma,*
Selenites when they are not needed are given an opiate that
puts them to sleep until there is again a particular function for
them to perform. Cavor reasons that this procedure is "surely
far better than to expel [the worker] from his factory to wander
starving in the streets"; but he adds, "I still do not like the
memory of those prostrate forms amid those quiet, luminous
arcades of fleshy [fungoid] growth" (VI, 243).

The structure of Selenite society, in other words, seems to
embody what Wells only hints at in "The Empire of the Ants."
The Selenites "are not merely colossally superior to ants, but,
according to Cavor, colossally, in intelligence, morality, and social wisdom, higher than men" (VI, 227). The reader has no
sense, however, that in either story Wells is advocating something like what was to become his plan for a world state. It is
true that the ants as well as the Selenites are admired to some
degree; but this admiration has its source largely, if not wholly,
in contrast to the irrationality of men and human institutions,
as many of Cavor's remarks explicitly make clear. Whatever
change of mind Wells may have had between the publication
of *The First Men* and his writing of *A Modern Utopia* (1905),
he does not view Selenite society as an absolute ideal, though
some aspects of that social order may be ideal relative to their
terrestrial counterparts.

That Wells does not look with favor on the possibility of
realizing a formicary world is evidenced by the difference in
rhetorical purposes to which the "ants" are put in *The First
Men* as compared with "The Empire of the Ants." In the short
story, as in *War of the Worlds* and "The Sea Raiders," the
strange species that calls itself to man's attention functions to
challenge his complacent assumptions about his place and
destiny in the world. The army of ants depicted in the process
of overrunning South America embodies the otherness of
nature, nature in its defiantly unanthropomorphic aspect,

opposed to all that man is and prides himself in being. The Selenites share some of this otherness, particularly as they present a satiric contrast to man's irrationality; but their society is not the militant negation of industrialized society on earth. Accordingly, they offer no threat of invasion, imminent or not: Cavorite, the antigravitational substance that allows Bedford and Cavor to get to the moon, remains for the Selenites a "practical impossibility" (VI, 264). Besides, they are so far from being bellicose that the Grand Lunar, that giant ganglion, reacts with the horror of a King of Brobdingnag to Cavor's account of human strife.[5]

Thus the Selenite world, like the world of 802,701 in *The Time Machine,* is at once the antithesis of an earthly state of affairs and the "working to a logical conclusion" (*TTM,* I, 64) of a tendency observable in the present—in this instance, the tendency toward increased specialization. It is this last-mentioned aspect of the myth of the Selenites, the details derived, as the Time Traveller explains, by "proceeding from the problems of our own age" (I, 63), that Wells deals with satirically. And in the sense that the formicary projects the consequences of specialized technology, *The First Men* gives "the broad outlines of the state of that other world so near, so akin, and yet so dissimilar to our own" (VI, 220).

Synoptic Satire: The Poetry of Science

The recapitulation in *The First Men* of various situations and incidents from his earlier science fiction shows Wells to have been conscious of the myths he had previously created. Some of the allusions need only be pointed out; others help to clarify features of the myths they are reminiscent of and require some comment. First, however, the character of the two witnesses who relate the romance should be established.

Bedford represents Wells's poetic observer; but he is also the paradigm of the irrational and often violent element in various

[5] Compare *Gulliver's Travels,* Bk. II, Ch. vii. Mark R. Hillegas, "Cosmic Pessimism," *Papers of the Michigan Academy of Science, Arts and Letters,* XLVI (1961), 662-663 n., also mentions the similarity between Gulliver's and Cavor's interviews.

personages in the early science fiction, especially among Wells's narrators. Like the Time Traveller, Prendick, the Invisible Man, and the alienated antihero from whose point of view most of *The War of the Worlds* is told, Bedford at some time gives way to the murderous impulse to kill or mutilate creatures with whom he cannot or dare not identify. He incorporates the component that in *The First Men* Wells has, as it were, excised from his scientist: that component in, say, the Time Traveller or Griffin which involves each of them emotionally and personally in his situation. The result is that Cavor, who fairly consistently is Bedford's antithesis, becomes the almost completely detached and disinterested scientific observer. He is uninvolved enough in the crises of the lunar expedition to radio to earth (after Bedford has returned safely in the Cavorite sphere) a report of his companion's imprudent inebriety and mad behavior. In contrast to Bedford, who schemes for material profit—whether that profit be gained by patenting Cavorite or mining gold in the moon—Cavor is only concerned with attaining knowledge; as Bedford incredulously reports at one point, "It wasn't that he intended to make use of these things: he simply wanted to know them" (VI, 129). Unlike his partner, Cavor is quite innocent in worldly matters, innocent by choice: "I cannot consent for one moment to add the burden of practical consideration to my theorising," he informs Bedford (VI, 31).

To be sure, Cavor's disinterestedness and impracticality—in his case the two appear to be inextricable from one another—have their drawbacks. For one thing, these characteristics paralyze any will to act, thereby surrendering control of any situation to Bedford or the Selenites. More importantly, these traits commit Cavor to the indiscretion of telling the Grand Lunar about war, and thus prove to be his undoing.

Bedford's desire for gain prompts him to become Cavor's partner, but his philistine attitude toward science blinds him to the realities of space travel and exploration. Thus like the Reverend Elijah Cook, the shadowy figure in *The Chronic Argonauts* who is compelled by circumstance to join the scientist Moses Nebogipfel on a voyage into time, Bedford encounters hardships that he had not counted on. After the Selenites have made them prisoners, Bedford asks Cavor:

> "What did we come here for? What are we after? What was
> the moon to us, or we to the moon? . . . We ought to have started
> the little things first. It was you proposed the moon! Those
> Cavorite spring blinds! I am certain we could have worked
> them for terrestrial purposes. . . ."
> "Look here, Bedford," said Cavor. "You came on this expedi-
> tion of your own free will."
> "You said to me—'Call it prospecting.' "
> "There are always risks in prospecting."
> "Especially when you do it unarmed and without thinking
> out every possibility." (VI, 111-112)

Obviously C. S. Lewis's *Out of the Silent Planet* portrays the
Bedford syndrome accurately in the characters of Weston and
Devine, the unscrupulous adventurers out to despoil Mars.

If Bedford's misgivings resemble slightly those only hinted
at in *The Chronic Argonauts*, the outcome of the first experiment with Cavorite much more certainly recalls another of
Wells's stories, "The Man Who Could Work Miracles." The
hero of that whimsical tale, one George McWhirter Forther-
ingay, carelessly and without foreknowledge of the consequences, upon finding that he can suspend at will some of the
laws of nature, wishes that the world stop. It does, and Fother-
ingay confronts an apocalyptic whirlwind and a "wilderness of
disorder" ("Miracles," X, 372). Similarly, the successful creation of a substance impervious to the force of gravity also results in temporary chaos. In this instance when one of the laws
of nature is abrogated, it seems to Bedford as if "the whole
face of the world had changed."

> The tranquil sunset had vanished, the sky was dark with
> scurrying clouds, everything was flattened and swaying with the
> gale. I glanced back to see if my bungalow was still in a gen-
> eral way standing, then staggered forward towards the trees
> among which Cavor had vanished, and through whose tall and
> leaf-denuded branches shone the flames of his burning house.
> (VI, 26)

As often happens in Wells's fiction, local or widespread destruction accompanies liberation from any sort of environmental constraint and the face of the world is, at least temporarily, transformed. (Such transformations dramatize the fact that any rebellious impulse against the established scheme of things disorders that scheme and makes an innovative ordering, or reordering, possible).

The romance that the lunar world, as described by Bedford, most prominently suggests is of course *The Time Machine*. The subterranean world of the Selenites—a world pulsating with the throb of machinery—is the "under-world" of the Morlocks revisited and more thoroughly explored. The Selenites, like the Morlocks, have become habituated to their world of relative darkness. The former creatures now completely control the upper, pastoral world; the mooncalves are literally —what the Time Traveller conjectures the Eloi to be—"fatted cattle, which the ant-like Morlocks preserved and preyed upon . . . saw to the breeding of" (*TTM*, I, 81).[6]

The significant difference between the Morlocks and the Selenites does not really stand out in Bedford's narrative. But Cavor's messages, which Bedford edits, make that difference patent. Whereas the Morlocks are a degenerate species, bound to their underground machinery without any real control over their destiny or environment, the Selenites comprise a civilization at an advanced technological level. The immediate tendencies of industrialized society, as Wells accurately perceived them, apparently caused him to revise his original vision.

Despite their technological progress, however, the Selenites are not without their absurdities. Specialization has made many of them machine-tickling aphids—to invoke Samuel Butler's prophecy of man's becoming "a parasite upon the machines" (*Erewhon*, II, 183). Still other Selenites suggest to Cavor the sort of caricature of humanity that the Beast People represent in *The Island of Doctor Moreau*.

They differed in shape, they differed in size! Some bulged

---

[6] I should point out that the epithet "ant-like" is not descriptive of the appearance of the Morlocks but rather alludes to their resemblance to leaf-cutter ants, which keep "herds" of aphids.

and overhung, some ran among the feet of their fellows. . . . All of them had the grotesque and disquieting suggestion of an insect that has somehow contrived to burlesque humanity; all seemed to present an incredible exaggeration of some particular feature: . . . one seemed all leg, poised, as it were, on stilts; another protruded an enormous nose-like organ beside a sharply speculative eye that made him startlingly human until one saw his expressionless mouth. (VI, 229-230)

The similarity between these burlesques of humanity and that earlier "travesty of humanity" (*IDM*, II, 99), the beasts that Moreau contrives to transform into men, is also a similarity in the satiric function of the two. And if the takeoff of the Cavorite sphere felt to Bedford "not like the beginning of a journey" but rather "the beginning of a dream" (VI, 49), clearly the dream has by this point turned into a nightmare.

A Farewell to the Poetry of Science

Bedford's experiences among the Selenites and during his escape from the moon call to mind one last important allusion in *The First Men*—namely, to *The War of the Worlds*—and also anticipate the dichotomy between poetry and science implicit in what follows. Some characteristics of the Selenites, particularly their reliance on machines and those anatomical peculiarities of theirs which make them "in form and function, in structure and habit different beyond the most bizarre imaginings of nightmare" from the creatures man has been acquainted with, of course associate them with Wells's Martians, and hence with the creatures in his various essays and short stories which prefigure those invaders from outer space (see pp. 29-31). In addition, Bedford's alienation from the Selenites and his subsequent alienation from himself on his return journey to earth constitute still another connection between the two full-length fantasies. But Bedford goes further in his disintegration than the antiheroic narrator in *War of the Worlds*. The passage describing this disintegration in *The First Men* is quite remarkable and runs in part:

I became, if I may so express it, dissociate from Bedford, I looked down on Bedford as a trivial incidental thing with which I chanced to be connected, I saw Bedford in many relations—as an ass or as a poor beast where I had hitherto been inclined to regard him with quiet pride as a very spirited and rather forcible person. I saw him not only as an ass, but as the son of many generations of asses. . . . I had that extraordinary persuasion that as a matter of fact I was no more Bedford than I was any one else, but only a mind floating in the still serenity of space. . . .

For a time I struggled against this really very grotesque delusion. I tried to summon the memory of vivid moments, of tender or intense emotions to my assistance; I felt that if I could recall one genuine twinge of feeling the growing rupture would be stopped. But I could not do it. (VI, 190-191)[7]

Overwhelmed by his own insignificance, Bedford views himself "as one might . . . an ant in the sand. . . . I regret that something of that period of lucidity still hangs about me."

Here is an instance of what T. S. Eliot called a "dissociation of sensibility" if ever there was one. Moreover, this dissociation of thought from feeling that Bedford temporarily experiences is already inherent in the opposition of Cavor and Bedford and can be perceived on a larger scale in the structure of *The First Men* itself. The separate accounts given by Bedford and Cavor are worlds apart in tone and spirit, the one histrionic to the point of melodrama, the other dispassionate and detached, a veritable "Natural History of the Selenites."[8]

The structural disjunction between Bedford's fiction, with its poetic descriptions of the lunar landscape and its concentration on the adventure in the enterprise, and Cavor's natural history, a factual and by and large undramatic presentation of life on the moon, is not to be found in Wells's previous fiction —certainly not in the same degree. The alternative Bedford offers to readers of *The First Men*—"If the world will not have it as fact, then the world may take it as fiction" (VI, 209)—

---

[7] Compare with this passage the opening pages of Theodore Sturgeon, *Venus Plus X* (New York, 1960).
[8] This is the heading of chap. 23 of *The First Men*.

while it vaguely echoes the Time Traveller's "Take it as a lie —or a prophecy" (*TTM*, I, 112), in the later romance points to an inescapable and unresolvable dichotomy. Bedford's part of the narrative, concluding with the remark as to how it can be taken, is as it were, the fictive part; Cavor's natural history, antithetically, is the factual. It is as if Wells were admitting that he could no longer create that fusion of poetry and science so uniquely his own;[9] as if, furthermore, in admitting this, he felt obliged to recall those earlier romances in which he had fused these Victorian antinomies so memorably.

To be sure, it is still possible to put the pieces of *The First Men in the Moon* together, despite the structural division between the two sections of the narrative; but at the end of the fantasy Bedford and Cavor, poetry and science, fiction and fact are—symbolically it seems to me—worlds away from one another—as if even their conjunction (not fusion) in this, the last of Wells's great science fantasies, were forced and must inevitably break apart. As Cavor's final message to earth is interrupted, Bedford envisions the regimented creatures of the formicary closing in upon the scientist, who is "being forced backward step by step out of all speech or sign of his fellows, for evermore into the Unknown—into the dark, into that silence that has no end" (VI, 267).

Conclusion

Wells's science fantasies, as I have indicated in the course of this study, are in many ways the culmination of a tradition that in English can be traced back to Francis Godwin. They are also the nexus between the strategies, and the mythic and thematic preoccupations, established prior to *The Time Machine* and the science fiction of the twentieth century. Wells was aware of the genre as a strategy for mythic displacement— what he called "prophecy"—in addition to its rhetorical tech-

---

[9] This, in retrospect, turned out to be the case; his two last scientific romances, *Food of the Gods* (1904) and *Men like Gods* (1923) can hardly be considered poetic, though they make some slight concession to scientific plausibility.

niques for using a more or less scientific rationale to provide
a transition between fact and fiction. Some of his science fantasies also elaborate a philosophy of "as if" by way of recognizing myth as myth. Finally, his *First Men in the Moon* draws
upon and epitomizes many of the myths he had given form to
in his earlier fiction, and thus consolidates what he had learned
from his precursors and his own previous achievements at the
same time that it points to the increasing difficulty of harmoniz-
ing poetic and scientific views of the world—the contemporary problem of somehow assimilating science and poetry, fact
and fantasy.

   Besides extending the range of science fictional "inventions"
and applying a science fictional strategy of presentation to
various kinds of fantasy, Wells anticipates the dilemma of
technological progress and the alternative responses of more
recent writers of science fiction to it.[10] He was one of the first
to foresee that a collision of technocratic objectives and traditional human values would lead to disastrous consequences.
He fiercely criticizes those consequences and clearly deplores
a world devoid of freedom and initiative; but he implies in
The Time Machine, and makes it explicit in *A Story of the
Days to Come* (1897), that any idyllic daydream of a retreat
from technocracy to the bosom of Mother Nature constitutes
an irresponsible evasion of the real alternative: whether or
not humane ideals can direct the course of technological advance. His later polemical treatises, from this point of view,
represent a logical development from his early science fiction,
though their hortatory faith in reasonableness may not now
be shared.

   [10] See Hillegas, *The Future as Nightmare* (New York, 1967); and my review,
"Was Wells Anti-Wellsian?" *Carleton Miscellany,* IX, no. 1 (1968), 110-112.

Postscript:

The Machina Ratiocinatrix and the

Abolition of Man

> Young Rossum invented a worker
> with a minimum number of requirements.
> He had to simplify him. He rejected
> everything that did not contribute directly
> to the progress of work—everything that makes man
> more expensive. In fact, he rejected man
> and made the Robot. . . .Mechanically [Robots]
> are more perfect than we are,
> they have an enormously developed intelligence,
> but they have no soul.
>
> KAREL ČAPEK

> It has long been clear to me
> that the ultra-rapid computing machine
> was in principle an ideal nervous system
> to an apparatus for automatic control. . . .
> With the aid of strain-gauges or similar agencies
> to read the performance of the motor organs
> and to report, to "feed back," to the
> central control system as an artificial kinaesthetic sense,
> we are already in a position to construct . . .
> machines of almost any degree of
> elaborateness of performance.
>
> NORBERT WIENER

Karel Čapek did not invent the notion of the automaton;[1] but in bestowing on it the name "Robot," he clarified its range of meaning and its ambivalence as a concept. In *R.U.R.* (1920), Robot specifically designates an anthropomorphic *machina laborans* behaviorally similar to a human being except that, through a lack of inwardness, its motivating directives are unimpeded by interference from anything like human feelings. Hence the term also implicates any system whose consummate values the robot embodies, as in the state engineered to achieve the ideals of efficiency and economic utility without regard for the well-being of its citizens. Such a state requires robots; that is, it demands that human beings perform as if they were robots.

The point of *R.U.R.*, then, is not merely to show how machines differ from human beings, but, what is equally important, under what conditions those differences diminish in significance. Čapek's epilogue suggests that emotional sensitivity and aesthetic awareness can humanize a robot; but the metaphoric substance of the action preceding the epilogue imparts a converse notion: that the corporate state aiming at efficiency and obedience and subverting all values other than the purely utilitarian robotizes human beings. The technicians of the enterprise, having lost sight of man as an end in himself and having become, necessarily, insensitive to human feelings and moral values in their pursuit of efficiency for efficiency's sake, manage to reduce themselves to inhuman mechanisms. They eventually find that they can no longer control the situation that they have brought about and are as caught up in the mechanical logic of events as the "robots" over whom they are supposed to have mastery. The entrepreneurs in *R.U.R.*, Rossum's successors, thus face essentially the same predicament as the people in the mechanized subterranean world of E. M. Forster's *The Machine Stops* (1928): "Year by year [the Machine] was served with increased efficiency and decreased intelligence. The better a man knew his own duties upon it, the less he understood the duties of his neighbour, and

---

[1] The automaton, or "android," appears in several science fictional tales of the last century; see H. Bruce Franklin, *Future Perfect: American Science Fiction of the Nineteenth Century* (New York, 1966), pp. 141-143 ff., 166-167 ff.

in all the world there was not one who understood the monster as a whole."[2]

By a simple extension of Capek's idea, the robot state can be thought of as being analogous to the *machina ratiocinatrix,* the computer, as well as the computerized blueprint for a system epitomizing efficient material productivity. Once it has been supplied with a set of rules by which to process data, the computer can be programmed to project the possible ways whereby the data can be made to lead to a desired end, and it can correct its calculations to accommodate changes in the data fed back through its system; but it cannot assess the premises of its own operation, the logical rules of its procedure,[3] nor can it alter the rules built into it. In other words, it cannot, to use the metaphors of Franz Kafka's "In the Penal Colony" (1919), judge its master without destroying itself. The robot state, the computerized technocracy, shares this limitation: its probable directions all proceed within a fairly well-defined, and hence predictable, range, and any radical overhaul of its premises is excluded as a possibility within the system. In this sense, the computer metaphorically generates the all-too-verisimilar antiutopias of Kurt Vonnegut's *Player Piano* (1952) and Jean-Luc Godard's film *Alphaville* (1965), in both of which a computer also functions as the brain of the technocracy.

The robot state sets up its own antinomies, which happen to be the alternatives that Dostoevski dramatizes in his *Notes from Underground* and "The Grand Inquisitor" from *The Brothers Karamazov.*[4] If the power of reasoning were the highest purpose of man, he could be replaced by the *machina ratiocinatrix,* which is, after all, much more perfect than he: it is more consistent and efficient in its level of performance than

[2] E. M. Foster, *The Machine Stops,* in *The Eternal Moment and Other Stories* (New York, 1956), p. 69.

[3] Compare J. R. Lucas, "Minds, Machines and Gödel," in *Minds and Machines,* ed. Alan Ross Anderson (Englewood Cliffs, 1964), wherein Lucas concludes: "a conscious being can deal with Gödelian questions in a way in which a machine cannot, because a conscious being can consider both itself and its performance and yet not be other than that which did the performance" (p. 57).

[4] On the relation between the alternative of "The Grand Inquisitor" and antiutopian fiction, see also Robert C. Elliott, "The Fear of Utopia," *Centennial Review,* VII (1963), 242 ff.

the human brain, logically less fallible, and, in case of break-
down, more easily repaired. Therefore, man must be unique
by virtue of his irrationality: possessing the capacity to reason,
he can nevertheless *choose* not to be rational, an option not
available to the machine.

From this capacity for choice emanates the second alternative, that of happiness or freedom (again I adapt Dostoevski's
logic to the concepts of the present argument). The technocracy can provide the requisites for material well-being; but
for this kind of well-being to be equivalent to the fulfillment
of all man's needs necessitates lobotomizing the desires of man's
spirit, or translating and reducing them to cravings for com-
modities.[5] The translation may bring about what Herbert
Marcuse ironically terms the "happy consciousness";[6] but it
does so at the cost of abolishing man's dimension of inwardness, which is to say his freedom.

The sacrifice of freedom in the attainment of utopia is
commonplace in the antiutopian fiction of the last fifty years.
Though often the point of view focuses on the unhappy misfits in the utopia instead of the contented masses, thus attenu-
ating the dichotomy between happiness and freedom, the basic
disjunction of the rationally regulated euphoria of the robot
state versus the primitive freedom of unreason in the state of
nature abides. The one dialectically calls forth the other; and
while the retreat to nature from the computerized technocracy
is not represented as a practical alternate way of surviving in a
world dominated by the totalitarian technocracy, it is a com-
pensatory gesture in the direction of pointing out the institu-
tionalized imbalance in the insanely rational utopia. Nature,
that is, becomes the scene of a life of emotional and instinctual
expression as opposed to the repression in the rational state.[7]

---

[5] Accordingly, diverse forms of thought control are pervasive in the nightmare fantasies of modern science fiction: biological and psychological conditioning in Aldous Huxley's *Brave New World;* creatures that attach themselves to, and take over, a man's nervous system in Robert Heinlein's *The
Puppet Masters* (1951); subliminal advertising in Frederik Pohl and C. M.
Kornbluth's *The Space Merchants* (1953); electronic devices inserted in the
brain in Kurt Vonnegut's *The Sirens of Titan* (1959); and so forth.

[6] Herbert Marcuse, *One-Dimensional Man* (Boston, 1964) pp. 76-79.

[7] Some idea of the uses of the natural scene as a counterfoil to the utopian
state is conveyed by a few instances: Eugene Zamiatin's *We* (1920), George

In this sense, as Aldous Huxley retrospectively remarked of *Brave New World*, a *tertium datur* is implicit in the unacceptable alternative of rational totalitarianism or primitive savagery.[8] Whether that third possibility, of a sane and free civilized society, is realizable in fact is quite another question.

What I am suggesting is that the notion of the individual and the state as machines generates the myths of a number of twentieth-century science fantasies. By analyzing the cybernetic model and the dichotomies it entails, I have tried to supply the conceptual coordinates for mapping an important and extensive sector of modern science fiction.

Orwell's *1984* (1949), and Kurt Vonnegut's *Player Piano* (1952). The discussion above readily applies to Orwell; in *We*, the diarist, D-503, associates the natural scene behind the Green Wall with the square root of minus one, that is, the irrational; and Paul Proteus, the central and protean character in *Player Piano*, entertains an atavistic impulse to quit his job as a technocrat and turn to farming. On the relation of the pastoral ideal to the machine, compare Leo Marx, *The Machine in the Garden* (New York, 1964).

[8] Foreword to *Brave New World* (Harmondsworth, 1955), pp. 7-9.

Selective Bibliography

I have divided this bibliography into: (A) bibliographical sources; (B) primary works relating to the development of science fiction in England through the end of the nineteenth century, together with a brief description of those works not mentioned in my text or notes (exceptions to this procedure are the works of Jules Verne, summaries of which can be found in Hillegas' "Annotated Bibliography" [see the citation below]); and (C) selected critical works, not necessarily critical of science fiction as such, along with miscellaneous sources of information. Some entries that might properly be placed in both categories (A) and (C) I have listed only in (A).

Bibliographical Sources

Amis, Kingsley. *New Maps of Hell: A Survey of Science Fiction*. New York, 1960.
Bailey, J[ames] O[stler]. *Pilgrims Through Space and Time*. New York, 1955.
Bleiler, Everett F., ed. *The Checklist of Fantastic Literature*. Chicago, 1948.
Bloomfield, P[aul]. *Imaginary Worlds; or, The Evolution of Utopia*. London, 1932.
Clarke, I[gnatius] F. *The Tale of the Future* [1664-1960]. London, 1961.
Crawford, Joseph H. et al. *'333': A Bibliography of the Science Fantasy Novel*. Providence, 1953.
Franklin, H. Bruce. *Future Perfect: American Science Fiction of the Nineteenth Century*. New York, 1966.
Gove, Philip Babcock. *The Imaginary Voyage in Prose Fiction*. New York, 1941.
Green, Roger Lancelyn. *Into Other Worlds*. London, 1957.
Hillegas, Mark R. "An Annotated Bibliography of Jules Verne's *Voy-*

ages Extraordinaires," Extrapolation, III (1962), 32-47.

——. "A Bibliography of Secondary Materials on Jules Verne," *Extrapolation,* II (1960), 5-16.

Nicolson, Marjorie Hope. *Voyages to the Moon.* New York, 1948.

Ray, Gordon N. "H. G. Wells's Contributions to the *Saturday Review," The Library,* 5th series, XVI (1961), 29-36.

Wells, Geoffrey. *H. G. Wells: A Bibliography.* London, 1925.

Primary works through the end of the nineteenth century

Abbott, Edwin. *Flatland: A Romance of Many Dimensions.* 2d ed. rev. London, 1884.

Allen, Grant. *Strange Stories.* London, 1884. [Allen claims, without justi-fiction, it seems to me, that "almost all the stories . . . have their germ or prime motive in some scientific or quasiscientific idea" (p. v). The story in this collection which comes closest to being science fiction is "Pausodyne: A Great Chemical Discovery," concerning a man who anesthetizes himself and sleeps for a hundred years.]

[Anonymous]. *The Aerostatic Spy: Or, Excursions with an Air Balloon.* 2 vols. London, 1785.

——. *The History of a Voyage to the Moon . . . an Exhumed Narrative, Supposed to have been Ejected from a Lunar Volcano.* London, 1864. [Two students discover "repellante" and utilize its repulsive force to propel their "flying greenhouse" (p. 54) to the moon.]

——. *The Man in the Moon, Discovering a World of Knavery under the Sunne.* [n.p.], 1649.

——. *The Modern Atalantis; or, The Devil in an Air Balloon . . .* London, 1784.

——. *Politics and Life on Mars.* London, 1883.

——. *A Voyage to the World in the Centre of the Earth. Giving an Account of the Manners, Customs, Laws, Government and Religion of the Inhabitants . . .* London, 1755.

Aratus, *pseud. A Voyage to the Moon.* London, 1793. [A "lunar" satire of English politics.]

Beaman, Emeric Hulme. *The Experiment of Doctor Nevill.* London, 1900.

Brunt, Samuel, *pseud. A Voyage to Cacklogallinia. With a Description of the Religion, Policy, Customs and Manners of that Country . . .* Facsimile text. New York, 1940.

Butler, Samuel (1612-1680). *Hudibras.* Ed. A. R. Waller. Cambridge, 1905.

——. *Three Poems.* Augustan Reprint Society Pub. No. 88 (1961).

Butler, Samuel (1835-1902). *The Works of . . . .* Ed. Henry Festing Jones and A. T. Bartholomew. 20 vols. London, 1923-24. [The Shrewsbury Edition.]

Cromie, Robert. *The Crack of Doom.* London, 1895.

——. *A Plunge into Space.* 2d ed. London, 1891.

Cyrano de Bergerac, Savinien. *The Comical History of the States and Empires of the Worlds of the Moon and the Sun.* Tr. A. Lovell. London, 1687.

——. *Les Oeuvres Libertines.* Ed. Frédéric Lachèvre. 2 vols. Paris, 1921.

——. *Other Worlds.* Tr. Geoffrey Strachan. London, 1965.

——. *Voyages to the Moon and the Sun.* Tr. Richard Aldington. London, [n.d.].

Daniel, Gabriel. *Voyage au Monde de Descartes.* Paris, 1960.

——. *A Voyage to the World of Cartesius.* Tr. T. Taylor. London, 1692.

Defoe, Daniel. *The Consolidator: or Memoirs of Sundry Transactions from the World in the Moon* . . . London, 1705.

——. *A Journey to the World in the Moon.* London, 1705.

Donne, John. *Ignatius his Conclave* . . . Facsimile Text Society Pub. No. 53. New York, 1941.

D'Urfey, Thomas. *Wonders in the Sun, or, The Kingdom of the Birds.* Augustan Reprint Society Pub. No. 104 (1964). [An operatic adaptation of Cyrano's *L'Autre Monde.*]

Godwin, Francis. *The Man in the Moone and Nuncius Inanimatus.* Ed. Grant McColley. Smith College Studies in Modern Languages, XIX (1937).

——. *The Man in the Moone; or A Discourse of a Voyage thither. By Domingo Gonsales* . . . London, 1638.

Greer, Tom, *pseud. A Modern Dædalus.* London, 1885.

Greg, Percy. *Across the Zodiac: The Story of a Wrecked Record.* 2 vols. London, 1880. [A man travels by rocketship to Mars and finds an advanced, but materialistic, society there.]

Griffith, George C[hetwyn]. *The Great Pirate Syndicate.* London, 1899.

——. *The Outlaws of the Air.* London, 1895.

——. *The Romance of Golden Star.* London, 1897. [A Frankensteinian scientist, the villain in this melodramatic fantasy, revives a mumified Incan ruler.]

Hay, William Delisle. *Three Hundred Years Hence.* London, 1881.

Hinton, C. H. *Scientific Romances. First Series.* London, 1886.

Holberg, Ludwig. *A Journey to the World Under-Ground. By Nicolas Klimius.* Tr. anon. London, 1742.

——. *Nicolai Klimii Iter Subterraneum* . . . [n.p.], 1741.

Jane, Frederick T. *To Venus in Five Seconds.* London, 1897. [A woman who later reveals that she descends from the ancient Egyptians shanghais the narrator and takes him to Venus, where experiments are to be performed on him and other earthlings. His efforts to escape provoke an Armageddon between the "Thothens" (the Egyptians) and the Venusians ("a sort of compound of elephant, mosquito, and flea, a Thing seven feet high or more"; p. 47).]

Lach-Szyrma, W. S. *Aleriel; Or, A Voyage to Other Worlds.* London, 1883.

Laurie, A., *pseud.* [i.e., Pierre Grousset]. *The Conquest of the Moon. A Story of the Bayouda.* London, 1889.

Lear, John, ed. *Kepler's Dream.* Tr. Patricia Frueh Kirkwood. Los Angeles, 1965.

Lucian. *Certaine Select Dialogues of . . . Together with his True History.* Tr. Francis Hickes. Oxford, 1634.

Lytton, Edward Bulwer. *The Works of* . . . 32 vols. Boston, 1891-92.

[The Knebworth Edition.]

Maccoll, Hugh. *Mr. Stranger's Sealed Packet.* London, 1889. [Mr. Stranger takes a space ship to Mars, and there finds a civilization where "there was no struggle for existence" (p. 103). Another race inhabiting the planet, however, is determined to annihilate the pacific "Grensumin"; and Stranger has difficulty preventing them from doing so.]

McDermot, Murtagh, *pseud. A Trip to the Moon.* London, 1728.

[Morris, Ralph]. *The Life and Astonishing Adventures of John Daniel.* London, 1751.

Munro, John. *A Trip to Venus.* London, 1897. [A cosmic romance that includes a trip to Mercury as well as to Venus. The Venusians, as the travelers from earth discover, are almost divine; but the Mercurial landscape is diabolical (pp. 216-217).]

[Paltock, Robert]. *The Life and Adventures of Peter Wilkins.* London, 1751.

Rusen, David. *Iter Lunare: or, A Voyage to the Moon.* London, 1703.

Shadwell, Thomas. *The Virtuoso.* Ed. David Stuart Rodes. With an Introduction by Marjorie Hope Nicolson. Lincoln, 1966.

Shelley, Mary, *Frankenstein; or, The Modern Promotheus.* 2 vols. London, 1818.

——. *Frankenstein . . .* London, 1960.

Stevenson, Robert Louis. *The Works of . . .* 26 vols. London, 1922-1923. [The Vailima Edition.]

Stockton, Frank R. *The Great War Syndicate.* London, 1889.

Swift, Jonathan. *Gulliver's Travels.* Ed. Herbert Davis. With an Introduction by Harold Williams. Oxford, 1941.

Thomson, William. *The Man in the Moon; or Travels into the Lunar Regions by the Man of the People.* 2 vols. London, 1783.

Verne, Jules. *The Begum's Fortune.* Tr. W. H. G. Kingston. London, 1880 [1879].

——. *Clipper of the Clouds.* Tr. anon. London, 1887.

——. *Floating Island.* Tr. William J. Gordon. London, 1896.

——. *From the Earth to the Moon direct in 97 hours 20 minutes; and a Trip round it.* Tr. Louis Mercier and E. C. King. London, 1873.

——. *Hector Servadac.* Tr. E. E. Frewer. London, 1878.

——. *A Journey to the Centre of the Earth.* Tr. anon. London, 1872 [1871].

——. *The Master of the World.* Tr. anon. London, [n.d.].

——. *The Mysterious Island.* Tr. W. H. G. Kingston. 3 vols. London, 1875.

——. *The Purchase of the North Pole.* Tr. anon. London [190–].

——. *Twenty Thousand Leagues under the Sea.* Tr. H. Frith. London, 1876.

Voltaire. *Micromégas.* Ed. Ira O. Wade. Princeton, 1950.

——. *Migromégas: A Comic Romance . . .* Tr. anon. London, 1753.

Wells, Herbert George. "Bye-Products in Evolution," *Saturday Review,* LXXIX (Feb. 2, 1895), 155-156.

——. *Certain Personal Matters.* London, 1898 [1897].

——. "Human Evolution, An Artificial Process," *Fortnightly Review,*

LXVI (1896), 590-595.
———. "Intelligence on Mars," *Saturday Review,* LXXX (Apr. 4, 1896), 345-346.
———. "Morals and Civilisation," *Fortnightly Review,* LXVII (1897), 263-268.
———. "The Limits of Individual Plasticity," *Saturday Review,* LXXIX (Jan. 19, 1895), 89-90.
———. "On Extinction," *Chambers's Journal,* X (Sept. 30, 1893), 623-624.
———. "The Rediscovery of the Unique," *Fortnightly Review,* LVI (1891) 106-111.
———. "The Time Machine," *National Observer,* n.s. XI (1894), 446-447, 472-473, 499-500, 581-582, 606-608; and n.s. XII (1894), 14-15.
———. "The Time Machine," *New Review,* XII (1895), 98-112, 207-221, 329-343, 453-472, 577-588.
———. *The Works of* . . . 28 vols. London, 1924-26. [The Atlantic Edition.]
———. "Zoological Retrogression," *The Gentleman's Magazine* (Sept. 7, 1891), pp. 246-253.
Wilkins, John. *A Discourse concerning a New World and another Planet* . . . London, 1640.
———. *The Discovery of a World in the Moone* . . . London, 1638.

Selected critical works

Adams, Percy G. *Travellers and Travel Liars.* Berkeley and Los Angeles, 1962.
Aring, Charles D. 'The Case Becomes Less Strange," *American Scholar,* XXX (1960-61), 67-78.
Barber, W. H. "The Genesis of Voltaire's *Micromégas,*" *French Studies,* XI (1957), 1-15.
Barthes, Roland. *Mythologies.* Paris, 1957.
Bekker, W. G. *An Historical and Critical Review of Samuel Butler's* [1835-1902] *Literary Works.* New York, 1964.
Belgion, Montgomery. *H. G. Wells.* British Authors Series. London, 1953.
Bergonzi, Bernard. "Another Early Wells Item," *Nineteenth-Century Fiction,* XIII (1958), 72-73.
———. *The Early H. G. Wells: A Study of the Scientific Romances.* Toronto, 1961.
———. "The Publication of *The Time Machine* 1894-95," *Review of English Studies,* n.s. IX (1960), 42-51.
———. "*The Time Machine*: An Ironic Myth," *Critical Quarterly,* II (1959), 293-305.
Booth, Wayne C. *The Rhetoric of Fiction.* Chicago, 1961.
Bradbury, Ray. "A Happy Writer sees his Novel," *San Francisco Chronicle* (Nov. 22, 1966), p. 41.
Bretnor, Reginald, ed. *Modern Science Fiction. Its Meaning and Its Future,* New York, 1953.
Brome, Vincent. *H. G. Wells.* London, 1951.
Buckley, Jerome H[amilton]. *The Victorian Temper: A Study in Literary Culture.* Cambridge, Mass., 1951.

Burke, Kenneth. *A Grammar of Motives and a Rhetoric of Motives.* New York, 1962.

Bury, J. B. *The Idea of Progress.* London, 1928.

Butor, Michel. *Essais sur les modernes.* Paris, 1960.

——. "Science Fiction: The Crisis of its Growth." Tr. Richard Howard. *Partisan Review,* XXXIV (1967), 597-605.

Canseliet, Eugène. "Cyrano de Bergerac, Philosophe Hermétique," *Cahiers d'Hermès,* no. 1 (1947), pp. 65-82.

Caspar, Max and Walther von Dyck, eds. *Johannes Kepler in Seinen Briefen.* 2 vols. Munich, 1930.

Cassirer, Ernst. *Language and Myth.* Tr. Susanne Langer, New York, 1946.

Caudwell, Christopher, *pseud.* [i.e., Christopher St. John Sprigg]. *Studies in a Dying Culture.* London, 1938.

Cherpack, Clifton. "Proportion in *Micromégas,*" *MLN,* LXX (1955), 512-514.

Chesterton, Gilbert Keith. *Robert Louis Stevenson.* London, [n.d.].

Crispin, Edmund. "Science Fiction," *TLS,* Oct. 25, 1963, p. 865.

Crombie, A. C. *Medieval and Early Modern Science.* 2 vols. New York, 1959.

Davenport, Basil. *Inquiry into Science Fiction.* New York, 1955.

De la Mare, Walter. *Desert Islands and Robinson Crusoe.* London, 1932.

Dowse, R. E., and D. J. Palmer. " 'Frankenstein': A Moral Fable," *The Listener,* LXVIII (Aug. 23, 1962), 281, 284.

Doyle, Arthur Conan. "Mr. Stevenson's Methods in Fiction," *The Living Age,* CLXXXIV (1890), 417-424.

Dyson, A. E. "Swift: The Metamorphosis of Irony," *Essays and Studies,* n.s. XI (1958), 53-67.

Eddy, William A. *Gulliver's Travels: A Critical Study.* Princeton, 1923.

Edel, Leon, and Gordon N. Ray, eds. *Henry James and H. G. Wells.* Urbana, 1958.

Eigner, Edwin M. *Robert Louis Stevenson and the Romantic Tradition.* Princeton, 1966.

Elliott, Robert C. "The Fear of Utopia," *Centennial Review,* VII (1963), 237-251.

——. "Gulliver as Literary Artist," *ELH,* XIX (1952), 49-63.

——. *The Power of Satire.* Princeton, 1960.

Fradin, Joseph I. " 'The Absorbing Tyranny of Every-Day Life': Bulwer-Lytton's *A Strange Story,*" *Nineteenth Century Fiction,* XVI (1961) 1-16.

Franklin, H. Bruce. "Fictions of Science," *Southern Review,* n.s. III (1967), 1036-1049.

Freud, Sigmund. *The Interpretation of Dreams.* Tr. James Strachey. New York, 1961.

Frye, Northrop. *Anatomy of Criticism.* Princeton, 1957.

Furbank, P. N. *Samuel Butler (1836-1902).* Cambridge, 1948.

Gerber, Richard. *Utopian Fantasy: A Study of English Utopian Fiction Since the End of the Nineteenth Century.* London, 1955.

Godwin, William. *Enquiry Concerning Political Justice . . .* Ed. F. E. L. Priestly. 3 vols. Toronto, 1946.

Goldberg, M A. "Moral and Myth in Mrs. Shelley's *Frankenstein*," *Keats-Shelley Journal*, VIII (1959), 27-38.

Haight, Gordon S. "H. G. Wells's 'The Man of the Year Million,'" *Nineteenth Century Fiction*, XII (1958) 323-326.

Hammer, S. C. *Ludwig Holberg* . . . London, 1920.

Harrington, Michael. *The Accidental Century*. New York, 1965.

Hellman, George S. *The True Stevenson: A Study in Clarification*. Boston, 1925.

Hillegas, Mark R. "Cosmic Pessimism in H. G. Wells' Scientific Romances," *Papers of the Michigan Academy of Science, Arts and Letters*, XLVI (1961), 655-663.

——. "The First Invasion from Mars," *Michigan Alumnus Quarterly Review*, LXVI (1959), 107-112.

——. *The Future as Nightmare: H. G. Wells and the Anti-Utopians*. New York, 1967.

Holt, Lee Elbert. "Samuel Butler's Revisions of *Erewhon*," *Papers of the Bibliographical Society of America*, XXXVI (4th qtr., 1943) 22-23.

Houghton, Walter E. *The Victorian Frame of Mind*. New Haven, 1957.

Hughes, David Y. "H. G. Wells: Ironic Romancer," *Extrapolation*, VI (May, 1965), 32-38.

Jones, Henry Festing. *Samuel Butler; Author of Erewhon (1835-1902): A Memoir*. 2 vols. London, 1919.

Kagarlitski, J. *The Life and Thought of H. G. Wells*. Tr. Moura Budberg. New York, 1966.

Kahane, Ernest. "Micromégas et l'Anticipation Scientifique," *Europe* (May-June, 1959), pp. 129-136.

Kermode, Frank. *The Sense of an Ending*. New York, 1967.

Kiely, Robert. *Robert Louis Stevenson and the Fiction of Adventure*. Cambridge, Mass., 1964.

Koestler, Arthur. *The Ghost in the Machine*. New York, 1968.

Koyré, Alexandre. *From the Closed World to the Infinite Universe*. New York, 1957.

Lascelles, Mary. "*Rasselas* Reconsidered," *Essays and Studies*, n.s. IV (1951), 37-52.

Lavers, A. "La Croyance à l'Unité de la Science dans 'L'Autre Monde' de Cyrano de Bergerac," *Cahiers du Sud*, no. 349 (1959), pp. 406-416.

Lawton, Harold W. "Bishop Godwin's *Man in the Moone*," *Review of English Studies*, VII (1931), 23-55.

Le Fanu, T. P. "Catalogue of Dean Swift's Library in 1715," *Proceedings of the Irish Royal Academy*, XXXVII, Sect. C, no. 13 (1927), 263-275.

Lewis, Clive Staples. *The Discarded Image*. Cambridge, 1964.

——. *An Experiment in Criticism*. Cambridge, 1961.

Liger, Christian. "Les Cinq Envols de Cyrano." *NRF*, XIII (1965), 242-256, 427-442.

Lloyd, Claude, "Shadwell and the Virtuosi," *PMLA*, XLIV (1929), 472-494.

Lund, Mary Graham. "Mary Godwin Shelley and the Monster," *University of Kansas City Review*, XXVIII (1962), 253-258.

McColley, Grant. "The Date of Godwin's *Domingo Gonsales*," *Modern*

Philology, XXXV (1937), 47-60.

Mannheim, Karl. *Ideology and Utopia.* Tr. Louis Wirth and Edward Shils. New York, 1936.

Marcuse, Herbert. *One-Dimensional Man.* Boston, 1964.

Moré, Marcel. "Hasard et Providence chez Jules Verne," *Critique,* no. 180 (May 1962), pp. 417-431.

————. "Les Jeux de Mots dans l'Oeuvre de Jules Verne," *Lettres Nouvelles* (1957), pp. 711-730.

————. *Le Très Curieux Jules Verne.* Paris, 1960.

Nauert, Charles G., Jr. *Agrippa and the Crisis of Renaissance Thought.* Urbana, 1965.

Newton, Sir Isaac. *Mathematical Principles of Natural Philosophy.* Tr. Andrew Motte. 2 vols. London, 1729.

————. *Philosophiae Naturalis Principia Mathematica.* 2 vols. Cambridge, 1713.

Nicolson, Marjorie Hope. "Cosmic Voyages," *ELH,* VII (1940), 83-107.

————. "Kepler, the *Somnium,* and John Donne," *Journal of the History of Ideas,* I (1940), 259-280.

————. "The 'New Astronomy' and the English Literary Imagination," *Studies in Philology,* XXXII (1935), 428-462.

————. *Science and Imagination.* New York, 1956.

————. "The Telescope and Imagination," *Modern Philology,* XXXII (1935), 233-260.

————. *A World in the Moon* . . . Smith College Studies in Modern Languages, XVII (1936).

Nicolson, Marjorie Hope, and Nora Mohler. "The Scientific Background of Swift's *Voyage to Laputa,*" *Annals of Science,* II (1937), 299-334.

————. "Swift's 'Flying Island' in the *Voyage to Laputa,*" *Annals of Science,* II (1937), 405-430.

Potter, George Reuben. "Swift and Natural Science," *Philological Quarterly,* XX (1941), 97-118.

Prideaux, W. F. *A Bibliography of the Works of Robert Louis Stevenson.* Rev. ed. London, 1917.

Pritchett, V. S. *The Living Novel.* London, 1946.

Quintana, Ricardo. *The Mind and Art of Jonathan Swift.* Oxford, 1936.

Raknem, Ingvald. *H. G. Wells and his Critics.* Norway: Universitetsforlaget, 1962.

Ridgely, Beverly S. "A Sixteenth-Century French Cosmic Voyage: *Nouvelles des Regions de la Lune,*" *Studies in the Renaissance,* IV (1957), 169-189.

Rieger, James. "Dr. Polidori and the Genesis of *Frankenstein,*" *Studies in English Literature,* III (1963), 461-472.

Roppen, Georg. *Evolution and Poetic Belief: A Study in some Victorian and Modern Writers.* Oslo, 1956.

Schwonke, Martin. *Vom Staatsroman zur Science Fiction.* Stuttgart, 1957.

Shelley, Percy Bysshe. *The Complete Works of* . . . Ed. Roger Lugpen and Walter E. Peck. 10 vols. New York, 1965.

Shoenberg, Robert E. "The Literal-Mindedness of Samuel Butler," *Studies in English Literature,* IV (1964), 601-616.

Simpson, George Gaylord. "Lamarck, Darwin, and Butler," *American Scholar*, XXX (1961) 238-249.

Singer, Dorothea Waley. *Giordano Bruno: His Life and Work*. New York, 1950.

Smith, Godfrey. "An Outline of H. G. Wells," *N.Y. Times Magazine*, Aug. 21, 1966, pp. 30-31, 39-40, 42, 44.

Spark, Muriel. *Child of Light*. Hadleigh, 1951.

———. "Mary Shelley: A Prophetic Novelist," *The Listener*, XLV (Feb. 22, 1951), 305-306.

Spink, J. S. *French Free-Thought from Gassendi to Voltaire*. London, 1960.

Stanley, Henry M[orton]. *The Congo and the Founding of its Free State*. 2 vols. New York, 1885.

Stevenson, Robert Louis. *The Letters of* . . . Ed. Sidney Colvin, 4 vols. New York, 1911.

———. "Robert Louis Stevenson on Realism and Idealism," *Living Age*, CLXXXVIII (1891), 768.

Strathdee, R. B. "Robert Louis Stevenson as a Scientist," *Aberdeen University Review*, XXXVI (1956), 268-275.

Sutherland, John H. "A Reconsideration of Gulliver's Third Voyage," *Studies in Philology*, LIV (1957), 45-52.

Swift, Jonathan. *The Correspondence of* . . . . Ed. Harold Williams. 5 vols. Oxford, 1963.

Taylor, Aline Mackenzie. "Cyrano de Bergerac and Gulliver's *Voyage to Brobdingnag*," *Tulane Studies in English*, V (1955), 83-102.

Traugott, John. "A Voyage to Nowhere with Thomas More and Jonathan Swift: *Utopia* and *The Voyage to the Houyhnhnms*," *Sewanee Review*, LXIX (1961), 534-565.

Trousson, R. "Voltaire et la Mythologie," *Bulletin de l'Association Guillaume Bude*, no. 2 (1962), pp. 222-229.

Vaihinger, Hans. *The Philosophy of "As If"*. Tr. C. K. Ogden. New York, 1924.

Vandenberg, Stephen G. "Great Expectations or the Future of Psychology (as seen in Science Fiction)," *American Psychologist*, XI (1956,) 339-342.

Wade, Ira O. "Voltaire's Quarrel with Science," *Bucknell Review*, VIII (1959), 287-298.

Walker, D. P. "Moonshine," *N. Y. Review of Books*. Sept. 22, 1966, pp. 10-12.

Wasiolek, Edward. "Relativity in *Gulliver's Travels*," *Philological Quarterly*, XXXVII (1958), 110-116.

Weeks, Robert P. "Disentanglement as a Theme in H. G. Wells' Fiction," *Papers of the Michigan Academy of Science, Arts and Letters*, XXXIX (1954), 439-444.

Wells, H[erbert] G[eorge]. Preface to *The Scientific Romances of* . . . London, 1933. Pp. vii-ix.

Wiener, Norbert. *Cybernetics*. New York, 1948.

Williams, Harold. *Dean Swift's Library*. Cambridge, 1932.

Yates, Frances. *The Art of Memory*. Chicago, 1966.

———. *Giordano Bruno and the Hermetic Tradition*. Chicago, 1964.

Index